SHADOW IN SERENITY

WITHDRAWN

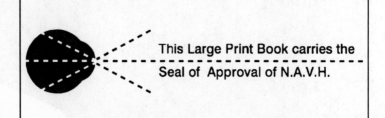

This Large Print Book carries the
Seal of Approval of N.A.V.H.

SHADOW IN SERENITY

TERRI BLACKSTOCK

CHRISTIAN LARGE PRINT
A part of Gale, Cengage Learning

GALE
CENGAGE Learning

Detroit • New York • San Francisco • New Haven, Conn • Waterville, Maine • London

GALE
CENGAGE Learning·

LIBRARY OF CONGRESS CATALOGING-IN-PUBLICATION DATA

Blackstock, Terri, 1957–
    Shadow in Serenity / by Terri Blackstock.
        pages ; cm. — (Thorndike Press large print Christian fiction)
        ISBN 978-1-4104-4363-2 (hardcover) — ISBN 1-4104-4363-9 (hardcover)
        1. Strangers—Fiction. 2. Texas—Fiction. 3. Large type books. I. Title.
    PS3552.L34285S46 2012
    813'.54—dc23   2011048835

ISBN 13: 978-1-59415-415-7 (pbk. : alk. paper)
ISBN 10: 1-59415-415-5 (pbk. : alk. paper)

Published in 2012 by arrangement with The Zondervan Corporation LLC.

Printed in the United States of America
1 2 3 4 5   16 15 14 13 12
FD045

*This book is lovingly
dedicated to the Nazarene*

ACKNOWLEDGMENTS

Many years ago I published a version of this book in the general market under another title and with a pseudonym. (You can read more about that in my "Note From the Author" at the end of this book.) It was my last book to be published before I changed to the Christian market, where I could write books that impacted lives in an eternal way. When I submitted proposals for my first suspense novels to Zondervan back in 1994, Dave Lambert was the editor who offered me a four-book contract. He has since edited almost all of my books. And when I decided to rewrite and update this one, he edited it too.

Another person who's been in my life since I left the general market is Sue Brower at Zondervan, who used to market my books and currently serves as Acquisitions Editor. She's the one who decides which of my ideas will make it to print.

Both of these people have been constant encouragers, teachers, and friends over the years. I should thank them in every book, but especially this one, since this book marks a full-circle moment in my career.

Thanks from the bottom of my heart, Dave and Sue. I couldn't have done any of what I do without your support and guidance.

ONE

Logan Brisco had the people of Serenity, Texas, eating out of his hand, and that was just where he wanted them.

He worked hard to cultivate the smile of a traveling evangelist, the confidence of a busy capitalist, the secrecy of a government spy, and the charisma of a pied piper. No one in town knew where he'd come from or why he was there, and he wasn't talking. But he made sure they knew he was on a mission, and that it was something big.

From the moment he drove his Navigator in, wearing his thousand-dollar suit and Italian shoes, tongues began wagging. Rumor had it that Logan Brisco was a movie producer scouting talent for his latest picture. But the weekly patrons of the Clippety Doo Dah Salon were sure he was a billionaire-in-hiding, looking for a wife. And the men at Slade Hampton's Barbershop buzzed about the money he was likely to invest in the community.

Two days after he arrived, the UPS man delivered two large boxes marked "Fragile" and addressed to "Brisco, c/o The Welcome Inn." One of the boxes had the return address of a prominent bank in Dallas. The other was marked "Hollywood, California." The gossip grew more frenzied.

For two weeks, he chatted with the people of the town, ate in its restaurants, shopped in its stores, bonded with its men, flirted with its women. As soon as speculation peaked, Logan would be ready to go in for the kill.

This one might be his biggest score yet.

The next step would be to hold one of his seminars, the kind where people came in with bundles of cash and left with empty pockets and heads full of dreams. That was what he was best at. Building dreams and taking money.

On his second Saturday in town — which consisted mostly of four streets of shops, offices, and restaurants — the sun shone brightly after a week of rain. It was the day Serenity's citizens filled the streets, catching up on errands and chores. Perfect.

His first stop that morning was at Peabody's Print Shop, where yesterday he had talked Julia Peabody into printing a thousand fliers for him on credit. "I'm not authorized to spend money on this project without the signatures of my major investors," he'd told her in a conspiratorial voice. "Can you just bill me at the Welcome Inn?"

Julia, the pretty daughter of the print shop owner, glanced over her shoulder to see if her father was near. "Well, we're not supposed to give credit, Mr. Brisco."

He leaned on the counter. "Logan, please."

"Logan," she said, blushing. "I mean . . . couldn't you just write a check or use a credit card and let your investors pay you back?"

"I'm in the process of opening a bank account here," he said with the hint of a grin sparkling in his eyes. "Thing is, I opened it yesterday, but they told me not to write any checks on it until my money is transferred from my Dallas bank. Now, if I were to write you a check and ask you to hold it, that would be exactly the same thing as your giving me credit, wouldn't it?"

"Well, yes, I guess it would," she said.

He smiled and paused for a moment, as though he'd lost his train of thought. "You know, they sure do grow the women pretty in Serenity."

Julia breathed a laugh and rolled her eyes.

"Oh, I'm sorry," Logan said. "I changed the subject, didn't I?"

"That's okay."

"So . . . would you prefer a postdated check or credit?" While she was thinking it over, he dropped the timbre of his voice and said, "By the way, are you planning to be at the bingo hall tomorrow night?"

"I think so."

"Good," he said. "I was hoping you would."

Flustered, she had taken his order. "All right, Logan, I'll give you credit. You don't look like the type who would make me sorry."

"Just look into these eyes, Julia. Tell me you don't see pure, grade-A honesty."

Today, when he went back in to pick up the fliers, he turned the charm up a notch. "Not only are you the prettiest girl in Serenity, but you're the most talented too. These are excellent fliers."

Julia giggled and touched her hair. "Uh, Logan . . . I meant to ask you . . . what project is it that you're working on? I looked all over it, but the flier didn't say."

He shot her a you-devil grin and brought his index finger to his lips. "I can't tell you before I tell the rest of the townsfolk, now can I? It wouldn't be fair to cut you in before anybody else has had a chance."

"Oh, I wouldn't tell anyone," she promised. "Discretion is my middle name. Secrets come through this shop all the time, and I never say a word. Politicians, clergymen, whatnot. Everybody in town knows they can trust me."

Chuckling, he handed her back one of the fliers. "Come to the bingo hall early tonight, and you'll hear everything you want to know. Now don't forget to send me that bill."

With a wink he was out the door, leaving her staring after him with a wistful look.

Stepping out into the cool sunlight of the May day, he looked down at the box of fliers. It shouldn't be hard to pass all of them out by tonight. And having the seminar at the bingo hall in the town's community center was a stroke of genius. That place drew hundreds of people on Saturday nights, and tonight they would just come an hour earlier to hear him. By tomorrow, he'd be riding high.

He would hit the hardware store next, since it seemed inordinately busy today. Easy marks there — he'd hook every one of them.

He stopped, waited for a car to pass, then started to dart across the street. The sound of a Harley hog stopped him. It growled its warning as it tore its way up the street, breaking the relative quiet that he had come to associate with the town. He stepped back when it passed, but when its wheel cut through a puddle, it splashed mud onto the shins of his pants.

"Hey!" he yelled. The driver apparently didn't hear. Logan stared after the bike, which carried a woman and a little boy. The petite biker's shoulder-length blonde hair stuck out from under her tangerine helmet, softening the impression created by the powerful bike. As she went up the street, people looked her way and waved, apparently pleased to see her rather than annoyed at the disruption.

Logan tried to rein in his temper as she pulled into a parking space and cut off the loud engine. It wouldn't pay to ruin the image he'd so carefully cultivated here by throttling the first woman who had the gall to ruffle his feathers. It was an accident, he told himself. An accident she would probably be glad to apologize for.

As she got off the bike, he approached her. "Excuse me, ma'am. I'm not one to hold grudges, but you just splashed mud all over my pants."

The woman pulled off her helmet, revealing a head full of baby-blonde hair. She looked like that little actress Kristin Chenoweth, with a flash of fire in her eyes.

First, she eyed him with curiosity, then glanced down at his muddy legs. "Sorry. Why were you standing next to a puddle?"

He shifted the fliers from one arm to the other and gaped at the woman as her boy got off the bike. She didn't seem to have the stature to hold up a Harley, much less ride one, but she stepped on the kickstand with little effort.

"I wasn't standing next to a puddle — I was crossing the street," he said. "I paid a fortune for these pants!"

"You know, I bet it would come off with a little water, if you don't stand here and let them dry. A little mud never hurt anyone, though. Did it, Jason?"

"Nope. It washes right off. I get into it all the time." The child, who looked no more than seven, held up his own feet and showed Logan the splashed mud on the bottoms of his jeans. "Hey, are you the movie producer guy?"

Still frowning, Logan nodded. "Yeah. I mean, no. Where'd you get that idea?"

"Everybody's talking," Jason said. "I've had the flu, so we haven't been to town, but we heard all about you."

15

With effort, Logan swallowed his ire and flashed the boy that political grin. "Well, I guess they are. Maybe I've been a little too secretive. My name's Logan Brisco." He reached out to shake the woman's hand, but she seemed not to notice. He settled for shaking the boy's.

"I'm Jason Sullivan," the kid said. "And this is my mom."

"Mrs. Sullivan," he said, nodding and searching those eyes for some sign of admiration. When he addressed them formally, women usually corrected him and told him their first names. But not this one. She couldn't have been less interested. "You know, if everybody's so curious, they'll be able to find out tonight what I'm doing in town. Six o'clock, at the bingo hall. Hope you'll both be there. And here . . . I'll give you a few of these fliers to pass out, if you wouldn't mind."

The woman didn't take the fliers, but the boy grabbed the stack he offered.

"Me too? Do I get to come?" the kid asked.

"Sure. This affects everybody in town."

"What does?" The woman took one of the fliers out of her son's hand and scanned it. "It doesn't say here what your seminar is about."

Dipping his head to her ear, he said in his most confidential voice, "It's about making all your dreams come true."

She wasn't moved. "My dreams have already come true."

That was a new one, he thought, stepping back. No one had ever told him that. "Then let me show you how to make the most of them," he said in the mesmerizing tone that had made him such a success. "Let me show you how to maximize your potential and minimize your risk, how to build your fortune the way everybody else in this town is going to, how to make your mark in the world."

A smile transformed her face, and she met his eyes. "Really? You could do that? I could get rich?"

Now he had her. "It's practically a guarantee."

"Wow," she said, pulling her purse out of a compartment on her bike. "How much will it cost me? I can write you a check right now. Two hundred? Two *thousand?* Maybe my life's savings? Do you take debit cards?"

He chuckled, not certain how to take her.

Suddenly, that ditzy smile vanished, and she stood a little taller. "Let me give you a warning, Mr. Brisco, if that's your real name. Not everyone in this town is fooled

17

by that act. It only takes one person to blow your cover, and I'm the one who's going to do it."

His smile crashed. "What makes you think there's a cover to blow?"

Her cool smile told him there was no doubt in her mind. "I know your kind," she said. "I knew it the first time one of my neighbors waxed poetic about the new man in town. You're a two-bit con artist, and you think you can ride into Serenity and milk these people for everything they're worth. This town has enough problems. I won't let you do it."

She turned to walk away. Following her, he said, "You're pretty sure of yourself, aren't you?"

"That's right."

"What if you're wrong, and you miss out on your chance to get richer than you ever imagined?"

"I'm never wrong," she said. "Ask anybody." Holding her helmet by the chin strap, she headed up the sidewalk.

Logan watched her stroll away from him, her son at her heels. Clearly, she didn't need or want Logan's attention. He would have staked everything on the probability that she drew men's gazes wherever she went. When she reached the hardware store, she

18

grabbed Jason's fliers and glanced back, as if to make sure Logan was watching as she dropped them into the trash.

Logan grinned. This would be even more fun than he'd thought. He might have to stay longer than he'd planned, just to meet the challenge of the little lady whose first name he didn't know.

The ladies of the Clippety Doo Dah Salon cackled and fluttered as Logan stepped inside, breathing in the scent of hair spray and peroxide and trying not to cough. "Hello, ladies," he said with his best grin.

A dozen gals crooned back their hellos and preened with their rollers, their rods, and their teased tresses, as if he could see past them to the beauty that lay just moments away. Across the room, he saw Julia Peabody sitting in front of the hair dryers, where she had the attention of at least five women. *Perfect,* Logan thought. She had to be talking about him.

"Mr. Brisco!" Lahoma Kirtland called from the sink where she was dyeing the head of Mildred Smith. Abandoning her client, she held her gloved, red-dyed hands up like a surgeon and made a beeline across the shop.

"Please, darlin'. My daddy was Mr. Brisco. I'm just Logan." He looked around the room. "I was just strolling through town, wondering where all the prettiest ladies were. And lo and behold, I think I've found them all right here."

The women giggled and exchanged delighted looks. "It's so nice to see you," Lahoma said. "We were just talking about you, weren't we, girls?"

"Were you now? Nothing bad, I hope." He glanced through the arch that separated the main part of the salon from the room with the dryers. Julia Peabody had a deer-in-the-headlights look. He chuckled. "Julia, honey. You aren't giving away all my secrets now, are you?"

Julia popped to her feet. "I was just spreading word about your seminar. Everyone's so excited."

"Well, good," he said, reaching into his box and pulling out a handful of fliers. "I hope you'll tell your friends, and your friends' friends, and your enemies, and your sweethearts, and . . ."

A titter of giggles made its way around the shop as he put a flier into each lady's hand.

"Tell them all that this could be the most important meeting of their lives. Years from now, you'll all look back and remember how your lives were changed when Logan Brisco blew into town."

The door clanged open behind him and closed with a tinkling bell. He turned around and saw the biker chick bouncing her son on her back as she cut across the salon toward Lahoma's station, zigzagging and swaying, pretending she might drop the boy. Holding on for dear life, he giggled and shouted for her to stop.

Spotting Lahoma across the shop, she spun around, inciting a scream from the child. "Lahoma," she shouted over his giggles, "have you got time to give Jason a haircut? Slade's too busy down at the barbershop."

"We can work him in, honey, as soon as one of the girls is finished," Lahoma said. "Come on over here and get one of Logan's fliers."

The blonde's eyes met his, and contempt hardened her features again. Letting her son slide down her back, she blew her wispy bangs out of her eyes and came toward the beautician, who held his flier with her rubber gloves still wet with red dye.

"I already got one," she said. "I put it in an appropriate place."

Grinning, Logan turned back to the patrons. "Now if you ladies wouldn't mind passing some out," he said, "I'll give you a

21

few extra fliers."

"I'll take some," a woman beneath a dryer called.

Mildred sat up, the red dye forgotten in her hair. "I'll take some too."

"Anybody else?" Logan asked. "You won't regret it. Anybody you talk into coming will owe you a lifelong debt."

"Sold," his nemesis said, her eyes dancing. "Give me the whole stack. I'll be rid of them in five minutes."

He chuckled and withheld them from her. "I don't think so. Besides, you've got that haircut to wait for. And this place is chock-full of lovely young ladies who'd be more than willing to come to the aid of a newcomer in town."

"Oh, brother." She grabbed her son's hand and headed back to the door. "Come on, Jason, let's go."

"Aren't you going to get him his haircut?" Lahoma called after her.

"I think I'll go wait for Slade," she said. "The air's a little hot in here. And Lahoma, you should really finish Mildred's hair before that peroxide eats through her scalp."

The door clanged shut behind her, and Lahoma slapped her red hands on her face. "Oh, my word, I forgot!" She ran to where Mildred sat with dye dripping down her forehead, hastily pushed the red head back into the sink, and turned the water on.

Logan grinned and watched out the window as the blonde woman ambled up the sidewalk. "I don't think she likes me."

"Sure she does," Lahoma said. "Carny gets along with everybody. You just have to get used to her. She's been a breath of fresh air to this town."

"Carny?" he asked. "What kind of name is that?"

"She was brought up in a carnival," Lahoma replied.

So that was it. She had street smarts. That might get in his way.

Mildred's eyes rolled back in her head as Lahoma scrubbed her scalp, and in a voice just short of a groan, she said, "Carny Sullivan. She moved here when she married Bev's boy, Abe."

"Then she isn't a native of Serenity?"

"Carny?" Lahoma chuckled. "Heavens, no. But she's sure brought life to it. Abe was no good, though. He lit out a year after he brought her here. Wound up dead in Amarillo. Barroom brawl, they said."

"And she stayed?"

"Of course she did. She's one of us now. We love her, even if she does do her own hair."

Laughing, Logan offered his goodbyes to the ladies and went back outside. Carny and her son sat on the bench outside the barbershop, a block down. He strolled toward them as if in no particular hurry.

She was probably in her late twenties. That savvy edge she had, that mature expression on her face, that lack of innocence only made her more attractive to him.

Stay away, Logan, he warned himself. That had been Montague's first rule. Never let a woman get under your skin — especially one who had the goods on you. It could be the kiss of death. Yet he liked a challenge, and he couldn't resist confronting her again . . . just one more time.

She gave him a smug look as he approached. "Bet you didn't pay for those fliers."

"Of course I did," he said, surprised.

She laughed and pulled her foot up to the edge of the bench. "No, you didn't. You conned her into giving you credit, didn't you? And you probably haven't let go of a cent at the Welcome Inn yet."

He set the box on the end of the bench, trying to look unruffled. "How did you know where I'm staying?"

She smiled. "I'm a genius. That, and the fact that it's the only motel in town. So how are you planning to hoodwink the men in the barbershop? Can't flirt with them like you did the ladies. But you can still flatter them, can't you? Touch on their misfortune. Plant ideas in their minds. You've probably learned enough about the people here in two weeks to know all their Achilles' heels."

His smile faded. Setting his mud-splattered foot on the edge of the bench, he leaned toward her. "I don't know yours."

She met his eyes boldly. "That's because I don't have one."

Why did her comeback delight him so? Was it that she stared back at him, undaunted and unflattered by his close scrutiny? Or that she had his number, or thought she did, and wasn't going to let him get away with a thing?

She glanced away when she heard Jason's name being called from inside, and nodded for the boy to go in. "Tell him to cut it shorter around the ears. And I want to be able to see your eyebrows."

"Aw, Mom!"

"Go," she said, shooing him away.

When he was gone, she brought her gaze back to Logan and stared at him as if waiting for him to explain why he was standing there with his foot on her bench.

"Look, I don't know why you're out to

get me," he said. "I haven't done anything to you. I'm just here trying to do these people a favor."

"A favor?" She laughed. "That's rich. You came here because you heard there was money here. That the local oil boom a few decades ago left these people sitting pretty. Then the wells played out, the factories closed, the hardest hit lost their farms — and everybody who still has money is waiting for a hero to show them how to grow it."

"Is that why *you* came here, Carny?"

She didn't ask how he knew her name. "It's none of your business why I came."

"Maybe it is," he said. "Maybe you're feeling threatened. Maybe you're the one with the scam, and you're afraid I'll horn in on it. You know what they say. You can't con a con."

"They're right, whoever they are," she said, standing and starting toward the barbershop door. Just before she went in, she looked over her shoulder and added, "And you can't con the *daughter* of a con, either. You've got your work cut out for you here, Brisco."

Logan didn't know whether that was meant as a threat or a challenge, but something about it delighted him more than

26

anything had in years.

Grinning, he picked up his fliers and started up the street. He wasn't just going to get rich in Serenity. He was also going to have the time of his life, with this little fireball who called herself Carny.

TWO

That night, Jason slipped out the truck's door and rushed away before Carny had even had time to pull into a parking space. Sighing, she watched him catch up to his friends entering the bingo hall like herded cattle. This Logan fellow was good, she admitted, cutting off her truck engine. She had to give him that. He had the town in a fever, and he could probably sell them Romania tonight if he tried. The fact that it wasn't for sale wouldn't even cross their minds.

That's why she had come.

She slid out of the pickup.

"Hey, Carny," Paul Dillard called across the parking lot.

She waved and waited for the man who'd had his eye on her since Abe died. "Not you too, Paul. You're not buying what this guy's selling, are you?"

"I don't *know* what he's selling," he said.

"Never hurts to listen."

"Yeah, well, just don't give him any money tonight, okay? No matter what he says, *don't* give him any money."

"If you're so doggone sure he's up to no good, why are you here?"

"Somebody sane has to be here. I think I'm the only one in town who's thinking straight about this guy."

"You're not giving us much credit," Paul said, opening the door for her as they reached the aluminum building. "We're not stupid. But it doesn't hurt to listen. Lighten up — you're too suspicious."

"There's a difference between suspicious and savvy," she said. "I've been around, Paul. I know when things aren't right."

"Well, maybe tonight he'll prove to you he's on the up-and-up."

Carny caught Logan's eye as she and Paul entered the packed room, and when he flashed her that devil-may-care smile, she shook her head. "I don't think he can, Paul."

She left Paul and wove through the townspeople she had come to know well over the past nine years. She couldn't believe how many of them had turned out for this. This definitely wasn't the usual Saturday-night bingo crowd; they didn't get this big a crowd at church on Sunday mornings, or at

29

the Fourth of July picnic, or at the Christmas pageant. And the nervous, excited hum over the room was something she hadn't experienced since she'd settled here.

But she had experienced it before.

It was the same anticipation that the marks had at the carnival. The same fervor that her father and mother inspired when they were setting up their own little scams. Carny had even been a part of those scams, years ago. Following her parents' orders, she'd picked her share of pockets, created her share of diversions, acted in her share of schemes. And the more excited the marks became at whatever the grift happened to be, the more her parents believed they deserved what they were getting.

But the people of Serenity didn't deserve anything of the kind.

A few of the men offered her their seats, but standing empowered her.

She watched as the man who had drawn this crowd walked up to the bingo hall's podium. That charm-packed grin gave him an ironic look of innocence as he scanned the room. "Well, now. I knew the people of Serenity had above-average intelligence, but there's more intellect here than I would have guessed."

His gaze landed on Carny as the crowd

gave a light round of applause, and she knew what he was thinking — that she had been too curious to stay away, that he was winning her over. That she was just like all the other easy marks in the room.

But soon enough, he would see what she was made of. If he was going to run a scam on this town, he'd have her to contend with first.

"Ladies and gentlemen," he said in a soft accent that came from somewhere in the South. *Real or fake?* she wondered. "I thank you all for coming. And I promise you won't regret it. I've grown pretty fond of many of you over the last two weeks. Slade, who gives the best haircuts this side of the Mississippi. Bonnie at the cafe, who makes the best lemon icebox pie I've ever put in my mouth. And Agnes and Tommy Slater at the hardware store, and the Sheaffers over at the post office . . . well, I could go on and on. Suffice it to say that I've never met a warmer town. And because you've all touched me in such a personal way, I want to give something back now."

Here it comes. Carny's stomach tightened.

Logan cleared his throat. "Many of you have wondered why I've been so secretive over the last two weeks. Well, I suppose you have a right to be curious. But the truth is that I work for a company called King Enterprises, located in Dallas. The company has alliances with a number of very creative high-tech firms and investors with money to burn. I've spent the last several months scouting the rural parts of the state, trying to find the best location for a particular venture we have in mind. Serenity wasn't at the top of our list of sites, but it was worth checking out. There's a lot of fallow land on the western side of town, acres and acres of foreclosed property that's being used for absolutely nothing. That's what makes it right for our project."

He leaned on the podium then, getting personal with the people of Serenity, meeting them one at a time with direct looks. *He's good,* Carny thought with a sick feeling. *Awfully good.*

"Now I'm a businessman, and I don't usually let personal feelings get in the way of sound decision-making. But having gotten to know the people of Serenity — well, I have to tell you, I don't think I have to look any further."

Applause erupted over the crowd, and Carny looked around, appalled. He hadn't even told them what he was doing, and already they'd given him hearty approval.

"There are a lot of citizens in Serenity

who, through no fault of their own, have lost their farms. The banks own them now, and good farmers have had to turn to factory work in Odessa to support their families. Those of you who are more fortunate, the ones lucky enough to have made a lot of money from oil leases on your land, are still getting nervous. Your wells are playing out. The money's not coming in like it used to. It's time for all of you, whatever your economic status is currently — farmers, factory workers, business owners, sales clerks, secretaries, and oil boomers — to find something else to put your hopes and dreams into, something else that can make Serenity the prosperous town it once was."

Again, thunderous applause filled the bingo hall.

"Here's the bottom line," he said. "My investors are going to build a multi-billion-dollar amusement park somewhere in Texas. It's going to make Astroworld look like a state fair and put Six Flags out of business. In fact, it will be on the same scale as Disney World. King Enterprises is building a team of engineers — some even worked for Disney, so they know their stuff — to create the kind of theme park that people will plan their vacations around, and they'll fly their families in just to experience it."

Oohs and ahhs rose over the crowd, then turned into applause.

"Whatever community we choose is going to get sopping rich," Logan went on. "The citizens of Serenity who own their own businesses will see unbelievable increases in their profits, and there will be thousands of new jobs. But the best thing about this endeavor is that we're willing to cut the community in. You invest in this project and you'll get a percentage of the profits. No matter how much or how little you put in, you'll get your cut. And ladies and gentlemen, I think there'd have to be something wrong with anybody who'd pass up a chance like this. You just can't lose."

An amusement park, Carny thought as the crowd roared in approval. Perfect. He'd rake in his profits tonight, taking everything anyone would give him, and then he'd be on the highway out of town before the sun came up tomorrow.

Anger shot through her as she stood looking around at the excitement, the fever, on everyone's face. Without another thought, she pushed through those standing on the sides of the room and made her way to the front. As the applause died enough for her to be heard, she darted in front of Logan Brisco, grabbed the microphone, and shouted, "Wait a minute! I have something to say!"

For the first time that night, his grin waned, but he quickly rallied. "Be my guest," he said. "This is a big venture. It's going to require a little discussion. Carny . . ." He gestured toward the microphone, surrendering it completely.

"First of all," she said, "I think it's important that we think about what's going on here. This man has been in town for two weeks. Two weeks! We know virtually nothing about him, yet most of you are already reaching for your checkbooks. What's wrong with this picture?"

A moan of protest swept over the crowd, and she raised her hand to stop them. "You all know about my background, so you know why I can spot a con man from ten miles away. My dad used to say that the people he conned deserved it, because their greed made them gullible. Are you people going to let greed drive you? Brother Tommy preached on that last Sunday. God was probably preparing us for this night, for this pitch. Remember what Jesus said? That you can't serve God and money? I stayed in this town because so many of you are good people who love the Lord. But, as Brother Tommy said, when you give in to greed, you

35

step out of God's blessing and protection. You don't want that, do you?"

"Carny," someone yelled, "this ain't greed, it's business. It ain't a sin to make investments."

"Yeah," another voice added. "Quit tryin' to lay a guilt trip on us!"

Carny groaned. "Will you at least promise me you'll pray about it? Not the God-stop-me-if-you-don't-want-this kind of prayer, because God doesn't play that way. But real prayer, seeking his will. Can you go home and do that before handing over your life's savings?"

Several nodded grudgingly. It made her feel a little better. "Beyond the greed, even if this isn't a scam, would we really *want* an amusement park in this town? I came here for the peace and stability the town offered me, and I love it just the way it is. I never dreamed I'd run from one carnival lifestyle to another. If we were to build this here, nothing would ever be the same again. We'd have tourists coming through all the time, and that draws lowlifes and thieves. Crime would go up, and the quality of life would go down. Are we willing to sell out our beautiful little town for that?"

Slade Hampton from the barbershop stood up, his dog, Jack, wagging his tail beside him. "Carny, the town's in trouble. We need *some*thing. This could be the answer to our prayers."

"If Logan Brisco is the answer to your prayers, Slade, then I'm Mother Teresa's long-lost daughter. Listen to me. I know what I'm talking about."

"Excuse me," Logan said, commandeering the microphone again. "I hope I didn't make any of you think that the policies of the park would be dictated to you. On the contrary, your own county government would establish the policies. If you build this park here, you can set limitations on how it's to be done. You can protect this town from the elements Carny is talking about, if you put your heads together. The hotels the tourists will need could be put outside town. You pick the areas for gift shops, tourist areas, new restaurants. You could divert all the traffic away from the main part of town, if you wanted. Ladies and gentlemen, it can be done to your satisfaction. Some of you will even be on the planning board. This will be your baby as much as mine."

Hugh Berkstrom, the richest man in town, got to his feet. "Mr. Brisco, your idea is intriguing. But I'm wondering about zoning issues, the influx of new children into our school system, noise, water pollution . . . Serenity may not have the infrastructure to support a project like this."

"You trying to talk me out of Serenity?" Logan asked with a chuckle.

More protests erupted.

"Not at all," Hugh said. "I'm just trying to be realistic. It's not just an amusement park we'd be building, but a new airport, hotels, restaurants, new neighborhoods, schools, utilities, water treatment plants . . ."

"Are you suggesting these things will be *bad* for the local economy?" Logan asked.

"No, of course not. But Carny has a point. If you're serious about this, then all those things would have to be considered. Do you have a business plan? Have you met with local officials about what needs to be done to get this thing under way?"

"A lot of the preliminary work is done. The rest of it is coming. One thing builds on another. I'll be sharing the details with my company and our investors as we go. But tonight I wanted to give you an overview."

"What size investments are you looking for, Logan?" someone asked from the back of the room.

"The bigger, the better," he answered, "but there's no amount too small. You'll each be paid dividends based on what you invest. If we get enough investors here, we may not have to offer it as public stock. That means more profit for all of you."

Carny gaped at her friends and neighbors. Their excitement was growing. No one was tearing out checks just yet, but from the looks on their faces, they soon would.

"Do we have time to go to the ATM down the street?" someone shouted.

"Of course," Logan said. "I'll be here signing up investors for the next few hours. That is, if the bingo players don't mind me taking one table for that purpose."

B. C. Jenkins, the town's bingo caller, nodded.

Flabbergasted, Carny snatched the microphone from Logan again. "Wait a minute! Please, everybody, just hold on." No one seemed to be listening, so she raised her voice. "What's the big hurry? The first sign of a con artist is that he wants his money immediately. Trust me, people, I know. If this guy's legitimate, then he'll give you time to think about how much you can afford to lose, to check out his company and the people in it. Where are the plans for the park? Which banks are behind this? Is there any such company as King Enterprises? And if he won't give you the information you need to make an informed decision, then you'd better kiss your money goodbye, because you'll never see it again."

The room had grown quiet, and a few people began to nod and whisper in agreement. Carny looked up at Logan. The look he returned had no trace of his usual amusement. She was ruining it for him, and he didn't like it.

Pursing his lips, he took the microphone back and looked into the crowd. Slowly, that smile returned to his face. He deserved an Oscar for this performance.

"You know, ladies and gentlemen, she's right," he said. "This is a big decision, probably one of the biggest you'll ever make. You do need to think and pray about it, and heaven knows, I don't want any regrets later on. As I said, I don't even have approval yet to put the park in Serenity. But the number of investors I get here this week as an indication of community support will swing things in your favor. I'll be happy to show you the plans for the park as soon as they're ready, and I'll speak to my investors about revealing their names as soon as they've chosen a town. Transparency is the name of the game. No hurry. Put your money away."

The crowd buzzed, and Carny stared at him, surprised at the new twist. She hadn't expected this.

"I'll be staying at the Welcome Inn, and starting tomorrow, anyone who wants to meet with me and discuss making an investment can do that. But I'm not here to rob anyone. I don't want your grocery money or your kids' college funds. I don't want anybody making an investment they can't afford. Think about it, and if you think you want to be a part of an endeavor that has the potential to set your family up for generations of prosperity, then we'll talk. But I won't take your money tonight."

He set the mike back in its stand and flashed Carny that amused grin. "You want the first appointment?"

She crossed her arms. The roar of the crowd rose again. She turned away from the mike so that only he could hear. "I'm impressed," she said quietly. "But I'm still not fooled. Just be prepared. I'm going to fight you every inch of the way."

He bent to her ear. "I'll look forward to it," he said. "Can't wait to change your mind."

"You won't," she said. "And you won't change my town, either, not if I have anything to say about it." She stepped off the stage. "Better not let your guard down, Brisco. I'm watching every move you make."

THREE

Logan's motel room was cold when he returned to it that night. He'd left the air-conditioner on to combat the damp muskiness of the room, and now it felt like a meat locker. Locking the door behind him, he dropped his briefcase on one of the hard, tightly made beds and got out his laptop. He sank onto the other bed and booted it up.

He looked dismally around the room. It ought to feel like home, as many motel rooms as he'd stayed in over the years. But no matter how many times he came back to a room like this, it felt empty.

Quickly, he shook the counterproductive thought from his head. Montague wouldn't have stood for it.

Just as he wouldn't have stood for what had happened tonight. Montague would be packing his bags right now, ready to hightail it out of town, knowing that the odds were against his scam working against such a strong challenger. If Montague were living, he would have accused Logan of falling prey to Carny's challenge.

Lying down, Logan stretched his arms behind his head and closed his eyes. "You're right, old buddy. But I'm not you. I never have been."

As many rules as Montague had taught him about the line of work he'd fallen into, there was one rule that had served him better than any other over the years. Follow your gut. And tonight, his gut said to stay in Serenity, play this one out, and face the challenge Carny Sullivan had thrown at him.

He didn't like being thought of as a two-bit con artist. He didn't like being called a liar. And he especially didn't like having his integrity questioned.

Even if everything she suspected about him was true.

It wasn't as if he ever really hurt anyone. As Montague had always said, you can't cheat an honest man. Logan considered himself something of a teacher — a teacher of the hard lessons that people needed to learn. Better from him than from some mean-spirited criminal who would leave them unable to recover.

Logan's scams were always clean and neat. He came, he squeezed, he left. End of story. No attachments, no regrets, and no real consequences.

He'd already paid his dues long ago.

Logan had learned the first of life's dirty lessons when he became a ward of the state of Alabama at the age of five. He had never known his father, and no one explained to him why his mother had vanished from his life. Each night, after he was sent to a strange bed in a strange home, he would lie awake for hours, remembering bedtime stories and whispered prayers, songs his mother had sung while she bathed him, the laughter in the house where they'd lived. She had never left him before, except at a babysitter's while she worked, and he had always trusted that she would come back for him.

Until the day she didn't.

By the time he was six, he'd stopped looking for her in crowds. When he turned seven, he'd forgotten what she looked like. At eight, he learned to curse her for leaving him alone, and by the time he was nine, her memory was just a numbness in the center of his heart. He had neither expectations nor answers.

By the time he was ten, he had learned that no one — especially his mother — really wanted him, and that he was nothing more than an unwelcome burden to the string of families who'd taken him in.

In his foster homes, his brightness wasn't seen as an attribute. Instead, he came across as sarcastic and smart-mouthed. His youthful inquiries into the workings of the world often landed him in the attic or basement for punishment. When his third foster mother withheld meals from him for an entire day because of what she considered a "sassy mouth," he stole five dollars from her purse, climbed out the bathroom window, and went to the corner convenience store, where he bought a bag of potato chips and a soda.

It had been the perfect crime — until the worried store clerk, not accustomed to seeing children out so late, reported it to his foster father, who was a regular in the store. When his punishment resulted in a beating, and his teachers reported his bruises, Logan was moved once again.

As Logan grew older, he channeled his intelligence into surviving. He knew that he had been denied the blessings that other children his age took for granted, and that good things weren't likely to come his way unless he found a way to take them.

Taking those things landed him in more than his share of trouble and got him thrown out of every home he was dumped into. By the time he was eleven, he'd given up on the idea that anyone would ever love him and began to rely on his size and intellect to get him out of scrapes. He looked at least three years older than he was, and that number seemed to multiply exponentially as he got older.

At the age of twelve, standing five feet eight inches tall, he went to live with the Millers. Evelyn Miller, a small woman with a pallid complexion and a perpetual scowl, embraced martyrdom and never missed an opportunity to tell anyone within earshot how miserable her existence was. Her husband, Scotty, was a foul-mouthed ex-construction worker with a bad back that kept him from holding a job.

That Scotty lived next door to the local pool hall was no coincidence, Logan discovered. Scotty spent every night there, drinking with his cronies and shooting pool — bad back or not — laying down bets that he usually won. For the first time in his life, Logan found himself fascinated by something. As time went on, he found it increasingly difficult to stay away from the pool hall when Scotty was playing. But Evelyn fought hard to keep Logan away from the place, afraid that if the state found out, they would close down the Millers' foster home and stop sending the checks they so badly needed.

So every night, Logan hung around the house, listening to Evelyn stomp around quoting Scripture under her breath and sweeping up cigarette butts, yelling at the five children in her care to get out of her way and go to bed. Logan was always the first to oblige. As soon as the lights were turned out, he slipped out the window and crept over to the pool hall. Scotty never sent him home.

Logan was a quick study in deception, and after watching Scotty's techniques for some time, he realized the man was a hustler. Scotty would engage every newcomer who entered the pool hall and challenge him to a game. The first game Scotty would always lose, as his opponent expected, and then while the poor soul was counting his money, Scotty would suggest a triple-or-nothing playoff. Inevitably, he'd sweep the table clean in his first few shots, and would always go home the richer for it.

Logan practiced pool until he became even better at it than Scotty — and rehearsed the con. If people continually underestimated Scotty's talent, they would certainly underestimate the talent of a kid.

Before long, Logan took the hustle to new levels, and spent his afternoons hitting the other pool halls in town, engaging other boys in games, the first few of which he would lose. Then he would turn things around and blow them away in a winner-take-all coup. When he had taken the crowds in the area pool halls for all they were worth and was well known in each, he decided it was time to move on to greener pastures. There was no sense being dependent on the Millers or the state of Alabama anymore. He was fourteen but looked older, and had a pocketful of money and a lucrative vocation.

For a while, Logan hustled his way from one town to another, stopping in every pool hall along the way and swindling the regulars. Not accustomed to losing so much money to a kid, his marks often got angry. Logan made many an escape out the men's room window, the fire-exit door, or down an alley, with a posse of pool-cue-waving losers on his tail.

One night when he burst out the front doors of a combination bowling alley/pool hall, running from two irate opponents, a van screeched to a halt in front of the building. The passenger door flew open and a man's voice shouted, "Get in, son!"

Since the only alternative was to be beaten senseless by the pool players he'd bested, Logan dove into the front seat without a moment's thought. The car skidded away, leaving the men behind, cursing and vowing to get even.

Catching his breath, Logan sat up and glanced at his rescuer. He recognized the man immediately as one he'd noticed earlier, sitting at a table between the bowling alley and the pool tables, watching him hustle. Something about the man had made him uneasy; he had a white mustache and sucked on a pipe, a knowing look in his eyes as if he recognized a hustle when he saw one. He wore a three-piece suit with a paisley tie. In the bowling alley, he'd worn gold-rimmed reading glasses, and Logan remembered thinking that he looked like a nineteenth-century banker from one of those western flicks.

"I don't know who you are, mister," he said. "But you probably saved my life. Thanks."

"You have a few things yet to learn, my boy," the man told Logan in a heavy English accent. "Your technique is excellent, but your style needs a great deal of work. And your escape leaves quite a lot to be desired. How old are you, boy?"

"Nineteen," Logan lied. "I'll be twenty next month."

"You're twelve if you're a day," the man said.

"I am not!" Logan protested. "I'm fourteen!"

The man smiled. "That's more like it." He extended his hand across the seat. "My name's Montague Shelton. And yours?"

Logan briefly considered lying, but decided there was no purpose in it. "Logan Brisco."

"Logan Brisco," the man said, rolling the name over his tongue. "Sounds like a cowboy name. You Americans love cowboys, don't you? Outlaws and cutthroats and such?"

Logan shrugged. "It's just a name."

"Where are your parents?"

"Dead."

"How convenient," Montague said. "The parents of all runaways are dead."

"I'm not a runaway," Logan said, growing uneasy. "I haven't seen my mother since I was five, and I never knew my father."

"I don't know a great deal about your American laws," Montague said in a gruff yet polished voice that was growing gentler by the moment. "But I do know that they don't throw children out on the street when they reach fourteen."

"Yeah, well, maybe I'm mature for my age. Maybe they knew I could support myself."

"Hustling pool? Yes, I can understand why they'd send you out on your own."

Logan looked at him. "Are you gonna turn me in or what?"

"Why shouldn't I?"

"Because I'll just run away again. I don't belong with the Millers. They probably haven't even noticed I'm gone yet. They'll be mad when the social worker stops paying 'em, but other than that it won't matter."

"Did they beat you?"

Logan almost laughed. "Scotty? No. He yelled a lot, but he has a bad back. He was scared that if he hit me, I'd hit him back. And Mrs. Miller yelled at me every hour on the hour, but she wouldn't dare raise her hand to a kid bigger than she was."

"Where are you sleeping tonight?" the man asked.

"I don't know. I have money. I could stay in a motel, if I wanted. But sometimes I just sleep in a parked car in an apartment complex or something."

Montague eyed him. "This is your lucky

day, young man. I just happen to have a hotel suite myself. You're welcome to sleep in the extra room."

Logan wasn't used to handouts, and he was suspicious of generosity. "What's in it for you?"

"I could use a business associate," the man said. "We shall see how things look in the morning."

Logan didn't know what he meant by that, but a good night's sleep sounded enticing, and if the man tried anything funny, Logan was pretty sure he could hold him off. Montague was big, but he was old. At least fifty.

Except for the man's snoring, which he found tolerable compared to Scotty Miller's, Logan found the sleeping conditions more than suitable that night. The next morning, as he headed out the door, Montague stopped him.

"Young man, how would you like to go from making pocket change to real money?"

Logan shrugged. "Who wouldn't?"

Montague placed his glasses back on his nose and stood up. Stroking his mustache, he strolled around Logan, studying him. "You have promise, boy. I think dressed in the right clothes, with the right haircut, you could probably pass for twenty." He took off the glasses and kept talking while he wiped the lenses on his lapel. "Not that I mind youngsters, you understand. They just have no place in my organization. But I *could* use a partner."

"What organization?" Logan asked.

"My traveling enterprises," he said. "I'm a businessman. I need someone of executive caliber, someone who looks fit and trim in a suit, someone who has a talent for making money."

"I don't have a suit," Logan said.

"We'll get you one, lad. If you stick with me, you'll wear the finest clothes, eat the finest meals, sleep in the finest hotels. I'll make you a rich man. Are you interested?"

Logan shrugged. "I don't have anything better to do."

"Excellent," Montague said. "We'll have you fitted in Atlanta tomorrow, at which time, we'll get you a new birth certificate, inflating your age just a wee bit, and perhaps a driver's license. You can drive, can't you?"

Logan nodded, though he'd never been behind the wheel. He'd worry about that later.

They loaded the car with Montague's belongings — a computer, a small printer, and several boxes of paper of various sizes and colors. "Where'd you get all this?"

Logan asked. "Are you in the printing business?"

"I once was," Montague said. "I consider myself something of an expert in printing, and these machines help tremendously in my work. They are to be treated with the best of care. Without them, my business is greatly handicapped."

When they were on their way, Logan asked, "Are we heading for Atlanta today?"

"After one brief stop by the bowling alley," the man said. "I was taking care of some business when I ran into you last night. I must conclude it this morning."

Logan worried that the men he'd hustled last night would be there this morning, but it was still early, so he decided he'd risk it. They pulled into the parking space near the door, and Montague sat still a moment. "Are you a man of honor?" he asked Logan.

"Well — sure, I guess."

"You must be, if you're to travel with me. Honor and loyalty. I expect you to support me in any of my endeavors, and I will do the same for you. Is that clear?"

Logan nodded. "I guess so."

"No guessing, young man. You must be decisive. You must know what you want and how to get it. Indecision is the kiss of death in this business."

Logan squinted at him. "What business did you say it was, again?"

"Moneymaking," Montague said, dropping his keys into his pocket. "Now, come along. You're my assistant, here to help me carry the load. I do the talking."

Logan nodded and fell in behind Montague. The man walked with purpose, and the moment they were in the bowling alley, he went directly to an automatic teller machine against the wall. Putting his glasses on the tip of his nose, he punched a few numbers into the machine's computer, nodded his head at the string of numbers that filled the screen, and turned around as if looking for someone. Logan hung back as Montague cut across to the front desk.

"Hello, sir. My name is Sidney Moore, of the First Federal Bank of Birmingham. We installed this ATM machine late yesterday, but we had several complaints throughout the night on our twenty-four-hour line. I understand it isn't working properly."

"Yeah, it took a bunch of people's cards. Told 'em they had insufficient funds. One or two I could believe, but I doubt everybody who came in here was in the red. And on a Friday, too, when they just got paid."

"Hmm," Montague said, fingering his mustache. "I'm going to have to remove it

55

and take it in for repair. We'll make every effort to have a replacement here later today."

"Sure thing," the manager said. "We got along without it just fine until yesterday."

"Please tell your customers that their cards will be sent back to them in today's mail."

The man nodded and turned to a customer needing bowling shoes. Montague strode back to Logan and the ATM machine. "All right, son, let's load it up."

"Load it?" Logan asked. "Load it where?"

"In the back of my van," he said. "I assure you that it fits."

"But it must weigh a ton. And isn't it built into the wall or something?"

Montague winked and slid the machine easily away from the wall. Unplugging it, he said, "It's no heavier than a small computer. But help me so that it looks heavier."

Logan lifted his side and found that it didn't weigh more than twenty pounds. Together, they carried it out to Montague's van and slid it in. Before closing the back door, Montague leaned in, opened a compartment on the back of the ATM box, and retrieved two dozen or so ATM cards. Then, tearing off a printout at the back of the box, he nodded for Logan to get into the car.

As they slowly pulled out of the parking lot, Montague handed him the cards and the printout. "You see, my boy, having someone else's ATM card means nothing if you don't have their PIN numbers." He reached over the backseat and patted the box affectionately. "But my friend here just took care of that for us. Look for the account numbers and match them to the PIN numbers the people punched in with them. The printout has it all. Then put the cards in order."

Quietly, Logan did as he was told.

"We'll have to hurry," Montague said. "Since it's Saturday, the banks aren't open, but we mustn't take chances."

Montague pulled into a bank parking lot and idled the car for a moment. Logan watched, astounded, as he donned a big baseball cap, a pair of dark glasses, and a mouthpiece complete with a black mustache and beard. Tossing Logan a wig, he said, "Here, put this on. Just for the camera. We don't want to be identifiable."

Logan pulled the wig on, and Montague pulled up to the drive-through ATM machine. "First card," he told him.

Logan handed him the top card.

"PIN number?" Montague asked.

"Three-two-nine-five," Logan read.

Montague slid the card into the machine, waited for it to respond, then typed in the number. The computer asked him what amount he'd like to withdraw. Logan followed Montague's fingers as he punched in two hundred fifty dollars.

Holding his breath, he watched, amazed, as the machine rolled out two hundred fifty dollars. "One more," his mentor said, reaching for another card.

They repeated the steps and got two hundred fifty dollars more.

That morning, they hit ten more banks and drew two hundred fifty dollars out of twenty different accounts. By the time they were on the highway toward Atlanta, they had five thousand dollars.

Logan was charmed. "Do you do this all the time?"

"Absolutely not," Montague said with a note of pride. "I have many other ventures. With my knowledge of computers and printing, I virtually have people handing me money wherever I go. Don't ever let anyone tell you that knowledge isn't a wonderful thing. It's your key, young man, to anywhere you want to go."

When Montague handed him his cut — one thousand dollars — Logan decided he wanted to know everything Montague knew.

Over the next few years, Logan traveled with Montague under several aliases, and watched, ever amazed, as the man posed as an airline pilot, complete with a Delta uniform, and paraded around airports cashing counterfeit checks at the terminal desks. Then he and Logan went to the hotels that housed the pilots, checked in for the night on Delta's tab, cashed another check the next morning, and went on their merry way. Some of them were payroll checks on Delta's account, others were personal checks in the name of Lawrence Cartland, but they had all been created with Montague's printer.

Sometimes Montague would dress in a bank security guard's uniform, complete with an unloaded gun. As he proudly explained, white-collar criminals did not carry loaded guns. He would padlock the night depository at airports and collect all the receipts of the day by simply standing beside the depository, looking official, and explaining to everyone who came to make a deposit that there had been several break-ins at the depository. He had been ordered to collect the receipts personally, he said. And they believed him.

Montague made Logan several fake birth certificates under various names and ages, which enabled him to get driver's licenses in several states, and Logan became his getaway driver, his assistant in carrying machines and bags of money, his diversion when one was needed. He also learned how to counterfeit the most detailed documents as well as Montague.

But they both specialized in cashing counterfeit checks, with routing numbers at the bottom that would make the banks' computers send them to banks all over the country before anyone realized the checks weren't good. By then, he and Montague would be long gone.

They were victimless crimes, Montague always said. Crimes against airlines, corporations, banks. In the few cases where actual individuals took the losses, as in the ATM withdrawals, Montague kept their thefts to a minimum.

In one case, when the police had been close on their trail and Montague was desperate to escape, he had convinced a stranger he befriended in an airport bar to cash a check for five hundred dollars. The check was phony, but he'd saved the man's business card, and when they reached their next destination, he'd sent the man a money order for the full amount plus interest.

Montague's code of honor was strict, and

by the time Logan was old enough to pull his own stings, his friend's unwritten "commandments" had been drilled into his mind.

1. *Never fall in love.* The moment a woman got under your skin, you were to leave town. There was nothing more dangerous to their chosen career, Montague maintained, than the brain damage a woman could inflict on a man. It caused him to take unnecessary chances and make serious mistakes. That would jeopardize everything they'd worked for.

2. *Only take from those who deserve it.* Honorable men only took from those who could afford to lose something or those who were insured. But after that rule always came the qualifying caveat — "You can't cheat an honest man." Logan assumed that meant that anyone who fell for their schemes actually did deserve it.

3. *Never stay in one place too long.* They had to assume that the Feds were always on their scent, just a town behind them. One day too long could make the difference between freedom and years of incarceration.

4. *Never let your conscience slow you down.* There was no room for guilt or regret in this line of work. On the few occasions when Logan expressed those feelings, Montague

made it clear he had little patience for it.

5. *Never allow your picture to be taken, except for counterfeit IDs or passports.* All it would take was one photograph sent to the authorities by a suspicious mark and shown to a past victim to land them behind bars.

6. *Always travel light.* Accumulation could be fatal. In their business, one had to be able to leave things — and people — behind without regret.

7. *You can be forgiven any crime if you commit it with class.* Montague had outfitted Logan in a wardrobe fit for a Trump, forcing him to discard all his jeans, tennis shoes, and T-shirts. They were always to dress and carry themselves with class, and they slept in the finest accommodations and ate the richest food. "People will believe you are whatever you appear to be, my boy. Your life is a blank slate, and you must imagine your past and future to be as grand as you wish it," Montague said.

Armed with those rules, Logan concocted his first original scam at age sixteen. Posing as a twenty-one-year-old, which was believable since he now stood over six feet tall, he went into a tax-filing office carrying a fake W - 2 form and a stolen Social Security number and had his tax return done. When it was finished and his sizable refund was calculated, he requested "fast cash," an immediate refund offered by the company at a nominal interest rate, much like a loan. Logan walked out with two thousand dollars in his pocket. When Montague tried the same scam, he netted even more.

The heady feeling Logan got from charming his way through his own scam was addictive, and soon he had more ideas. For each, he spent hours at the library, researching the ins and outs of the businesses he intended to sting, making phone calls and talking to people, and analyzing the ways that he could pull off the most lucrative con.

Montague was clearly pleased with Logan's progress, and as Logan grew closer to adulthood, Montague became the closest thing Logan had ever had to a father. As the years passed, Logan realized that he hadn't been that much help to Montague in the early days; rather, the man had wanted him along to combat loneliness. Their friendship served both of them well.

The older Logan got, the higher he lived, and the more money he and Montague needed to maintain their lifestyle. Logan put his mind to work on bigger schemes, looking for ways to sweep a town of all its spare cash and move on without looking back.

The idea came to him when he was lounging in a hot tub one Sunday afternoon, watching television. He saw a documercial for a real-estate venture. "That's it," he said aloud.

Montague, who seemed to be sleeping in the bubbling tub, opened his eyes. "Did I miss something?"

"Seminars," Logan said. "We need to give some seminars. You know. On real estate, or investments. Let's say we come into a town, hold a seminar laying out some get-rich-quick schemes that would have the greediest people salivating. We tell them they have to invest that night, or it'll be too late. Then we tell them that we have to go to the site — you know, Brazil or somewhere — and that we'll be back with their deeds. Give them time to have their checks clear before they get suspicious."

"Seminars," Montague repeated, thinking it over. "My boy, I believe you may have something there."

They did their first real-estate scam in Picayune, Mississippi, a small town near the Gulf Coast, where the residents showed up at their seminar, checkbooks in hand, ready to make the investment of their lifetime. They sold property in Brazil that would allegedly be developed into one of the most sought-after resorts in the southern hemisphere. They walked away that night with fifty thousand dollars.

It was the first of many. Montague lent a touch of integrity and regality to the act, and Logan offered unabashed enthusiasm, along with a zealous passion for his product, whatever it might be. Together, they couldn't lose.

"This is the caper that could help us retire from this nefarious life we lead," Montague said with a grin one night as he stacked his money into bundles and packed them into a suitcase.

Logan laughed. "*You,* retire? What would you do?"

"Buy a ranch in the Southwest," Montague said without hesitation. "Find myself a nice little bride. Raise horses."

"I can't see you on a ranch, Montague," Logan said. "I've always imagined you usurping a prince and taking over his castle."

"Much too high profile for me," Montague said. "When I retire, it will be quietly. I'll put it all behind me and hope the hounds never catch up."

But the hounds — better known as the FBI — were always on their trail, inching ever closer, gathering more ammunition for the day they caught them. The pair had returned to their hotel more than once to find police waiting at their door, and once, as agents banged on the front door, they'd escaped out the back. It kept them moving, and it kept them careful. And it kept Logan tired, even though he found more happiness with Montague than he'd ever known since he was five.

But those happy times were soon to end. On Logan's nineteenth birthday, just before they were to pull off one of the biggest scams of their career, Montague collapsed on the hotel room floor. Logan fell to his knees at Montague's side, eyes locked with his mentor's, crying, "What's wrong?" Alarm colored Montague's face, then confusion, then terror. Before Logan could decide what to do, his friend was unconscious. He was dead before Logan could get him to a hospital.

Logan buried his friend in the town they had been about to sting, then disappeared into the night alone, not sure where he would go, but eager to get there. For some reason, he wound up returning to his hometown. A little research led him to an aunt, his mother's sister, who was not at all happy to see him. When he realized that she, his mother's only relative, had known he was abandoned and allowed him to go into the foster care system at five years old, a deeper loneliness than he'd ever known set in.

He couldn't remember another time since he was five that he had cried, for that kind of weakness made him too vulnerable. But that night, as he drove across the country in Montague's car, with no destination and no ties, he wept like a baby. For years, he had felt like an adult, been treated as an adult, been paid as an adult. But that night, he felt like a child who'd just been abandoned for the second time.

For a while, he lived off the money that he and Montague had acquired — money they had stashed in several safe-deposit boxes across the South. When several months had passed and the grief was not so profound, he tried to formulate a plan. But try as he might, he couldn't make himself carry out any of the scams that came to mind.

It didn't matter, because the FBI had a long memory. When they finally tracked him down, they made him pay. His sentence was fifteen years in a federal penitentiary under the name that was on his current driver's license — Lawrence Cartland. His bankroll was confiscated to make restitution to those he'd robbed.

Even in prison, Logan knew how to work a room. He made friends with all the guards and worked with gusto at every job given him, and he was paroled after serving half his sentence.

As much as Logan deserved to be called a criminal, he hated the label. So when he was free again, he decided to turn over a new leaf. He'd lost nearly eight years in prison, and he had no desire to lose any more. Montague had shown him that he had brains and that he could do just about anything he set his mind to. Maybe he needed legitimate work. Maybe it was time to get a real education.

He worked as a fry cook while studying for his GED and aced the test the first time he took it. He immediately applied for a grant to a nearby university, using his real name — Logan Brisco. He lived four years in the college dorm. Montague had taught him that one should never forget his assets, and Logan's happened to be a handsome face and a wizard's tongue. He could sell slab beef to a vegetarian and make her feel she'd gotten a deal. With minimal study, he charmed all his teachers into thinking he was their most gifted student, and he wound up with a transcript full of A's and a degree — his first and only legitimate credential.

Logan's first job after he graduated was in computer sales. He earned phenomenal commissions, for he was the best salesman the company had ever had. Always eager to find a new angle, he researched every aspect of the products and his customers and used every resource available to move the merchandise.

But when his boss began cheating him out of his commissions, he realized that con artists existed even within the bounds of legitimate enterprise. If that were the case, he'd rather do things Montague's way.

One night he watched an episode of *20/20* about the effect of the economy on the Mayberry-like town of Serenity, Texas, a former oil boomtown whose wells were drying up. What could be more perfect? Decent bank accounts from the boom days coupled with desperation about the future. They would be his first marks.

It took a few months of preparation and planning, but the payoff would be worth it. He'd planned to spend two weeks laying the groundwork, hit them with the so-called seminar, sweep up all the cash they gave him, and leave town before anyone had second thoughts.

Then he met Carny Sullivan, and found that there was an even greater game than pulling off this scam. To Logan, success lay not in the money, but in the degree of challenge. Even if it broke all of his old friend's rules, he was going to see this through.

FOUR

Jason always got off the school bus with a smile on his face that suggested he had a secret. But today, his smile was not secretive, but exuberant, as he bounded into the house, dropped his backpack on the floor, and ran to find his mother. "Mom! Mom! We're gonna be rich! Did you hear?"

Carny came out of the back of the house and caught her son. "What?"

"That man. Logan Brisco. He came to school today." Pushing past her, he ran into his room. "He's gonna give us free passes."

Carny watched as he grabbed his piggy bank and shook it, dumping pennies and nickels all over his dresser. "Passes to what? What are you talking about?"

"I'll give him everything I've got, Mom! How much do I have?"

"Slow down!" Carny turned her son around and forced him to look at her. "Let's go over this now. You're telling me that

71

Logan Brisco came to your school today?"

"Yeah. They let him talk during assembly. And he said he's gonna hold workshops for us kids after school, so he can explain the whole park to us and get our ideas and stuff. And if we get our parents to give him money, we'll be part owners!"

Carny let her son go, and he turned back to his pennies. "Jason, he's a crook. A thief. You can't give him your money."

"Mom! Everybody else believes him."

"Everybody else is going to get stung."

"Oh, yeah?" Jason swung around. "Then how come he didn't just take the money the other night? Lots of people were ready to help him, until you stopped them. If he was a crook, he would have taken their money then."

"Is that what he told you?"

"Yep. And after he talked to us, when the kids were going back to class, he came up to me and remembered my name! He's a nice guy. I like him. You're wrong about him, Mom."

As he spoke, Jason arranged his pennies into little stacks of ten, and Carny grabbed his hand. "Jason, I don't want you talking to him anymore. Do you hear me? And I won't let you give him one cent!"

"But Mom!"

"End of discussion." Making her oversized shirt into a catchall, she raked the pennies into it and headed to the kitchen.

"But Mom! That's not fair! It's my money!"

She dumped the pennies into a bowl on the counter, then grabbed the phone book. "You'll keep your money, Jason," she said, flipping through for a number. "You can keep saving for that four-wheeler you want. I'm not taking it away from you. But neither is he." She picked up the phone.

"Who are you calling?"

"The school," she said. "I'm going to tell Mr. Anderson to keep that man away from you kids. He's a thief, and he shouldn't be on campus."

"But Mom! People will hate you if you keep messing him up! Don't you want us to have a park?"

"There isn't going to be a park," she said. "Don't you hear what I'm saying? It's a scam! He's a con artist!"

Sarah Jenkins, the school secretary, answered, and Carny took a deep breath. "Sarah, this is Carny Sullivan. Is Mr. Anderson there?"

"Sure he is, Carny, honey. But before I transfer you, let me tell you that I think your intentions were good Saturday night with that Mr. Brisco fella, but you're wrong. I can just feel it. I have feelings like that, you know. Just sensations, but they're usually right. I can sometimes just see things, feel people's thoughts, that sort of thing. I think during my last abduction those aliens gave me some kind of psychic ability."

Carny closed her eyes and decided not to touch the subject of Sarah's infamous alien abductions. "Then why haven't you won the lottery, Sarah?"

The woman gasped. "Well, I never said I knew everything."

"And how many con artists have you known in your life?"

"Well, certainly none. But I'm sure I'd know if —"

"I've known dozens," Carny cut in. "I know their lines, I know their techniques, I know how they smile and how they walk. And I know how they make people believe them."

"Just because your parents are dishonest doesn't mean everyone else is."

She grunted. "Sarah, it's not just my parents. It's all the carnies who work for them. People I grew up learning from. I moved to Serenity because the people here are honest and good, even if they are a little naive. I won't let him brainwash you or

74

anyone else — we'll leave that to your aliens. Now, may I please speak to Mr. Anderson?"

Mumbling something incoherent, Sarah transferred the call.

The moment the principal answered, Carny could tell he was in a bad mood. "Hello?"

"Mr. Anderson, this is Carny Sullivan. I understand that you allowed Logan Brisco to indoctrinate our children today. My son came home ready to give him every cent he has."

"Now, Carny," Mr. Anderson said in a condescending tone, "I didn't let him speak. I had a dentist appointment this morning, and Sarah, who had good intentions, let the man have the stage. I wouldn't have. But now that he's shown us that several school projects can come out of his work, I'm thinking maybe it didn't hurt anything. It might be good for the children to get involved. They'll see what goes into a business enterprise like this."

"He's a liar, Mr. Anderson. I don't want him within a hundred yards of my son."

"Come on, Carny. You're overreacting. He strikes me as someone who knows what he's doing. He's not just trying to grab people's money and leave town. He's taking his time, giving people a chance to think about it.

I'm beginning to think that maybe this could improve our town."

"I can't believe you! Serenity has everything. It's the sweetest, cleanest, most peaceful town I've ever seen, and I've seen plenty. Mr. Anderson, let's just say he *is* telling the truth and there *is* going to be a park — which I'm absolutely positive there isn't — don't you realize that it would ruin this town?"

"This town could use a few changes," he said. "Mr. Brisco is bringing us hope. All he wants is a little cooperation."

"And a lot of money."

"He doesn't have to build the park here, Carny. If we give him too much trouble, he'll take his plans somewhere else. Hugh Berkstrom had a meeting with him this morning. Hugh has a good head for investments. He wouldn't even be considering it if it was a scam."

"Oh, no," Carny groaned. Surely the richest man in town had more sense than that! "Why won't any of you listen? You all know where I came from. You know how I was raised." She took a calming breath and tried again. "Look, Mr. Anderson, what if — just what *if* — I'm right, and Logan Brisco *is* a con artist? What if he got everybody in town, including the children, all worked up, and managed to walk out of here with all our money? It could ruin us. We'd never recover. This town has so many blessings from God, but if we do something stupid out of greed, we could destroy those blessings. Don't you see how high the stakes are in this?"

"And what if he's honest?" Anderson replied. "What if he gets impatient with us and goes somewhere else, and the next thing we know some other town is getting the park and everybody there is getting rich instead of us?"

"Then we'd find another way to stimulate our economy. But we'd still have this beautiful little town and all the good people in it, and our spirits would be intact, and so would our savings. We could do the *right* thing to help our people, not something that will completely break them."

"That's not good enough for me," Anderson said. "And it's not good enough for most of us here. Please. Just stay out of it."

Frustrated, Carny hung up and threw herself on the couch as her son came back through the room at a clipped pace, lugging his backpack. "Where are you going?" she asked.

"To Nathan's."

"What's in the backpack?"

He gave her an exaggerated look of innocence, which appeared more than a little guilty. "My homework."

She got up and took the backpack from him. "This must weigh thirty pounds," she said, unzipping it. "What a surprise. Money. The same money I just poured into that bowl." Glancing toward the bowl, she slapped her forehead. "And now the bowl's empty."

"Mom! You're ruining my dreams! I just want to be a part of it!"

"Over my dead body." She put the backpack on top of the refrigerator. "I have to go somewhere for a few minutes. You stay at Nathan's until I get back."

"Mom, are you going to cause trouble for him?"

"You bet I am," she said, grabbing her keys. "Logan Brisco has met his match."

FIVE

Carny shut off her Harley outside the motel and ran her fingers through her windblown hair. She hated wearing a helmet and only put the thing on when her son was riding with her. Someone from the sheriff's department pulled her over at least once a week and slapped her with a warning, but she hadn't yet gotten a ticket. The truth was, half the deputies had a crush on her and the other half considered her their little sister. None of them was about to get tough with her.

But Carny didn't take advantage of that often. It was nice to know that so many nice guys lived in Serenity. If Abe Sullivan hadn't ruined her stomach for relationships, she might even consider some of them dating material.

She walked into the office of "Doc" Carraway — so named not because he was a doctor, but because he'd flunked out of a

South American med school. He'd chosen hotel management as an alternative occupation. Leaning on the counter, she said, "Hey, Doc. What room is Logan Brisco in?"

Doc looked up and instantly smoothed down his hair. "Uh . . . he's in 210. I ain't really supposed to tell you, but since folks have been comin' in and out of there all day, I don't guess it's a secret."

Dread flashed through her. "Don't tell me they've been bringing him money."

"If they're smart," Doc said. "Hugh Berkstrom got here at seven-thirty this morning."

"Did he invest?" she asked. "Tell me he didn't."

"I don't know. But I'll tell you this much. Hugh didn't make his fortune with careless investments. If he invests with Logan Brisco, then far as I'm concerned, there's no better investment. And some of the folks who've come by this morning have been trying to make deals with him to put shops and restaurants inside the park."

"Doc, there isn't going to be a park."

He just smiled. "We'll see, won't we?"

Exasperated, she headed up the stairwell to room 210 and knocked firmly on the door.

Logan opened the door wearing well-cut

slacks and a white shirt with the sleeves rolled up. It was the first time she'd seen him without his jacket.

He grinned as if he'd been expecting her. "Well, well."

"We have to talk," she said, pushing into his room. She stopped cold when she saw her in-laws, Bev and J. R. Sullivan, getting up from the table. Her heart sank. "Oh, no. Not you too."

"Don't start, Carny," J.R. said. "We know what we're doin'."

"Not if you gave him any money, you don't."

Bev shot a nervous glance at Logan. "Carny, please. We'll talk about it later."

For the first time in years, Carny felt the ache of tears behind her eyes. But she wouldn't cry in front of this man. That would give him too much power.

"Look at me, Bev," she said, her voice shaking slightly. "You know me better than anybody else in town does. Have you ever known me to say anything that wasn't true?"

"No, of course not," her mother-in-law replied.

J.R. looked up at her with weary eyes. "Honey, your past sometimes colors your thinkin'."

"It sure does. If I can't learn from my

81

past, J.R., then I'd be pretty stupid, wouldn't I?"

Logan leaned against the wall, arms folded, and from the amused look in his eyes, she knew he was enjoying every minute of this.

"You haven't even prayed about this, J.R.," she said. "If you had, you wouldn't be doing it."

"Honey, we can talk later," J.R. said, and he and Bev stood to go.

Carny gritted her teeth and stared at Logan as the couple closed the door behind them. "Jail is too good for you. You should be shot."

He broadened that maddening smile. "Did you come to invest too?"

"No, I did not," she said through her teeth. "I came to warn you to stay away from my son. Duping the adults of this town is bad enough, but when you start conning little kids —"

"Excuse me," he said, turning to his table as she spoke and opening a logbook. "You don't mind if I make a few notations in here, do you? It's important that I log in every penny I get, so I can register the shares and get the profits paid out accordingly."

"Give me a break!" She jerked the logbook away from him and caught her breath at the number of investments he'd already logged there. "Nice prop," she said. "Looks real legitimate."

He shook his head, still grinning. "You're determined to make me out to be a liar, aren't you?"

"No," she said, leaning over the table. "I'm determined to get you out of town. But first you're going to give back all the money you've already gotten. What was the take today, Brisco? Ten thousand dollars? Twenty?"

Logan got up wearily, and crossing his arms, looked down at her. "What are you so hostile about?"

"You think this is hostility? Oh, no, this isn't hostility. You haven't seen hostility yet."

He dropped onto the couch and patted the spot next to him. "Sit down."

She gave a short laugh. "Yeah, right."

"No, really. If we're going to talk like two adults, then I'd prefer that you sit down."

"I don't really care what you prefer," she said. "I didn't come here to have a nice, cozy chat with you."

"No, you came to show me how tough you are." He stood back up and leaned against the wall. "So why didn't your husband come? Why does he let you fight these battles all alone?"

"Brisco, by now I'm pretty sure that you've found out everything there is to know about me. I'm your biggest stumbling block in this town. So I'm sure you know that I'm a widow."

"Well, that explains how vulnerable your son is. He's hungry for a man's attention. I noticed that right away."

"Of course you did. It's your job to spot people's weaknesses. And right now you think Jason is my weakness. But it won't work. If you insist on staying here until you've stolen all the town's money, I'm going to make you sorry you ever took up crime as a profession. I've seen more cons than you've ever dreamed of. I've even been part of some. I'm not wrong."

"Oh, so that's it," he said. "You're so distrustful because *you* can't be trusted. You think I'm like you."

"You're *nothing* like me," she bit out. "I made something of my life in spite of my background. God washed me clean of all the garbage in my life, and these good people loved on me. I'll fight tooth and nail to keep you from ruining them!"

His expression was serious as he stared at her, and for a moment she thought she might be getting through to him. Then he took a long breath and said, "You're really cute when you have that look in your eye. Do you know that?"

She fought the impulse to slug him. "Give it up, Brisco. I can't be charmed."

His eyes danced with the challenge. "Want to lay odds on that?"

"I don't gamble, but if I did I'd take that bet."

He laughed. "A hundred bucks says you'll be chasing me before the month is up." His eyes twinkled. "Winner take all."

For a moment, she stared at him, incredulous. What arrogance! This might even be fun. Winner take all, indeed. Lock, stock, and ego. "Like I said, I'm not a gambler." Heading for the door, she looked back over her shoulder. "If you come near my son again, Brisco, I'll hurt you."

Then she slammed out of his room.

Six

Logan was grinning when she closed the door behind her. Slowly, he ambled to the window and watched her march down the steps to her motorcycle.

Still chuckling, he went back to his logbook and flipped until he came to the pages of notes he'd taken about her — the pages he was glad she hadn't seen. It was as complete as a dossier, and he was proud of it. He'd learned a lot about her today. Much more than he'd expected to. The citizens of Serenity didn't even know they were being pumped for information. But Montague had taught him years ago that there was one difference between a successful huckster and a jailbird. And that was research.

That was why he'd wound up in Serenity in the first place. After watching the *20/20* episode, he had researched all of western Texas, soaking up information about the farms that had reverted to the banks, about the oil wells drying up, and about the people, most of whom had lived here all their lives.

He'd sought out a town that was down on its luck, a town that needed a dream or two. But it also had to be a town that still had resources. Preferably green resources — the kind that kept him in the lifestyle to which he was accustomed. He had researched the building of amusement parks so that he'd be able to speak intelligently on the subject and answer any questions from the most astute of the populace without babbling or stumbling.

Then, after he'd come to the town, he researched the people, one at a time, deciding who would be the easiest marks, who had the most money, who were the entrepreneurs of the community, and who had the least to lose.

And today, he had researched Carny Sullivan.

Pulling out the chair at his desk, he sat down and went back over the things he'd learned about her. The facts about her — from birth until today — still surprised him, and he couldn't help feeling an affinity for her. Whether she liked it or not, the two of them had a lot in common.

Carny had been a con artist until she was

seventeen, pushed that way by both heredity and upbringing. According to Lahoma — whose brain he'd picked during her appointment this morning — Carny had been raised by two small-time frauds in a traveling carnival. Someone else had told him she was born in the back of a Winnebago in a carnival's convoy, somewhere between Shreveport and Monroe, Louisiana. She'd been named after her family's lifestyle and trained to follow in her parents' footsteps.

The town's accounts of Carny's past had been colorful and detailed. She'd dazzled many of them with tales of her childhood over the nine years she'd lived in Serenity. Her in-laws had told Logan about Ruth, the carnival's fat lady and Carny's tutor, who had the IQ of a genius and a table full of computers in her own RV, and spent every morning tutoring Carny to such an extent that Carny probably knew more about a broader range of subjects than any college graduate.

From Blue Simpson, he learned how Carny had spent afternoons with her parents — learning card tricks instead of ballet, rigging games instead of playing them, and creating diversions for their cons. And from Eloise Trellis, whose deceased husband had launched Carny's current career, Logan heard about the little girl walking alone each evening through the carnival while her father picked pockets and her mother guessed ages and weight.

He sat back and tried to imagine the details he hadn't been told. It wasn't hard — his own childhood had left him with plenty of images to fill in the blanks of Carny's life. In his mind, he could see a little towheaded girl with huge, beautiful eyes, dark circles under them from staying up too late and eating too much junk. She probably wandered through the carnival, following happy families with normal children who went to school and sang in choirs and had best friends. Did she imagine staying behind as one of those happy children after the rides were broken down and the booths were loaded back onto their trailers? Leaning his head back on the seat, he rubbed his eyes and wondered if, in her darkest hours, she had dreamed of starting over with normal parents who went to church and had barbecues and coached softball.

God knew, he had, until he'd grown too hardened to allow himself such painful indulgences.

For a moment, he allowed himself to sink into the mire of self-pity, a luxury he rarely afforded himself. For a split second, he was that abandoned child again, firmly believing that his mother would return, not under-standing why she hadn't. For a split second, he knew intimately that little girl wandering down the midway, looking for her fantasy family.

Turning the page, he read through the rest of his notes. There was much he hadn't written down yet. He hadn't recorded the part about her escape from her old life and how she had come to Serenity. But he had it all in his head. Her in-laws, two people who loved her as if she were their own, had told him, almost in apology, everything else he needed to know.

Carny, at age seventeen, had met Abe Sul-livan when the carnival came through Serenity. He was good-looking and seemed soft-spoken, clean-cut, the apple-pie-and-mom type. After a week-long romance, she had slipped out in the night with him and eloped, and the next morning when it was time for the carnival to tear down, she informed her parents that she was staying behind.

She had been just a child, according to Abe's parents, but Logan knew better. You never got to be a child in that kind of environment. He suspected that she'd behaved in ways much older than her years, and that the marriage had had as much to do with her fascination for the sweet little town itself as it had with the man she'd married. She had probably believed that, in the quiet little town of Serenity, she could have the kind of home she'd only dreamed of before. She was old enough to know what she wanted out of life, and young enough to fool herself into believing such things existed.

He suspected that now, nine years later, she was much more savvy about the goodness that existed — or failed to exist — in the world. According to Abe's father — who'd seemed disgusted even to recount the tale, but had been compelled to explain Carny's "rudeness" — Abe had taught Carny her first lesson about the grass being greener on the other side. Abe wasn't the sweet husband material Carny thought she was getting. He drank most of the time, had trouble holding a job, and stayed out too late. It amazed Logan that two such sweet, kind people could have raised such a son. But as Bev Sullivan had said with a tear in her eye, "There's such a thing as loving too much. We had him in church every time the doors were open, and tried to instill our Christian values in him. But he chose a different path. We spoiled him rotten. We blame ourselves. That's why we took Carny in when he ran out on her. We felt so responsible."

When Abe left her and her baby, then drank himself dead, Carny stayed with the Sullivans. Logan suspected that they'd given her the first nurturing love she'd ever known. The town, which had that Western quality of prizing rugged individualism, had rallied around her, something he found unusual for a community with relatively few newcomers. But the people he'd asked about her today had all voiced a deep love for the young woman, tinged with amusement.

She had a wild, unconventional streak, they said, and a free spirit that made them all smile, but since coming to Serenity she had turned into a God-fearing disciple of Jesus. She was a little of what everyone in town wished they could be. She hadn't meant to be rude at the bingo hall, they'd all said. She was just overly suspicious because of her past, and overly protective of the people she loved.

He envied their love for her. Carny had truly made herself a home here, while Logan was still running, looking for that pot of gold at the end of a self-made rainbow. Someday he'd come to the end of that rainbow.

But he doubted that there was a Serenity waiting at the end of his.

SEVEN

The Sullivans were waiting on the front porch when Carny pulled her motorcycle up her gravel driveway. She rode to her front steps and cut the engine off. "Y'all are making a terrible mistake."

"Carny, honey, you don't have to worry," her mother-in-law said. "We're not giving him more than we can afford."

J.R. stood up from the rocker. "But the folks in town who have already invested are afraid that you'll talk Logan out of building the park here, and we'll lose out. You've got to stop it, Carny. We need this park in Serenity."

Groaning, she got off her bike and went up the porch steps. Sitting down on the top one, she leaned back against the post and looked up at them. "You aren't hearing me. He's got all the earmarks of a pigeon dropper. Why can't you listen?"

"What's a pigeon dropper?" J.R. asked.

"A huckster. A shyster. A con man. J.R., if some big organization was considering building a park here the size of Disneyland, don't you think we'd have heard from the governor, the legislature, the bankers? Don't you think there would be some kind of public competition among the towns? Don't you think there would be some sort of legal process involved?"

"We're in on the ground floor," J.R. said. "All that will come later. But all Logan's doing is scouting around for the best place to build it. He's recommending us, and then I expect the governor will get involved. If he chooses to put it somewhere else, we can either get a full refund or still invest in the park wherever he does put it."

Carny closed her eyes. "Come on in, and I'll call Jason home."

As they went in, J.R. asked, "You still have a class tonight, don't you?"

"Of course," she said. "I won't quit teaching just because there's a criminal wreaking havoc on my town."

J.R. shook his head. "Lands, how you do exaggerate." He walked to the television, grabbed the remote control, and plopped into his favorite chair, which she had bought just for him since he spent so much time at her house spoiling his grandson.

She paused for a moment and regarded J.R., who was already switching from *Ultimate Fighting Championship* to *Dateline,* then back again. Bev made herself at home in the adjoining kitchen, putting a pot of coffee on.

Carny loved them, and because she did, she couldn't just sit still and let Logan deceive them this way. Overcome by a sense of helplessness, she stood for a moment, wishing for the right thing to say to make them proceed more cautiously. But for them, it was already too late.

"What will happen if you find out I'm right?" she asked them softly. "I don't know how much you gave, but what'll happen to the town if none of it works out?"

They both looked at her. Finally, J.R. said, "Honey, it'll be all right."

Sighing, she slipped the keys to the pickup into her pocket and started for the door. "It took me seventeen years to find this place, and now that I'm here, I'm a little protective of it. I don't know what I'd do if I lost it." Her voice broke, and she looked down at her feet. "Maybe I'm fighting him out of selfishness. I want to keep things safe for me . . . and for Jason."

"Oh, honey." Bev came across the room and embraced her, the way her own mother had rarely done. "We know why you're doing it. And we don't blame you. But that doesn't mean we agree with you about Logan."

"I'll have to prove it to you, I guess," she said. "Call Jason to come home, will you? The number's on the fridge. I'll be back around eight." Feeling herself losing control of her emotions, she hurried to the truck.

She drove two miles before the tears came to her eyes, but quickly, she wiped them away. Somehow, she would stop Logan before he hurt these people too much. She just hoped he wouldn't skip town tomorrow with the money.

She turned onto the road to her private airport, just on the outskirts of Serenity. Serenity Airport and Aviation School were her stake in this community. It was how she made her living, how she contributed to the town, and one of the ways she satisfied the wild streak she'd been born with. It hadn't been easy to settle into this tight little town, to become a part of it, to be trusted and loved.

In fact, there had been a lot of head-shaking when Abe Sullivan brought her home as his wife. Part of it had been that she was just seventeen, and they all knew Abe wasn't cut out to be a husband. But the other part, the part she had never quite forgotten, was that she had a checkered past. She knew she had something to prove to Serenity, so she made it her business to get to know everyone in town, from Jed who cleaned the factory after hours to Mayor Norman, who said she looked like his daughter who had moved to California.

At first she'd struggled with the dichotomy between her strong desire to settle down and her hungry spirit that craved adventure. Rather than moving on to satisfy that yearning, she opted to take flying lessons. That way, she reasoned, she could feed the gypsy lust bred into her and still have a hometown.

To support herself and finance her flight lessons, she took a job as teller in the only bank in town. As her pregnancy progressed, she got to know the townspeople and felt more a part of the town. The moment she got her pilot's license, Wendell Trellis, owner of the aviation school, the airport, and the air service that carried crucial deliveries from Serenity to wherever they needed to go, offered her a flying job. It paid considerably more than she had made at the bank, allowing her, three years later, to venture away from the Sullivans' home and get a place of her own for Jason and herself. She would never forget the lump in her throat the day she brought Jason to the old house she'd bought for them, the first real home she'd ever known. It had two bedrooms, a huge open kitchen that adjoined the den, a garage, and a white picket fence around the backyard.

Jason was mostly thrilled that there was a tire swing in the yard — he was far too young to grasp how much this home meant to Carny. Her unsavory childhood didn't matter anymore. What mattered now was that she was a good mother, making a good life for her son.

She'd been weepy that first day in her new house, ever aware that God had wiped her slate clean and turned the ashes of her life into beauty. She wanted the same transformation for her parents and those she'd left behind in the carnival. Instead, they all thought she'd been brainwashed by her Bible-thumping neighbors. Only one responded to the grace she saw in Carny's changed life. Ruth, the carnival's fat lady, followed Carny's immersion into Christianity. Though she stayed with the carnival to keep teaching the children, her newfound love of God led her to resign from the freak show. A child of God was never meant to be gawked at and mocked, especially not for money. Carny considered Ruth's changed life a fruit of her own.

And it was no small feat that Carny went from answering the phone for Wendell and making an occasional jaunt across the state, to actually buying the airport when he retired, and running the three related businesses herself. She was proud that the bank where she'd worked had approved her loan as a vote of confidence in her character. Her aviation classes were always full, and her freight schedule was always busy. She gave people free flights to Dallas or Houston for doctor's appointments and other crucial business, and had endeared herself to everyone in town. People needed her here, and they enjoyed her. She had never felt so good about herself.

Now, she pulled up to her hangar, threw the truck into park, and grabbed her bag full of papers. Already there was a car here, a dark Lincoln Navigator with blackened windows. Had Jess Stevens traded in his twenty-year-old Plymouth? She chuckled at the picture of the retired farmer letting go of a nickel he didn't absolutely have to. Or the Navigator might belong to Cass or Jacob Jordan, but they were both more the sports-car types. And it couldn't be either Brad Gillian's or Wayne Cash's, since they wouldn't be caught dead driving anything but pickup trucks. Since that ruled out all five of her students, she got out of the truck with a feeling of apprehension.

The SUV door opened, and Logan Brisco got out.

Her mouth dropped open. "What are you doing here?"

Logan's grin riled her as he stepped closer. "I wanted to see your facilities. I thought I might need your services for emergency deliveries."

"Deliveries of what?" she asked. "Large bundles of cash going to a Swiss bank?"

He laughed. "No. My company in Dallas will be spearheading the operation and sending contracts, payroll, that kind of thing."

"Save it, Brisco." She went inside, aware that he followed, and dropped her papers on her desk. "You're wasting your breath. How did you know where I work?"

"Everybody knows," he said. "I must have gotten ten different versions of your life story today."

"Good," she said. "Then you know I don't give up."

"I'd suspected." He turned a chair around backward and sat down. "Tell me something, Carny. What would it take for us to call a truce?"

"For you to be on the next train out of town."

He laughed. "No, I mean what would it take for you to give me some peace while I'm here?"

Crossing her arms, she cocked her head and faked a thoughtful expression. "Well, let's see . . . Atlantis rising from the ocean floor, Amelia Earhart landing on my runway, Jimmy Hoffa being discovered on an island paradise with Elvis . . ."

"Okay, I get the point," he said, still amused. "Maybe you and I just need to get to know each other a little better. How long's it been since you've been in a relationship?"

It was her turn to laugh. "I've had lots of relationships. But the odds of my ever having one with you are pretty much as likely as all the scenarios I just mentioned."

He tried to look wounded, but she wasn't buying. "Carny, I could have walked into town in a priest's collar waving a Bible and you still wouldn't have trusted me."

"You're right," she said. "My father posed as a priest once and made three thousand dollars a night 'healing' people. I was the little crippled girl he made walk. My mother was blind, until he mumbled a really loud prayer and made her see. I'm a tough sell, Brisco."

Logan seemed genuinely appalled. "And you think *I'm* a fraud? Your father sounds like a real prince, and if that's the kind of thing you grew up watching, I don't blame you for being paranoid now."

"What's your point? That you're better than my father because your scams are cleaner?"

She'd hit a nerve, and for a moment Logan only looked at her. "Carny, I realize that nothing short of my own miracle is going to persuade you to trust me," he said in a soft, almost convincing tone, "but I really want to do this for your town, because I think Serenity needs what I'm bringing it. And I think *you* need it. You're a woman who needs something she can trust . . . something to believe in."

"If that's what you think, then your conversations about me today weren't very productive. I happen to believe in a lot. I believe in God's ability to change people, and I believe in the goodness and purity that I've found here. And I believe in that kick in the gut that the Holy Spirit gives me when something isn't right."

"I call that instinct." He walked toward her, his face serious, and said, "Do some research on me, Carny. Check me out. Write for my college transcript. Talk to my teachers. I have a degree in marketing from Virginia State. Call A&R Marketing in Marietta, Georgia. Check out my employment records."

Doubt altered her expression. Con artists didn't often have college degrees, and they rarely had job histories. She whipped out a pad and pen, jotted down the two places, then looked up at him. "I'll call them tomorrow," she said. "And your company. What did you say it's called?"

"King Enterprises." He handed her his card. "You can call this number and verify my employment."

She wondered if she'd get a busy signal or if he'd gotten a cohort to answer the calls. "And what about Dallas banks that'll be financing this? Can you give me their names?"

He smiled calmly and shook his head. "I can't do that. It's still in the initial stages. If you were to start calling them and drilling them about the park, they'd get scared and pull out. It's my job to make everybody feel confident that this is going to work. Including my investors."

Smiling, she dropped her pen. "What else did I expect?"

He sighed and ran a hand through his dark hair, leaving it ruffled. "Look, I'm just curious. If you did trust me, if you had known me all your life and knew I had a sterling character, would you still be fighting me on this?"

"I sure would," she said.

"I thought so. Why?"

"I told you. I don't want my town ruined by a flow of tourists, criminals, and carnies."

"Tourists, I can understand. But what makes you think either criminals or carnies will come here?"

"Because they will." She heard a car drive up and glanced out the window. Her students, Cass and Jacob, were getting out of their car. "The criminals will come to rip off the tourists, and who do you think you'll get to run the park? Carnies, that's who!"

"Then work with me on this," he said. "Help me plan it so that we can avoid that. At Disney, they put a police station on the grounds. Hotels and malls can go way outside of town, near the park. Carny, if this works, your airport would benefit. We'd need to enlarge it for bigger planes. My investors could finance the expansion."

She lowered her voice as Cass and Jacob came closer. "Is that how you usually manage to pull off the gaff, Brisco? By making it personal? Telling each person in Serenity how they'll wake up rich one day, if they just give you all their money now? You're wasted in this line of work. With those talents you could run for president."

He stared at her as though it truly hurt.

She looked out as another of her students drove up. "Well, I've enjoyed this little conversation, Brisco, but I have a ground school class to teach."

He made no move to leave.

"Did you hear me? Time to go."

"Where do I sign up?" he asked suddenly.

She gaped at him. "Sign up for what?"

"For the class," he said. "I want to learn to fly."

She laughed. "You've got to be kidding."

"Why?" he asked. "I'll need to know how to fly once this park gets off the ground."

"My class is full."

"You can fit one more in."

"I don't want you here!"

He smiled. "I know you don't. But if you think about it, it would be the smart thing to do. That way you could keep your eye on me. Make sure I don't skip town."

"There's nothing that says you can't skip town just because you're taking a class."

"True. But I really do want to learn to fly,

Carny. It's always been a dream of mine. I've just been too busy. Come on, I'll pay you in advance. Cash. And I'm a quick learner."

She waved at her students assembling in her classroom. Well, he was right about at least one thing. She would be wise to keep an eye on him. And the more money she could take from him, the better. After all, his cash had come from the people of her town. Maybe she could use it to help out those who could least afford to lose it.

"All right, Brisco," she said. "I charge forty dollars an hour, plus plane rental. To get a private pilot's license, you'll need ground school plus at least twenty instructor hours in the plane, and at least twenty solo hours."

He smiled and pulled out his wallet. "And you call *me* a con artist."

"FAA rules. And that's cash in advance for you," she said. "And frankly, I wouldn't be comfortable letting you solo in my plane."

He looked insulted. "You think I'm going to steal your plane?"

"I'd rather not take chances. You can get your solo hours somewhere else."

He pulled out ten one-hundred-dollar bills

and dropped them in front of her. "How's that?"

Something tightened in her chest. Was she really going to have to teach him how to fly? Snatching the money angrily, she went into the classroom. He started to follow. "You can't start tonight," she said. "I only have enough materials for five students at a time, and besides, these people are halfway through ground school."

"When do you have another class?"

"I have one for kids after school on Tuesdays and adult classes on Saturday and Monday nights. But they're all in progress."

"Then I guess you'll have to start a new class just for me."

"The price I gave you wasn't for private lessons," she said.

He laughed and reached into his wallet. "Boy, your daddy taught you well."

Something in her snapped. She took a step closer, glaring into his eyes. "There's a difference between a con artist and a business person, Brisco, and you know it. If you don't like my rates, find another instructor."

He opened his wallet. "Why don't you just take what you need and give me back what's left?"

"Fine." Taking the wallet out of his hand,

she counted out the bills she needed, wondering if it added up to what her in-laws had given him. "That ought to do it."

He looked down at the few bills she gave back to him. "This better be good."

"Oh, it will be," she said. "I have a delivery to make in Sherman tomorrow, but I should be back by mid-morning. Meet me here at ten for your first lesson, Brisco."

EIGHT

Logan was right on time for his lesson the next day, and Carny launched into the first session of ground school, which was an overview of the parts of the plane. But Logan already knew most of them, what their uses were, and many aviation terms. Some of his knowledge applied more to commercial jets than to small single-engine planes. He'd posed as a pilot many times to cash Montague's homemade Delta payroll checks at the airport terminals. He'd claimed to have a degree from Embry-Riddle Aeronautical University in Daytona Beach, one of the leading schools for commercial pilots, so he'd learned enough to make that plausible. He'd deadheaded on many a flight, posing as a pilot catching a ride between airports, listening to the talk in the cockpit and watching the captains and first officers work. Now he'd have the chance to find out how to actually get the plane off the ground.

Halfway through the lesson, Carny put her hands on her hips. "How do you know all this stuff?" she asked him.

"I fly a lot," he told her.

"You don't pick this up sitting in coach," she said.

He shrugged. "Who says I fly coach?"

"You don't get it in first class, either. You already know how to fly, don't you? This is just another con."

"Well, if it is, it's your con. I'm the one who paid you an arm and a leg, remember?" He raised his right hand. "I promise I don't know how to fly. But I read a lot. There was a time when I thought I might want to be a professional pilot, so I did some research. I told you, I'm a quick learner."

She bristled. "Don't waste my time, okay?"

"I won't. When you check me out, see if I have a pilot's license."

Carny leaned back on her desk. "You know, I do intend to check you out, but I have no illusions that you're even using your real name. You could have the name and history of some other poor soul."

Logan had, indeed, used aliases before, and the time he'd served in prison was under Lawrence Cartland. He hadn't been the only one in prison using a fake name.

Many of the other inmates were arrested with false IDs and booked under those names. But he did have a couple of legitimate credentials under his real name, and no rap sheet. "Now how would I get identification with someone else's name?" he asked.

She laughed. "All it takes is a computer and a printer, and a little ingenuity. My father once got the birth certificate of an acquaintance who'd died, and with it, he was able to get a driver's license and a passport. But I would imagine you know all the tricks."

"You're the one with all the expertise. I should take notes."

"Yeah, I was raised to be a hawker, but you might say I departed from the ways of my kin. Were you raised to be a con artist, Brisco, or were your parents good, law-abiding citizens who had to answer to the cops for you?"

That hit a nerve. "Nobody answers for me."

"Well, there must be somebody back there in Virginia . . . isn't that where you said you were from?"

"I didn't say."

"Oh, excuse me. I should have known that was a secret."

Wearily, he stood up and began to gather his notes. "It's no secret, Carny. I was born in Alabama."

"And went to school in Virginia? Interesting."

"People go away to school all the time."

"Yes, they do. Logan Brisco. Logan's an interesting name. Is it a family name? Your mother's maiden name, maybe?"

He didn't like her talking about his mother. "My mother never married. Brisco was her maiden name."

"Oh." Carny hesitated, almost as if she sensed his discomfort. But she didn't back off. "So where did the name Logan come from?"

"I don't know," he said. "I never got the chance to ask her." He slammed the cover of his textbook shut. "Her name was Melissa Brisco, Carny, and she was born in Selma, Alabama. Happy hunting."

Her eyes softened, and he could almost see the wheels turning in her brain, wondering if this was another bluff.

"When's the next lesson?" he asked in a clipped voice.

"Next Monday? Same time?"

"What's wrong with tomorrow?"

"I'm all booked up with classes and deliveries through Saturday."

113

"Then what about Sunday?"

She shook her head. "Nope, I don't work on Sundays."

"Oh? Then what do you do on Sundays?"

"I go to church," she replied. "Have you ever gone to church, Brisco?"

He thought of the dead church that one of his foster mothers had made him attend. "Not without being dragged."

"You should give it another shot," she said. "It might change your life."

He managed to grin again. "Are you trying to convert me?"

She smiled. "Heavens, no. I'll leave that to Brother Tommy. He's worked miracles before. The real kind."

"With you, maybe?"

"Absolutely," she said, lifting her chin. "With me. Salvation is the biggest miracle of all. You want to really get to know the people of Serenity, Brisco, you have to go to their church."

His stomach felt a little sick. "And what church is that?"

"Half of Serenity goes to Deep Waters Christian Church. We're of the 'turn-the-other-cheek' ilk. Of the belief that if a man asks for your shirt, you should give him your cloak also. That's why we make easy targets for people like you."

114

He gave a defeated laugh and started for the door. "Why on earth would you want a lowlife like me in your church?"

"Because," she said, ignoring the sarcasm, "if I can't stop you myself, maybe God can at least reactivate that conscience of yours. Maybe seeing the goodness in these people will make you back off. But beware, Brisco. You might decide you like them too much to fleece them. It could cost you a huge score."

The woman knew which buttons to push. Irritated, he turned around. "You never give up, do you?"

"Nope." But her smile was less condemning, and he saw the slightest trace of warmth in it.

He shook off his discomfort. "Do the church folks go to the town dances?" he asked.

She shrugged. "Of course we do. Everybody goes."

"Really? I thought Christians were against dancing."

"Some are. But we're just fine with foot fellowships."

He laughed, and surprisingly, she joined him. No wonder the townspeople were so fond of her. "You want to start a scandal and show up with me at the dance?" he asked.

Her grin almost disarmed him. "No, Brisco. I doubt you'll still be in town a week from Friday."

"Wait and see," he said.

He closed the door behind him, and as he got into his car, he felt her watching him through the window.

Watching him drive away, Carny reflected on the anger and pain she'd seen flash across his face when she'd mentioned his mother. In spite of her efforts not to be moved by him, something about his reaction had touched her.

I never got the chance to ask her . . . Melissa Brisco . . . Selma, Alabama . . .

After her class, she went back in her office, sat behind her desk, and ran what he'd told her through her mind. Some of it sounded true, and her instincts were often right. But there was so much that didn't add up.

She flicked on her computer, pulled up her email. There was a message from Ruth, who sat in her trailer at her computer when she wasn't teaching the carnies' kids. She earned her living designing software and feeding her genius IQ while communicating

116

with people all across the world.

Carny smiled as she read.

Hey, baby. Haven't heard from you in a week. How's Jason? When are you bringing him to see us again?

Carny responded quickly.

Ruth, sorry I haven't written. I've been busy. Why don't you give me a call? I'll be at the hangar all afternoon. Jason's getting off the bus here at three. While you're at it, get Mama and Pop to call me too. I need to talk to all of you.

She sent the message, then waited for the phone to ring. In moments, it did.

"Serenity Aviation," she said.

"Hi, baby," Ruth said in a voice so thin, you'd never know she weighed five hundred pounds. "I got your message."

"I'm sorry I haven't emailed this week," Carny said. "It's just that this guy came to town, and I'm pretty sure he's trying to run a scam . . . and I've been a little distracted trying to expose him."

"Anybody I'd know?"

"Well, I don't know," she said. "That's why I wanted to talk to Mama and Pop. I thought they might have run into him."

"They're right here, darlin'. I'm gonna put on the speakerphone so we can all talk."

She switched over, and Carny heard her

mother. "Hey, sweetheart. How's it going?"

"Hi, Mama. Pop, are you there?"

"Right here, Carny. So how's that grandbaby of ours?"

"Growing like a weed. You wouldn't recognize him."

"When are you ever going to bring him to see us?" her mother asked. "You know we can't get away. We have carnivals booked all through the South for the next six months."

"I'll come soon, Mama. But I have to ask you something. There's a guy here who's trying to sell the town on building a huge amusement park. He's taking money from everybody, telling them they'll get rich."

"Good line. Are you in on it with him?" her father asked.

Carny wilted. "No, Pop, I'm not. I told you, I'm living a clean life here. And I don't want him messing up this town. I wondered if you might know him. The name he's going by here is Logan Brisco."

"Brisco," her mother said. "I don't believe I've heard that name."

"Don't know him," her father said. "What's he look like?"

"Tall, dark hair, relatively handsome, but not as good-looking as he thinks he is. Of course, all the women here practically swoon every time he walks by. It's downright sickening. And he's got an unusual smile. Real big, and real contagious."

"Are you sure you're not swooning too?" Ruth asked with a laugh.

Carny grunted. "I'd rather be hung up by my toenails in the town square," she said. "Does he sound familiar to any of you? He tells me he's from Alabama and went to school in Virginia, and he's also mentioned Marietta, Georgia."

"Was he a carny?" her mother asked.

"I don't think so. My gut tells me his are all white-collar scams."

"I'm sorry, honey, but none of what you've told us rings a bell."

She sighed. "All right, just thought I'd ask."

"By the way, Carny," her father said. "If it turns out not to be a scam, and there really is a park, I'd like to talk to him. I could set him up with some rides, and your mother and I could bring a bunch of our carnies and set up some flat stores."

Over my dead body, Carny thought, but instead, she said, "There's no way he's legit, Pop. And as soon as he realizes what a hard time I'm gonna give him, I'm sure he'll head out."

"So what's his line again?" he asked. "Building an amusement park? Telling them to invest and they'll get rich?"

Was her father taking notes? "Pop, don't."

"I was just askin', darlin'. That's all. Now, when can I see my grandson?"

"Soon," she said, but her promise was as weak as ever. The less time her parents had to influence Jason, the better.

After they hung up, she got on the Internet. In a few hours, she would know a lot more about Logan Brisco — hopefully, enough to expose him for exactly what he was.

NINE

Logan hadn't expected to be an honored guest at Deep Waters Christian Church, but when Brother Tommy, the preacher, spotted him before the service, he introduced him to the deacons he hadn't yet met.

It surprised him that the whole town actually set their alarms on Sunday mornings and showed up early enough for Sunday school. As they wandered in to find their places before the service, he was hit with the strange and unexpected feeling that they actually enjoyed being here. It was a social gathering, where people smiled and laughed and encouraged one another, where they wore their Sunday best and fixed their hair. Men who rarely shaved during the week were spit-polished this morning.

Logan didn't know what Montague would have said about his being here, but he suspected he would have approved. As mercenary as he was, his old friend had always admired honor and decency, traits Montague vowed to adopt as soon as he made enough money. And as Carny had pointed out, what better place for him to get to know people than in their church?

Someone tapped Logan on the shoulder, and he turned to find Slade Hampton, smiling like an old friend and waiting to shake his hand. Jack, his dog, was at his side.

Logan stood and shook Slade's hand, then bent to pet Jack. "They let you bring him in here?"

"Nobody's ever said nothing about it," Slade said. "I guess they're so used to seeing us together, they've mostly forgot he's not human. Besides, he enjoys it."

Logan could see that the dog did, indeed, enjoy it, for every child that came by stopped to speak to him. Slade slipped into the pew next to Logan, and Jack followed, curling up at his feet. As he and Slade talked, Logan watched the crowds coming through the doors from Sunday School, waved at all of those he knew. But the moment he spotted Carny, he realized the real reason he had come.

She wore an outfit that spoke more of southern gentility than biker chick — a long, flowing skirt that stopped just above the ankles and a silky lavender blouse.

Logan tore his gaze away as Julia Peabody approached him, and grinning his most flirtatious grin, he told the printer's daughter how glamorous she looked, complimented her dress — then glanced back at Carny. Her eyes briefly met his, then she looked down at Jason, walking at her side. It was almost as if she didn't care that Logan was here.

Mildred Smith, her hair glowing neon-red from the dye job Lahoma had given her, started to play the piano, and Logan watched Carny and Jason move through the crowd still coming in. Her hair was pulled up in a loose chignon, with tiny wisps around her face. He swallowed. Man, she was beautiful. She made every other woman in the room look like a poor imitation of femininity. She was the real thing.

Carny came up the aisle and stopped when she reached him. "So you decided to come, did you, Brisco?"

Like the gentleman Montague had taught him to be, Logan stood and smiled. "A man has to worship somewhere."

"I guess that depends on what he worships. Do yourself a favor and *listen* to Brother Tommy. You might learn something important." Then she slipped into the aisle across from him.

Logan didn't believe in God, and he rarely believed in goodness. And even though Carny clearly viewed Serenity as something of a paradise, he didn't believe in heaven.

Still, as the preacher spoke in mesmerizing tones about the fallen nature of the world and the pain that sin caused in the hearts of young and old, he couldn't help locking in. The man had a way of driving the point home.

As he stood to leave after the benediction, Logan realized that this was the first time he'd ever sat through a church service without nodding off. If he was still in town next Sunday, he might come back.

Monday afternoon, Carny sighed, almost disappointed, as she hung up from the last of the phone calls she'd made about Logan. Something was wrong. All the sources he'd told her to call — his former employer, his college, had all checked out. She hadn't been able to reach a human at King Enterprises, though. A recorded voice transferred her around, but all she got was voicemail. She left messages asking about Logan, but no one had called back yet.

Carny had spoken to the secretary at A&R Marketing, who still remembered Logan and described him in an awestruck voice, leaving little doubt that they were talking about the same man. She described him as the best salesperson they'd ever had, and in a near-whisper, told Carny he'd been cheated out of his pay, and she hadn't blamed him for leaving.

When Carny spoke to those of his professors who were still at the college, they'd described him to a T. Charming, with a devilish grin. Smart. Charismatic.

But it was the call to the Selma, Alabama, county clerk's office that had given her the most insight into the man. Just as Logan said, his mother's birth certificate was on file there, dated fifty-five years ago. When she'd asked the clerk about the woman's only recorded child, she'd been directed to Human Services.

Telling the woman at Human Services that she was investigating a case, Carny persuaded her to find Brisco's file. The woman read bits and pieces over the phone — enough to tell Carny that, from the age of five, Logan Brisco had been shuffled from one foster home to another until he'd run away at the age of fourteen.

That was the source of the pain in his eyes when she'd mentioned his mother. Carny couldn't help feeling a little ashamed of herself. That kind of pain never went away.

Pain like that had the power to mold a person into something he might never have been, to drive him toward the kind of life where he thought he was in control and created his own destiny. Where close attachments were rare, and abandonment was impossible.

Knowing about his childhood made her see him in a different light. For the first time, she allowed herself to wonder whether he really was the grifter she believed him to be. Nothing she had discovered about him suggested that he'd ever been on the wrong side of the law.

But there were giant holes in his life — from the time he'd run away at fourteen until he'd gone to college, and from his resignation from A&R until now.

She hadn't found any evidence of Brisco's duplicity. But as she gazed out her hangar window at Jason washing her Baron, she decided that didn't matter. She still didn't trust the man, and she couldn't let her sympathy for his difficult childhood color her thinking. She rarely doubted her instincts, and she wasn't about to give up on them now.

Jason was almost finished washing the plane. She smiled at the serious way he went about it, talking to himself the whole time, as his imagination rambled. She wondered what part he was playing today. Was it fighter pilot with his guns aimed at the enemy? Was it firefighter, putting out a monstrous blaze?

She went outside and headed toward him. When he saw her, he grinned and aimed the hose in her direction. Ducking, she reached for another hose coiled beside the hangar, turned on the water, and aimed her own spray at him.

Screaming and laughing, he ran behind the plane and sprayed at her over it. She ducked under it and got him good from behind. Squealing with laughter, he reciprocated by drenching her.

"I got you first!" he shouted. "If those had been bullets, you'd have been dead before you reached for your hose!"

"Flesh wounds, my boy," she said in a bad English accent. "Mere flesh wounds. But *your* wounds were fatal."

"I don't think so," he said. "I can take a few bullets without even feeling them."

"Good," she said, and pulled her hose back up into his face, spraying him at point-blank range. He screamed and wrestled with the nozzle, and by the time they collapsed on the tarmac laughing, they were both sopping wet.

"Tell me two things," she said, finally. "Tell me how I could have raised a little boy without guns, without toys that look like guns, and without allowing television shows or video games with guns, and you can still manage to make a gun out of a garden hose."

"You can make a pretend gun out of anything, Mom," he said matter-of-factly. "It's a guy thing."

"I guess so."

"What's the second thing you want me to tell you?"

She sat up. "How we're going to get home on that motorcycle soaking wet. We'll freeze to death."

"Nah. It's 80 degrees. Almost summer. Hey, you know what, Mom? This summer, Nathan's dad said he'd buy us the lumber and stuff, and we can build a fort between our houses. Won't that be cool?"

"It sure will. Can I help?"

"No way," he said, aggravated. "Girls don't know anything about building stuff."

"Sure we do," Carny said. "When I was growing up, we used to have to tear down the whole carnival everywhere we went, then put it back up when we got where we were going. I know a few things about construction. Come on," she said, tickling

128

him. "Let your old mom help!"

He squirmed and held back. "Sure, if I want my fort to look like a carnival booth. I don't think so."

"How'd you get to be such a male chauvinist at seven?"

"What's a male chauvinist?" he giggled, defending himself from her tickles.

"A guy who thinks building a fort is a guy thing. And I suppose if I don't get to help build it, I won't get to play in it, either, huh?"

Jason held her hands to stop the tickling and tried to catch his breath. "It's a boy's fort, Mom. No girls allowed."

"That's it," she said. "I'm suing."

"Mom!" he said. "You'd bump your head on the ceiling, anyway. It's for kids."

"Keep going. I've got two counts of discrimination so far. Gender and height. I can take you for everything you're worth. I'll probably even get the fort. I'll paint it pink and turn it into a doll house."

He giggled frantically. "Mom! That would be gross! Besides, you can't sue us for something that isn't even built!"

"Oh, yeah." She got up and wrung out the front of her shirt. "And if I die of pneumonia, I probably can't sue, either. This was all a clever ploy to intimidate me out of taking you to court, wasn't it?"

He laughed and popped his wet shirt away from his skin, then let it stick back. "Hey, Mom. Are we going to the dance Friday night?"

"Why? You got a date?"

"I sorta told Amber I'd meet her there. I might dance with her this time."

Carny made a face. "But she's a *girl!*"

"Girls are okay once in a while," he said, skipping behind her in the puddles as she turned off the hoses. "I mean, you can't have 'em coming in your forts and stuff, but they're okay to dance with. Are you going with Mr. Joey?"

Still chuckling, she shook her head. "Nope."

"He said you were. He told me you're his girlfriend."

"Joey's got a lot to learn. I never told him I'd go with him to the dance."

"Then who are you going with? Mr. Paul? Mr. Sam?"

"None of the above. I thought I'd just go as your date."

His face sobered. "Okay. I think that would be okay. Amber probably wouldn't mind if it was just you."

As he skipped into the hangar, Carny knew she couldn't do better than Jason as her date. He, after all, was the man of her dreams.

TEN

Thursday, Logan swung around in his chair at the Clippety Doo Dah, where he spent as much of his spare time as he could, buttering up the ladies. He grinned at the proprietor. "Tell me, Lahoma," he said, "do you consider yourself single-handedly responsible for the abundance of beauty in this town?"

Her laughter had a sweet, infectious ring to it. Eliza Martin, whose hair she was working on, hooted right along with her, and the ladies under the dryers chuckled as well, even though he doubted they'd heard his question.

"You're such a talker," Lahoma said in her deep southern drawl. "By the way, have you heard about the dance tomorrow night? Down at the bingo hall?"

"I sure have," he said, "and I intend to be there."

"And have you got a date?" Lahoma asked

with a wink.

He grinned. "You got somebody in mind?"

She blushed, then recovered. "Well, if I was fifteen years younger, I'd snap you up myself. Might anyway, now that I think about it."

The other ladies guffawed, and Lahoma preened in the mirror, proud of herself. "No, Logan, I had someone more your age in mind. My daughter, Mary Beth, doesn't have a date yet. Or there's Jean Miller, who works at the drugstore. Or Bonnie . . . you know, the little waitress in the diner? Take your pick. There's plenty of gals in Serenity who wouldn't mind going on your arm."

Grinning, he swung around in his chair again. "Well, you see, that's just the problem. There's so many I'd love to go with. It's hard to decide. I think I might just go stag so I can dance and flirt with all of them."

The women laughed again, as if that suited them just fine. Logan pulled up out of the seat and sighed. "Well, ladies, I've sure enjoyed shooting the breeze with you. And like I said, if any of you want an appointment with me, you know where you can find me. Time's running out, though. I have to have all my investors registered pretty soon, or we'll have to move on to another town. My employers don't like to be kept waiting. And the idea, of course, is to get the park started by the end of the year, so we're really under the gun here."

"My husband's gonna call you today, Logan," one of the ladies under the dryer said. "His name's Jess. When you hear from Jess, you'll know who he is. My husband."

Logan leaned down and took her hand. Kissing it, he said, "I sure will, ma'am. And if he's half as delightful as you, it'll be a pleasure going into partnership with him." He went to the next lady under the dryer, kissed her hand, then reached for the third. They all tittered like birds.

Then he grabbed Lahoma, pulled her into a waltz, and spun her. "Tomorrow night, you save a dance for me," he said, kissing her cheek.

"I will," she said, almost swooning. " 'Bye, Logan."

On the sidewalk, Logan checked his watch. He'd talked Carny into giving him a private lesson today, and he had just enough time before it to stop by the barbershop and shoot the breeze. It was these intimate little gab sessions, unscheduled and relaxed, that inspired the kind of trust he needed to make the people of Serenity part with their money.

He stood by the red-and-white barber

pole outside and looked in the window. Slade was cutting the mayor's hair, and Cecil was cutting that of a man Logan didn't know yet. There was one other man waiting, and they were all laughing.

Friendship. Camaraderie. It was something he'd missed terribly since Montague died. But he couldn't break Montague's rule of getting too close now, just because it felt good. A lot of things felt good, but they could also land him back in jail. The goal now was to get to know the folks as well as he could while still holding himself aloof from them. That was the trick. Fortunately, he was good at it. It was what made it easy to leave the towns behind.

Serenity was something else, though. *20/20* was right. It was just like Mayberry, for Pete's sake. And this was Floyd's Barber Shop, and the men in the chairs could have been Andy and Barney. He hadn't really believed such towns existed. No wonder Carny was protective of it. But he couldn't let that influence him. A man had to make a living, after all.

Logan slid his hands into his pockets and strolled inside. Everyone turned and greeted him. "Logan!"

Slade and Cecil shook his hand, and the mayor, almost completely hidden by a voluminous chair cloth, freed his hand and reached for Logan's too. As if he were the town celebrity, the other men introduced themselves and told him they had been at his town meeting.

Slade looked over at the chair where his dog sat, and said, "Jack, get up and let Logan sit down." The dog jumped down immediately and went to lie beside Slade's chair.

Laughing, Logan stooped to pet the dog. Jack sat up and licked Logan's hand. The gesture broke the shell of a memory Logan had kept stored away for years. Butch, a lab mix with big, soulful eyes — the dog he'd come to love in his first foster home. At five years old, Logan had curled up with Butch in bed every night, crying softly for his mother. Butch had been the only one who could comfort him.

When Logan was taken from that home, he'd begged to take Butch with him. But the family wouldn't give their dog to the homeless boy.

"Logan?" Slade said. "You need a haircut?"

Logan shook himself out of his reverie. "No thanks, Slade," he said as he stroked the dog. "I just had a few minutes to kill before my next meeting and thought I'd see what you fellows are up to."

Fellows. Wasn't that how they would have said it in Mayberry?

"Well, oddly enough, we were just talking about you."

"Oh yeah?" He looked up. They were smiling, so they hadn't been raking him over the coals. "I came just in time to defend myself then, didn't I?"

"Oh, you don't need defending. Not from us, anyways. From Carny Sullivan, maybe."

"Yeah, she's not so bad, though. I'm taking flying lessons from her. I figure when the park gets underway, I probably ought to buy a plane."

"Carny's teaching you?" The man who'd introduced himself as Joey, a younger man than the others, who had an enviable beard and was as big as a bear, gave him a surprised look.

"She sure is. She's a good lady. Just a little suspicious, and from what I've heard about her, you can't blame her. It's a shame about her childhood."

"So which class are you in?" Joey asked. "Her Monday night class?"

"No. She's teaching me privately. All the other classes were already in progress."

Joey got quiet, and Logan noticed something behind the man's eyes. Was it jealousy?

He couldn't afford to make any enemies in this town, so he tried to rally. "You're not the Joey she keeps mentioning, are you?"

His eyes lit up. "She talks about me?"

"Well, I guess it's you."

"What did she say?"

Logan laughed and bent down low to let the dog lick his face. "Well, now, whatever she said, it was in confidence. But I will tell you that she thinks a lot of you."

Joey smiled and looked off into space.

"How long have you had Jack, Slade?" Logan asked.

Slade put the finishing touches on the mayor's hair. "Ten years. He's been by my side almost every minute of that time. Goes everywhere I go, don't you, boy?" Slade went over to pat the dog's head, then resumed his cutting.

"He looks like a loyal pal." Logan patted the dog's coat one last time, and, as if he knew that meant a dismissal, Jack wandered over to the corner.

"So how are the plans for the park shaping up?" Mayor Norman asked.

Logan crossed his arms and looked the mayor straight in the eye. "Well, sir, I'll give the people of Serenity another week or so to get their investments in. Then I'm supposed to meet back with my employers and their big investors with my recommendation. I'm pretty sure that, if we can demonstrate enough support from Serenity, they'll choose this site for the park. In fact, I'd bet on it."

The mayor laughed. "The best thing to happen in this town in forty years, and it's during my administration. Who would have thought?"

"You're not tryin' to get credit for it, are you, Mayor?" Cecil asked, a twinkle in his eye.

The mayor shook his head. "Oh, no. No one would believe me. It's just kind of nice to be in office when so many good things are happening."

Slade swung the mayor's chair cloth out of the way and shook it out, and the mayor got to his feet. "I'm going to need an appointment with you myself, Logan," he said as he fished through his wallet for Slade's fee. "I'll call you later."

"I'm going your way, Mayor," Logan said, standing up and stretching. "I'll walk with you and we can nail down a time."

As if he had lived there all his life and knew them each as well as they knew one another, they all waved goodbye.

Logan's lesson with Carny that afternoon

went well, and he noticed an ever-so-slight change in her attitude. "So did you check on me yet?" he asked when the lesson was over. "Decided I'm legit?"

"I checked, Brisco," she said, consulting her appointment book for a time for the next lesson.

"Good. Then I should be cleared. You want me to make you an appointment so you can talk about investing?"

She shot him a look. "Your stories may have checked out, Brisco, but I'm still not convinced you're on the level."

Not convinced, he thought. Wasn't that better than before, when she'd been absolutely certain he wasn't? Still, it aggravated him that she hadn't considered his references positive enough to clear him. She was just too smart.

"What did I ever do to you?" he said, intending it as a joke, but his words came out sounding a little plaintive.

"Nothing," she said with a flip smile. "I just don't intend to sign my soul and my bank account over to you, like my friends and neighbors have. Don't get too secure, Brisco. I haven't given up trying to expose you."

"Carny, you have got to be the most stubborn woman I've ever met."

"I'll buy that," she said. "You've probably never met anyone like me."

"You've got that right."

"Good. Then you won't quite know how to handle me, will you? It looks like I'm the one who has the advantage here. I know exactly how to handle you."

That was a challenge if he'd ever heard one. "What if I'm one of the good guys, Carny? What if you're completely, absolutely wrong?"

"I'm not," she said simply. "Now, if you'll excuse me, I have a delivery to make. I have to hurry if I want to get back before Jason's out of school."

"You still going to the dance tomorrow night?"

"Yep." She jotted down the time for his Saturday afternoon class on the back of one of her business cards.

"Going with Joey?"

She stopped writing and looked up. "Boy, you don't miss anything, do you? No, I'm not going with Joey. I'm going alone."

"Oh, yeah?" He took the card from her, looked at it, and put it into his pocket. "Me too."

She slapped her hand against her forehead. "Say it isn't so. Logan Brisco, celebrity among us, has not got a date to the dance?"

141

"Oh, I could have gone with Lahoma's daughter, or Jean Miller, or Bonnie . . ."

She smirked. "Then why didn't you?"

"Because I wanted to be free to dance every dance with you."

She laughed. "You'll have to stand in line."

He liked that spunk. Grinning, he went to the door. "I will," he said. "See you tomorrow night."

She was still smiling when he closed the door behind him. Progress, he thought. He was making progress.

Eleven

High Five was the town's country-music band that played at all the local gatherings. It consisted of the postmaster, one of the grocers, a traffic engineer from Odessa, and the twins who ran the railroad depot.

The makeshift dance floor in the bingo hall was full. As Logan stepped into the room, smiling in answer to all the greetings he was immediately barraged with, he thought again that this surely was Mayberry. The dream town, where little boys named Opie grew up to be wholesome and good. Or little boys named Jason.

He caught Jason's wave across the crowd and saw that he was dancing with a pretty little girl in a frilly dress. He winked and flashed him a thumbs-up, and Jason blushed. Logan laughed and tried to remember being that age. Where had he been at age seven? With the Clements or the Legates? That was the year he'd been passed around to three different families. The sobering thought killed his smile, and he glanced away. His gaze immediately collided with Carny's. He might have known she'd be on the dance floor too. And he wasn't the only one watching her. A number of men on the edge of the crowd seemed to wait their turns.

Man, she was cute. That was the thing about her. A lot of women were pretty — in fact, a lot of the women right here in Serenity were pretty. But it was Carny's cuteness, her bounciness and playfulness, juxtaposed with her serious side, that made her impossible to purge from his mind. And he'd tried. He'd tried hard.

He watched as she strayed from her partner and found her son dancing with his friend. Tapping his partner on the shoulder, she got Jason to turn her way, and he took her hand. The two of them began to dance, and Logan couldn't escape the look of pleasure in her eyes or the look of delight in the boy's.

Someone tapped on Jason's back — Logan recognized him as Joey from the barbershop yesterday — and Jason deferred to him. Without batting an eye, Carny fell into step with him. She wasn't a tease, Logan thought. Lots of men would shower attention on her tonight, and while she didn't *need* that attention, she wouldn't make them feel small, either. He enjoyed watching her.

Something tugged at his leg, stealing his attention, and Logan looked down to see Jack looking up at him. "Hey, boy," Logan said, stooping to pet him. "What's a nice guy like you doing in a place like this?"

The dog closed his eyes and rolled his head into Logan's hand, clearly wanting a scratch. "Where's your old man, boy? Where's Slade?" Jack's ears perked up, and he looked toward where Slade stood with a group of men. "Not far, huh? I didn't think so."

The dog went back to his master's side, and Slade bent and rubbed the dog's head while he talked.

Logan thought of joining them, but he wasn't ready to take his attention from the dance floor. Carny seemed to have boundless energy. The other women dancing around her paled in comparison. Ironic that the only woman he was interested in in Serenity was the one who saw right through him.

Strolling along the outskirts of the crowd, he ran into Jean Miller, a pretty little redhead he'd heard was training to be a missionary. There was no doubt in his mind that, if he wanted to, he could make her forget her calling. But he wasn't that kind of man. He had always been diligent at keeping Montague's rule not to pursue innocent women.

He flirted with Jean just for show, but his eyes kept straying to Carny. She was pouring punch for herself and Jason. Jason was chattering about something, and Carny laughed as she listened.

"You've made quite an impression in this town," Jean said, dragging Logan's attention away. "I hope you plan to stay, even after the park is built."

"Thinking about it," he said with his most flirtatious grin. "I'm getting attached to Serenity." Though the statement rolled off his tongue with the fluidity of the rest of his spiel, he had to admit it was true. There had never been a town he'd be sorrier to say goodbye to.

"Don't let folks like Carny run you off," Jean said. "Carny marches to her own drummer. Everybody loves her, but we don't put a lot of stock in anything she says or does."

"She's the flighty type, huh?" he asked.

Catching his lame attempt at a pun, Jean burst into giggles.

Logan left Jean and ambled toward the punch table. The bowl held straight lemonade. Nothing alcoholic. This town . . .

His eyes gravitated back to Carny as he sipped.

Montague would have told him to pack his bags this very moment and leave town. There was nothing more likely to cloud a man's judgment than getting tangled up with the wrong woman. Bad judgment meant making mistakes, and mistakes led to jail, as Logan well knew.

Besides, he'd already scored enough cash to close the whole thing down.

But he couldn't go. Not yet.

He watched as Jason went to play a video game against the wall with some of his friends, and Carny stepped outside the bingo hall alone. Logan followed her. The moon was full, lighting the main street through town in silvery hues, and the lights from the windows and doorway spilled out, breaking up the darkness. He watched her walk up the sidewalk, fanning herself with her hand, then stop to get a drink out of the machine in front of the barbershop.

Logan stayed close to the buildings, not wanting to be seen just yet, and watched her lean against the wall, take a long sip of the Coke, then stare off into space.

He pushed away from the wall and strolled up the sidewalk. She saw him coming and flashed him a knowing grin.

"Well, well. You never know what might be lurking in the dark," she said.

He wanted to be sincere with her, but he wasn't sure how — he'd been faking it for so long. "I've been watching you," he said.

She smiled. "Oh, yeah? You must be pretty bored."

"Not at all." He braced his hand on the wall, just above her head, and leaned down over her. "There's nothing boring about you, Carny."

She laughed. "You can say that again. I've been accused of a lot of things, but never of being boring. You either, I'd imagine."

He shrugged. "I know you don't like to admit it, but we have a lot in common."

Her smile faded, and she looked up at him, her eyes soft and vulnerable, but still so savvy that he felt uneasy. "And what do you think we have in common?"

He breathed a laugh, but quickly his smile faded. "Loneliness."

The laughter that burst from her took him by surprise.

"What? What's so funny?"

"That's pretty good, Brisco," she said. "But you can do better than that."

He bristled. "What do you mean?"

"Oh, you know." She walked a few steps away, still grinning, and when she turned back to him, he saw that she was genuinely amused. "Touch on the struggles I've had as a single parent. Tell me you have an empty house in the Midwest with five bedrooms you dream of filling up. Or my disillusionment. Tell me you've had your share of the same, but that a woman like me could restore your faith . . ."

"What are you talking about?"

"Cons, Brisco," she said, stepping closer and grinning up at him. "Let's face it. The usual ones won't work on me. You'll have to be more creative."

"Lady, you're as hard as nails. It wasn't a con. It was a statement of fact. You're a lonely woman. It's written all over you."

Again, she laughed. "You think you can read me? Man, you're arrogant. You don't know the first thing about me. If you did, you'd know I don't need a man to be content."

"But a woman like you needs one to be happy. And you deserve to be happy, Carny."

"And you think happiness is falling for the likes of you?"

"No, I think happiness is falling for the

likes of *you*."

Again, she laughed, but this time it was a little more strained. She turned away, took a drink of her Coke, and kicked at a rock. "Let me tell you something, Brisco. There are at least a dozen eligible men in town who are attractive, productive, and decent. Why on earth would I choose you?"

"Because I'm different," he said. "Just like you. And for what it's worth, if I had a woman like you, I'd have stayed home every night. I wouldn't have gone out drinking and gotten killed in a drunken brawl."

He realized the moment he said it that he shouldn't have. Her cheeks reddened as if she'd been slapped. She pointed up at him. "Don't you say another word to me about my husband."

He swallowed. "I'm sorry. I didn't mean to offend you."

"Slamming my husband, who isn't here to defend himself? You didn't think that would offend me?"

"I was told you weren't happy in your marriage."

"My marriage is none of your business." She turned and looked out over the parking lot. "So you'll have to try a different angle."

"I'm really sorry. Bad call."

She crossed her arms and headed back

toward the bingo hall.

Logan watched as she went back in, and for a moment he listened to the sounds of the town, the sounds of friendship and family, the sounds of laughter and lightness, the sounds of somebody's home. Her home. But not his.

He'd never been lonelier in his life.

And the worst thing he could fault her with was that she was right. This would be even harder than he'd thought. The only way he'd ever convince her that he was legitimate was if he *became* legitimate. And maybe not even then.

What a thought. Going straight — for a woman. He could imagine Montague's incredulity, could hear that distant voice urging him to get out of here, telling him that he'd stayed too long already, that no man could carry out a scam for more than a couple of weeks. It was dangerous. It was ludicrous. It was suicide. With every day that he stayed, his position — and his freedom — would be jeopardized more.

But Logan had no desire to leave. There were challenges here he had yet to meet, and few of them had anything to do with money.

TWELVE

Carny wandered back into the dance. Jason was still playing video games. High Five was just about to crank up again. Her in-laws were clustered in a circle of friends, and she strolled toward them.

But someone grabbed her arm from behind, and she turned. Joey stood over her, his eyes looking wounded, and she gave an inward groan. "Hey, Joey."

"Were you out there with him?" He gestured toward the door, where Logan stood now.

Two women had already spotted him, Carny noticed, and were giggling and preening around him. His grin told her he ate it up. *Nothing lonely about that man,* she thought. "I was out there and he was out there."

"I thought you hated him."

"I don't much approve of him, but that

doesn't mean I can't breathe the same fresh air."

"I heard he was taking private lessons from you," Joey said. "Is he coming on to you?"

She chuckled then and looked back at Logan as the band struck up a new tune. He had swept one of the women into his arms and was tangoing his way to the dance floor with her. "Look at him, Joey. He comes on to everybody. It's part of the con. Blows into town, dazzles everybody he meets, makes the women fall in love with him, takes all their money, then cuts out. You haven't given him any, have you?"

"No, I don't think I like him."

"Well, good," she said, her eyes lighting up. "I'm proud of you. Come on, let's dance."

He was clearly pleased. He took her hand and pulled her to the dance floor. As always, she enjoyed dancing with him. He felt good, like a big teddy bear, and he had a good sense of rhythm. She just wished he was more her type.

Her gaze strayed to Logan, and she watched as he dipped his partner dramatically, making her squeal, then swept her up and spun her around. The dancers around them were all watching, impressed. She looked away.

"I really wanted to bring you to the dance tonight, Carny," Joey said. "Why wouldn't you come with me?"

She sighed. "I told you. You're getting too serious. You need to cool it a little."

"I don't want to cool it," Joey said. "I want to know when you're ready to marry me."

She tried to keep her voice soft. She didn't want to hurt him, but his proprietary attitude and his constant marriage proposals only pushed her further away. "I'm not marrying anybody. I've been there. I've done that."

"With the wrong guy."

"They're all the wrong guy once they get a ring on your finger."

He gazed down at her, and she had to look back up at him. He had sweet, sincere eyes, but they failed to move her. "Carny, what have I done wrong?"

"It's not you, Joey. It's me. I'm not your type. You deserve someone who is."

"You are my type, Carny. I love you."

She smiled and whispered, "I love you too. You're one of my best friends. But I'm not *in* love with you, or anybody else. Look at me, Joey. I ride a motorcycle. I fly planes for a living. I grew up in a carnival. You're sweet and safe, and I'm . . . well . . .

something of a wild child. I could never make you happy."

"No, I don't think that's it," he said. "Maybe it's more like I could never make *you* happy."

She knew that was true, but she would never have said it. Joey was the nice, quiet, settle-down type, and he would make someone a terrific husband. But married to him, she would be bored to death. She hated that about herself.

"Who are you attracted to, Carny? Seriously. Is there anybody in this town you're really attracted to?"

She looked at the couples dancing around them and wished they could have this conversation in private. "Why are you doing this?"

"I can take it," he whispered, though she knew better. "I've watched you shoot men down one at a time, politely and very sweetly, but I've never seen one that had a chance with you since Abe died. Who would, Carny? Him?"

She followed his gaze and saw that he referred to Logan, and suddenly she stopped dancing. "You know how I feel about him."

"I know how you're telling yourself to feel. But maybe he's just the adventurous type you need."

She broke free of him and stepped back. "You're making me mad now, Joey. I know how I feel, and I don't need any amateur analysis. You're a cop, not a psychiatrist."

"I'm sorry," he said quickly, reaching for her again. "I didn't mean it. You've just got me all bumfuzzled."

"I never meant to bumfuzzle you."

"I know you didn't, Carny. I think you just can't help yourself."

As the song ended, her gaze strayed to Logan again. He was holding the woman too close, looking too deeply into her eyes. Carny felt a sudden surge of rage and thought of jerking the girl away and telling her to run while she still had a clear head. He was poison. He was trouble. He was dangerous.

His eyes met hers across the girl's head, and his irreverent grin blossomed. He was taunting her, daring her to step in, teasing her into reacting.

She shook her head, then excused herself from Joey and went to find her son.

The moment Carny left the dance, Logan lost interest in being there. And that disturbed him.

He slipped out of the party, leaving behind the people who accepted him so readily and

156

made him feel like their friend, when he didn't dare call any of them friend. They were marks, and that was all. He should never forget that. And the women were marks too, the kind who threw themselves at him because they thought he was their dream bachelor, then kicked themselves when they were left with no money and nothing to show for it.

But as he strolled down the lonely street, looking in the windows of stores closed for the night, he realized that the irony of the whole thing was that, just maybe, he was the biggest mark of all. Carny's mark.

He could feel Montague rolling over in his grave.

THIRTEEN

Logan made more money the Saturday morning after the dance than he'd ever made in one day. Maybe the townspeople had seen him horsing around like one of them, fitting in, and had decided that he could be trusted with their investments.

The Trents had invited him over for lunch, and he decided to take them up on it. The fact that they lived next door to Carny had something to do with his enthusiasm. He hoped to run into her.

He was just finishing lunch and waiting for the Trents to write out their sizable check when Jason ran in. "Nathan! Come on! The fish are biting like crazy. Papa caught six this morning!"

David Trent intercepted Jason before he reached the kitchen. "Whoa, there, boy! Nathan's not here. He's at his grandmother's today."

"His grandmother's?" Jason asked, as if

the idea were ludicrous. "What did he want to go there for?"

David shot Logan an amused look. "He's helping his grandpa bathe the dogs."

Jason wilted. "And the fish are biting. Papa caught —"

"Six. I heard," David said. "Jason, you know Mr. Brisco, don't you?"

As if he only noticed him now, Jason looked at him directly. "Yeah. Hi, Logan. You fish?"

Logan laughed. "I've been known to." The truth, however, was that the only pole he'd ever held as a boy was a pool cue. "Who's Papa?"

"My grandpa."

David handed him the check, and Logan pocketed it as he got to his feet. "Where do you fish?"

"I have a secret place over at the lake," Jason said. "Only Nathan and I know where it is."

"Well, you can go without him, can't you?"

"Nah, that's no fun," Jason said. "Hey, Logan, why don't you go with me? Please? You'd like it, I promise. And I know you'll catch some fish. This morning my papa caught —"

"Six," David and Logan said simultaneously, and they both laughed.

"Well, I guess I could go with you for a little while," Logan said. "Not that I'm dressed for it."

Jason regarded his khaki pants, short-sleeved shirt, and Italian shoes. "That'll be fine," he said. "Honest. There's hardly any mud up there at all."

The boy's exuberance was contagious. "I don't have a pole," Logan said.

"He can use Nathan's, can't he, Mr. David? Please?"

"Sure, Logan," David said, feigning seriousness. "I'll get it if you want. There really is practically no mud."

Logan chuckled. "Okay. I think we've got a deal."

He thanked Janice for the meal, underscoring it with the most flattery he could pack into a sincere-sounding statement, and followed David out to the garage. The pole David got for him was his own instead of Nathan's, and Logan thanked him. He'd bring it back when he came to get his car, he said. Then, after tapping his pocket where he'd placed the check, he followed Jason through the woods behind the Trents' house.

"Shouldn't you tell your mother you're going?" Logan asked him.

"She knows," Jason said. "I told her I was

going with Nathan."

"She might not like that you're going with me."

Jason shrugged. "She doesn't want me talking about the park with you, but she didn't say I couldn't go *fishing* with you."

Logan grinned at the boy's rationale. It sounded much like his when he'd sneaked out the Millers' window to go to the pool hall. There were, indeed, some things a boy had to keep to himself.

Logan felt like Andy walking with Opie in the opening credits of the *Andy Griffith Show*. As they came to the edge of the woods behind the house and the lake came into view, he stopped for a moment. A summer breeze whispered through the leaves on the trees and swept across his face, and the water circled in gentle ripples where a fish jumped or a turtle swam.

It wasn't real life, he told himself as some distant, hollow memory rose inside him. It was only a script that he played out, just like all of his life. It was no more real than a television show.

But the television show it reminded him of was the only semblance of true family life, or innocent childhood, he had known since the age of five. And something about that disturbed him now.

Jason had gotten ahead of him. Now he turned back. "Come on. I'll take you to my secret place. But you can't tell anyone."

"A secret, huh? I won't tell."

"You have to promise," Jason said. "Because it's real important."

"Okay, I promise," Logan said, holding up his right hand. "Scout's honor."

Jason regarded him a moment, considering whether he could trust him, then finally said, "Okay. It's this way."

They wove through trees skirting the edge of the lake, and as they walked, Jason pointed out where he and Nathan liked to swing from the vines in the summer and drop into the lake, and where they had once found a dead bobcat, and where they'd caught a snapping turtle. The boy rambled on as if he'd known Logan all his life. Finally, they came to a small clearing with a stump where a tree had fallen adjacent to the lake, and Jason set his fishing gear down, stepped up onto the log, and held his arms out. "Well, whaddaya think?"

Logan looked around, envying the boy for having a place like this. If he'd had one as a kid, rather than the smoky pool hall, things might have turned out differently. With someplace to go to find peace, someplace that could have been his own, maybe he would have felt less of the turmoil he'd known in his childhood. Maybe he would have grown into someone who obeyed the law, settled down into a hometown of his own, and became a respectable member of society. Maybe a decent husband . . . a father . . .

Poisonous thoughts, came the voice from the back of his mind. Montague's voice would have reminded him who he was, kept him in focus and out of trouble.

"This is the best hangout any guy ever had," Logan said. "Look. You've even got a place for me to sit." He sat down on an evenly sawed stump near the water.

"Yeah, me and Nathan worked for a long time sawing that down. Before if you sat on it, you got splinters in your rump. I like to sit here on the log. One time we found a rabbit in the log, and we took it home, but Mom made us bring it back and let it go. She said its mother was probably looking for it. Did you ever have a rabbit?"

"Nope. I never had a pet of any kind. Not one of my own, anyway."

Jason dug through the dirt in the small bucket he carried. He pulled out a long worm and handed it to Logan. "No pets? How come?"

"I moved around a lot." Folding the worm

in half, Logan hooked it.

"Did you have a dad?"

Logan swallowed. How did he tell the kid that he didn't know his father's name? "No, no dad."

"I had one, but he died. Mom said he was real nice. That he used to hold me all the time."

That wasn't the way Logan had heard the story. The man sounded like a hard-drinking loser. Flinging the line out into the water, he glanced over at Jason, who was intent on getting his worm fastened. Finally the boy flung his line out as well. "I have three cats," he announced when he got the line where he wanted it. "And two goldfish, and a turtle, and a dog that kind of runs away whenever he wants but comes back when he gets hungry. They all stay outside, except for the turtle."

"Your mom must like animals."

"Yeah," he said. "She moved around a lot when she was a kid. She never got to have pets. So whenever I bring one home, she usually lets me keep it, except for a snapping turtle I found once. I wanted him to be friends with my other turtle, but she made me set him free. She doesn't like locking up something wild."

He wondered if that had anything to do

with Carny's free spirit. Did she ever feel locked up, confined to this tiny town? If she did, he hadn't yet seen any evidence of it.

"Your mom is a very special lady, Jason."

"I know," Jason said, matter-of-factly. "She's fun. She's not exactly like other moms."

"How do you mean?"

Jason shrugged. "Well, a lot of the guys are jealous because their moms don't ride motorcycles. They think she's cool."

"Has she taught you to fly?"

"We're working on the ground school," he said. "But I need to learn math a little better before I'll get good enough to fly. Maybe when I get in third grade." When Logan laughed, Jason said, "Really! It could happen. I saw a kid on TV who flew across the country when he was ten. If he can do it, I can! At least, if I get better at math."

"I'm pretty good at math. If you ever need any help . . ." Logan felt something tugging at his line, and he got to his feet quickly, reeled it in, and lifted it from the water. A big, floppy fish hung at the end it, and he laughed aloud as he grabbed the line and pulled it in. "Are you kidding me? I caught something?"

"All *right!* That's a bass, Logan! Big enough to eat for supper. I'll get Mom to cook it, and you can eat with us!"

Logan was too distracted by the flopping fish to respond, but when he'd wrestled it off the hook, Jason took it, hooked it on the stringer, and hung it in the water.

Some overwhelming feeling — pride, or maybe childish pleasure — came over Logan, and he sat back down. He couldn't remember ever feeling such a burst of pure excitement. Jason, however, took it all in stride and handed him the bucket. "Here, get another worm. We're gonna catch a million of those today."

Repeating that pleasure suddenly became Logan's immediate goal, and he dug out another worm and baited his hook again. "You do this all the time?"

"Every Saturday, almost," Jason said. "Sometimes Mom comes with me, but I don't bring her to this place because it's a secret. It wouldn't be a secret anymore if I brought my mom."

Logan threw his line back out and settled in to wait, watching an egret as it flew across the water. In the tree above him, birds chirped and sang, and the breeze whispered smoothly through the leaves, relaxing him more than a stiff drink ever had.

He regarded the child who sat quietly on his log and realized that it had been years

166

since he'd experienced a comfortable silence with another person. There was no sales pitch on the tip of his tongue, no scheme brewing in his mind, no new angle that he was trying out. There was no need for pretense, and the pretenses he'd started out with today — his Gucci loafers, Brooks Brothers sport shirt, and custom-tailored khakis — seemed awfully silly now.

"You know, Jason, I really appreciate your bringing me out here. But you shouldn't have."

Jason frowned at him. "Why? I thought you liked it."

"It's just dangerous, inviting strangers to a private place like this."

"You're not a stranger."

"Strangers like to pose as friends sometimes. The next guy you invite might not be as great a guy as me."

Jason grinned. "Okay, I won't invite anybody else. But since you already know about it, you can come back anytime."

Logan stared out over the water, suddenly uneasy. His facetious comment about being a great guy had been meant to amuse Jason, but instead, it brought Logan down. Jason was so trusting — but in truth, what Logan would do to this town would help destroy that innocence. "You sure we've got enough bait?" he asked finally.

"If we don't, we'll dig for more," Jason said. "But it should be enough. Mom told me to be home at three."

"Yeah," Logan said. "That's probably because I have a class with her at three thirty."

"You will come back and eat with us, won't you?"

Logan squinted into the sunlight and gave it a moment's thought. "Uh . . . no, I don't think so, Jason. Your mom doesn't like me much."

"I know," the boy admitted. "Why do you think that is? I mean, you're a nice guy. I wouldn't just take any old jerk fishing with me. Not to my secret place."

Logan smiled. "Well, maybe your mom has a different standard of judging people. She's just looking out for your best interests."

"I know, but she goes overboard sometimes. Everybody in town knows you're a good guy. The park is gonna be so great — oops, I'm not supposed to talk about that with you, am I?"

"I guess not." He studied the surface of the water, watching for a ripple. "So does your mom see anyone special?"

"What do you mean?"

"Does she have a boyfriend?"

"Lots of them. She's real pretty. That's another reason so many of my friends are jealous. Their moms don't look like mine."

"You can say that again."

"But I don't think she wants just one boyfriend. She doesn't go out on dates too much. Sometimes, when I spend the night at Nathan's, she might go to a movie with one of them. Mostly Nathan spends the night at my house, and we make popcorn and watch movies and stuff. Have you seen *Homeward Bound*?"

Logan's mind wandered as the boy rambled on about the movie, but Logan couldn't help dwelling on the fact that although Carny had lots of men after her, she preferred to stay home most of the time. And that, he was sure, was by choice. She wasn't looking for a relationship. She really was happy with her life as it was. He'd been wrong about her loneliness.

That he envied the way she lived surprised him, and he couldn't put his finger on why. In a few days he would be moving on, richer and wiser, and the town of Serenity would be nothing more than a distant memory that he could never return to. But for the first time in his life, he wished he could stay.

That was foolish. Montague would have

said, *You're getting too involved, my boy. You're letting the people con you, instead of the other way around. And worst of all, you're thinking too much.*

But as the day went on and the fish kept biting, Logan realized that leaving wasn't going to be as easy as he'd thought. Serenity lived up to its name. He wondered if it still would after he'd finished with it.

FOURTEEN

Carny watched through the window of her office next to the hangar as Logan's Navigator pulled up. She'd seen it parked at the Trents' earlier in the day, and that riled her. Apparently, David and Janice were buying into the scam. She had stewed about it all day, trying to think of a way to make the people of Serenity listen to her. But those who were gullible enough to give Logan their money didn't want to hear anything negative about him. Everyone's patience with her wore thin as soon as she got on her soapbox.

She turned to the plane parked in the hangar behind her. Jason sat in the cockpit, making flying noises and talking into the radio, a top gun who'd just seen the enemy. As long as she and Jason were safe from Logan's clutches, maybe she should just let it go. Let the town learn its lesson. As for her in-laws, well, she had put the money

Logan paid her for her class in a safe place, to return to them when he skipped town. She only hoped they hadn't given him more than that.

She watched Logan get out of the car and wave at her, grinning that grin. For a moment, she considered the possibility that she *was* wrong, that he wasn't a con artist, just a businessman about to change the face and heart of Serenity.

No, the image didn't fit. He was a crook, pure and simple.

Opening the door, Logan stuck his head into her office. "Are we still friends?"

She feigned distraction and headed for the classroom at the other end of the building. "We've never been friends, Brisco."

"Well, okay. Then are we still just mild enemies, or is it worse since last night?"

She frowned. "What are you talking about?"

He looked a little too smug as he came in and dropped his notebook and car keys on the table. His nose was the slightest bit sunburned, and vaguely, she wondered when he'd had time to get any sunshine since last night.

"You seemed a little disgusted at my attentions to the pretty Miss Miller. Isn't that why you left?"

She laughed then. "You thought I left because of you? Get real."

He leaned a hip against her desk as she straightened her papers, and crossed his arms. "I don't know. I noticed a definite chill when you looked at me on the dance floor."

She knew he was baiting her, so she came around the table and faced him squarely. "All right, Brisco. It did disgust me. There's not a woman in this town who deserves to be strung along by you, used, and then dumped when you disappear without a trace."

"And what if I stayed, Carny?" he asked, annoyed. "What if I actually did what I said I was going to do, and built the park, and made Serenity my home?"

"And what if the sky turned green, and grass was pink, and the Loch Ness monster turned up in our lake?"

He stared at her. "You think you've got everything all figured out, don't you? The possibility that you're wrong never even occurs to you, does it?"

"When I'm wrong I can admit it."

"Are you sure?"

She looked him dead in the eye. "Tell you what. When you prove me wrong, I'll prove I can admit it. Until then, we have nothing to talk about. Now, do you want to take your lesson or not?"

Logan sat down. Pulling his pen out of his pocket, he said, "Teach me. I'm listening."

Her heart hammered with anger as she launched into her lesson about federal air-traffic regulations. She wondered how much longer she'd have to endure this.

Logan didn't know what had provoked him more — Carny's dead-on attitude about him, or the tough questions the town's citizens had begun asking about the park. Now that they'd had more time to think through his "proposal," questions about infrastructure, permits, and the buy-in of county and state government kept popping up. By the middle of the week, those questions had driven him back to his motel room, where he reviewed the research he'd done to get a better working knowledge of theme parks. He memorized details about the inner workings of those parks, the people who had built them in the past, the impact on the towns around them, their potential revenue. As always when he researched a part he was playing, he found himself absorbed in the subject matter, meticulously planning out details and adding up figures. He had the facts worked out as clearly as he would have if he'd been legitimate.

The problem was, he'd been here too long already. In another week or two, everyone from Peabody's Printing to the Welcome Inn would realize his credit was no good, that he was a fraud.

That left him a week or so to finish the job and skip town. The checks he'd collected from the citizens so far had already cleared, and all he had to do was push those undecided investors over the hump, take their money, and disappear. It was so simple.

So why hadn't he called it a day already? *You're getting soft,* he imagined Montague saying, but Logan shook his head. He told himself that Carny Sullivan hadn't gotten under his skin, that Jason's fishing hole had made no difference. He was here to score, and score big.

And then what? Would he buy that ranch that had been Montague's dream and live there alone, isolated and hidden, so he wouldn't get caught? Or would he just keep moving, keep scoring, keep deceiving everyone he met for the rest of his life?

A knock on the door to his room startled him, as though he'd been caught with his incriminating thoughts. He glanced at the appointment calendar on his computer to see if he'd forgotten someone. He hadn't.

Tucking his shirt in and finger-combing his hair, he went to the door. Slade Hampton, the barber, waited there with Jack at his side. "Slade, come on in," Logan said, shaking the man's hand.

"I hope I'm not interrupting anything," Slade said. "I didn't have an appointment, but I just made my mind up this minute."

It was exactly the kind of thing Logan liked to hear. Bending down to pet Jack, he said, "What's on your mind?"

"My retirement," Slade said. "I think I told you that I've been planning for it for years. Saving a good portion of what I made, so that one day, I could retire in style and do some traveling, some gardening, some volunteering — the kinds of things I've never had the chance to do."

"Sounds like heaven," Logan said. "Are you planning to do it soon?"

Slade hesitated for a moment, then looked Logan squarely in the eye. "No. Actually, I've decided to keep working a while longer. I want to invest my retirement money into the park. When it starts paying me back, then I'll retire."

Logan stared at him for a moment, his conscience at war with his goal. This was what he'd come for — to take money from marks like this. Besides, Slade loved his work. He loved cutting hair, always having someone to talk to, always having a line of friends and neighbors waiting for his services. Retirement probably wouldn't suit him. He was the type who should work until he simply couldn't anymore.

And yet — the money Slade was offering him was his life savings, the money he'd earned and banked, the money that would allow him to finally do the things he deserved after a lifetime of working on his feet.

"So do you think that's realistic? That I'll earn it back, and then some, in time to retire?"

Something inside Logan — something that had never been there before, something unwelcome — prevented him from lying and making a quick killing. "I can't promise that you'll earn every penny back in the next ten years, Slade. In fact, I can almost promise you won't."

"But you said —"

"I know what I said, but it's a matter of timing." Logan went to his logbook, opened it up to a clean page. Sitting down, he wrote Slade's name at the top. "Everyone who invests stands to make a fortune. Just not overnight." He looked up at Slade and noted the disappointment on his face. "Look, don't give me the whole thing, Slade. Keep some back, just in case. I can promise you dividends enough to supplement your retirement. They'll grow every year, I know that."

Wearily, Slade sat down on the edge of the bed, his face pale. "I came here prepared to give you all I had."

"I know, but I can't take it. Not all of it."

Slade rubbed his face, slumping slightly. "You see, I'd like to have enough to live well on in retirement, but still leave something behind to my daughter and her husband. They don't expect anything, 'cause I've never been a rich man. But wouldn't it be nice if I could take care of their kids' educations, maybe a down payment on a house? I don't quite have enough for that as it is, Logan. But I might if I invest with you. I could leave them my share of the park, and that would be just as good."

Logan took a deep breath and leaned forward, planting his elbows on his knees. He tried to block out Montague's voice blaring through his ears, *Take it, boy! You're thinking too much. Stop it right now!*

Logan slammed the door on his conscience and gave in. "All right, Slade. I'll take whatever you're offering. And I'll do my best to see that it helps you reach your goals."

Slade smiled like a lottery winner as he fished the checkbook out of his back pocket and picked up a pen from Logan's table. "Thank you, Logan. You're practically saving this town, you know. You couldn't have come along at a better time."

Logan watched him tear the check out and hand it to him, and his heart jolted when he saw the amount — one hundred thousand dollars. It was enough, he thought. Enough to call the mission accomplished and get out of town. There was no point in being greedy. No point in waiting for more.

Excitement welled inside him as he made the careful log entry, trying to keep up the appearance of legitimacy. When he'd finished, he laid the check carefully on the log entry's page and closed the book. "Thank you, Slade. You won't regret it."

They shook hands. Slade's was unusually limp and clammy. Perspiration glistened over his lip and at his temples, and his face became even more pasty than it had been when he came in.

"Slade," Logan said softly, "are you feeling all right?"

Slade tried to chuckle, but the effort fell flat. "Just a little angina, I think," he said.

"Chest feels a little tight."

Alarmed, Logan got to his feet. "Do you . . . do you want me to call an ambulance?"

"No, no," Slade said. "I'll go up the street to see Dr. Peneke."

"Right now? Do you want me to drive you?"

He waved him off. "I'm fine, Logan. I can make it."

Logan hesitated at the door as Slade went through it, walking with a pained slump, but trying to hide it. When he stumbled and fell against the wall, Logan ran out and caught him. He eased Slade to the floor as Jack began to whimper. "Doc!" Logan yelled. "Help, Doc! We've got an emergency! Please! Somebody call an ambulance!"

In seconds, Doc, who had never been a real doctor, ran out of the office downstairs, looked up at Logan holding Slade, then dashed back inside to the phone.

As Slade clutched at his heart and winced in pain, Logan flashed back to Montague's heart attack. "You're gonna be okay, buddy. Just hold on." The memory of the teenaged kid he used to be, and the death of the only person in his life who had cared for him, reeled in a loop through Logan's frantic mind.

Jack began to whimper and lick Slade's face.

In moments that seemed to stretch into eternity, the area outside Logan's room was crowded with paramedics and machinery. But before they could get him on the gurney, Slade Hampton was dead.

FIFTEEN

The funeral home was crowded from the first moment of visitation. Flowers lined all four walls of the viewing room, where mourners clustered beside the coffin, paying their last respects to the barber who'd been such a vital part of the community. Logan felt a tinge of apprehension as he signed the guest book, and a great sadness fell over him as he noted how vastly different this was than it had been when Montague died.

He hadn't bothered with visitation for Montague, since they'd been in the town solely to score, and the only "friends" they'd made were marks who had believed them to be government employees selling surplus real-estate holdings dirt cheap. Since Montague had never spoken of family back home in England, Logan had arranged a small, private funeral at which the only guests were Logan and the preacher he'd hired. He had taken the money they'd made thus far on that score — several thousand dollars — and bought the best coffin he could afford and a headstone with Montague's final con — an epitaph that claimed he was "a pious man, beloved of all who knew him."

But it wasn't a con in Slade's case, for everyone who came by to pay their respects to Slade's daughter had tears in their eyes and stories to tell of special ways Slade had touched them. It was so sudden, they all said. So unexpected. He'd had so much living yet to do.

But no one felt that as vividly as Logan, as he waited for the small group at the coffin to break up. And when they did, there was Jack, curled up on the floor at the foot of the casket, looking as forlorn as an abandoned child.

Logan didn't know where the tears came from, but he blinked them back as he looked down at Slade's slumbering body. "You weren't supposed to die, you old fool," he whispered under his breath. He drew in a long, deep breath and turned away.

Carny stood behind him, looking up at him with uncertain eyes. "Carny."

"I heard he was with you when he died," she said, and though he expected it, he found no accusation in her voice.

"That's right."

She didn't say anything for a long moment, and he wondered when she would ask how much he'd gotten from the man before he collapsed. If she knew he held a check for a hundred thousand dollars in his pocket right now, she'd probably break her neck getting to a phone to call the police.

He looked back at Slade's body. "He was talking about retiring. Traveling. Doing all the things he'd never had time to do." His voice broke, and he cleared his throat.

Carny looked down at Slade's body, her eyes filling with tears. "Serenity won't be the same without him." Then she looked up at Logan. "Are you all right?"

The question threw him, and for a moment, he searched the words for hidden meaning. Why wasn't she condemning him, blaming him? "I . . . I'm fine." He looked down at the dog, still lying there. "Look at Jack. He won't leave Slade's side."

"It's gonna be awfully hard for him," Carny said.

Logan stooped next to the dog and scratched his ear. As he stroked Jack, Slade's daughter Betsy left the cluster of people surrounding her and approached them. "We don't know what we're going to do with Jack," she said, wiping her eyes. "He wouldn't leave Daddy's side all night. Mr. Nelson, the undertaker, said he had to lock him out of the building last night, but he slept right beside the door until he let him in this morning."

The image of Jack refusing to leave Slade's side touched Logan in a place that had been numb for as long as he could remember. "How do you explain death to a dog?" His eyes filled again, and he blinked back the sting of tears. "He'll just keep expecting him to come back."

Carny touched Betsy's shoulder. "Are you all right? Have you slept any?"

"Some," Betsy said. "It's been a shock, but . . . we'll make it. Mr. Brisco, I know he was with you when he died . . . I know you did everything you could . . ."

Logan looked at her. Where were these emotions coming from, the ones assaulting him from so many directions today? Coming to this town had been a mistake. A serious tactical error. Montague would have been long gone, and he'd have already cashed that hundred-thousand-dollar check.

But Logan wasn't Montague. Maybe he was just weak.

"He . . . he came to me that day to talk about an investment, Betsy," he said, and Carny's head snapped up. "He had a dream of retiring and traveling and doing whatever he wanted, but he still wanted to leave an inheritance to you to put your kids through college, help you financially . . . he wanted to invest his retirement into the park, so he could make it grow enough to do both of those things."

"He gave you money?" Carny asked.

"Yes," Logan said. "He gave me everything he had. A hundred thousand dollars."

Betsy gasped. Carny's mouth dropped open, but it was Betsy who got out the words.

"I had no idea . . . that he had . . ."

"He's been saving for years," Logan said. "Your father might not have made a lot of money, but he saved it well."

He could see the recriminations in Carny's eyes, the murderous accusations, the I-told-you-so's. But for now, she had too much decorum to vent those feelings in front of Slade's body, his grieving daughter, and a room full of mourners.

Logan looked into the young woman's eyes and realized he had two choices. He could keep the money and tell Betsy how much this investment was going to make for her and her family, or he could do the right thing, the thing Carny least expected. The thing he would never have expected of himself.

Reaching into his wallet, he pulled out the check, unfolded it, and handed it to Betsy. "I haven't cashed the check yet, Betsy. And in light of what happened to Slade, I can't do it in good conscience. This money should go to you."

Bursting into tears, Betsy took the check in trembling hands. Reaching up to hug him, she whispered, "Thank you, Logan. You're a good man." Then she disappeared back into the other room, leaving him with Slade's body, Jack, and Carny.

Carny looked speechless when she finally met her gaze. She'd clearly been ready to chew him out, and now she didn't seem to know what to say.

"What did you think I would do?" he asked. "Skip town with his life savings?"

She drew in a deep breath. "I thought I had you all figured out," she whispered.

"Yeah, well, life's full of surprises."

Unable to take another moment of her scrutiny, and unable to hold back his anger at himself, Logan made his way back through the crowd and left the funeral home. Instead of returning to the Welcome Inn, he just drove. What was happening to him? As he drove down the main street of town, mentally identifying every store by its owner, he found that he had warm feelings about each owner's family and the employees who worked there. Some of them had given him money, and others were on the verge.

He was getting too soft. Giving back that check had been inexplicable. Montague would have washed his hands of Logan right then and there.

He reached the outskirts of town, where the land lay empty and abandoned — the area he'd claimed would be developed into the park. And as he aimlessly followed the roads around it, he asked himself why he had given that check back. Was it for his own conscience, a conscience that had never spoken up before, no matter how much money he took? Or was it to impress Carny? If so, it was just another hustle.

He drove for over an hour before he realized he had no direction. No attachment. No home. Was the life in hiding Montague had dreamed of really so great? Montague had never attained his dream. He'd died in a strange town, and even his headstone was a sham. He hadn't been able to keep his fortune. What good had any of his clever schemes done him the day he dropped dead?

Logan wasn't sure he wanted the same

fate — to leave behind no legacy except that of being a fraud and a thief.

He didn't like the fact that it disturbed him so deeply. Why now, when it never had before? Logan pulled his car to the side of the road, left it idling, and tried to think. Never before had he allowed himself regrets about the people he'd scammed. Never before had he given a thought to what they would think of him when he was gone.

But this time, he cared deeply.

Jerking the car into gear, he turned around and headed back to Serenity. But his self-disgust stayed with him like the stench of a skunk. He had to see this through, because it was too late to turn back. But when it was over, there would be little joy in his success.

SIXTEEN

"Why do people have to die?"

Carny finished tying the knot in her son's tie and looked into his freckled face. Usually, she had a ready-made, carefully thought-out answer to these profound questions, but today she was at a loss. "I don't know, Jason. Maybe Slade had finished doing whatever God meant for him to do."

"Will he go to heaven?"

"I'm sure," she said, swallowing the lump in her throat. "He was a strong Christian. He loved Jesus and showed it every day."

"Do you think Logan will be at the funeral?"

The question seemed to come from left field, and Carny stood up and got her purse. "I don't know. Why?"

"Just wondered." He looked quietly at her, then said, "Mom, you look real pretty."

"Thanks, honey," she said, bending to kiss

his forehead. "But I don't think black is my color."

"You look pretty in any color," he said. "Logan thinks so too."

Frowning, she turned back to him. "Logan? When did he tell you that?"

Jason hesitated for a moment, then shrugged. "Maybe at church. No, it was at the dance. That must have been when."

The way he answered alerted her that something wasn't quite right, but they were going to be late, so she let it go. She was just about to ask him what else Logan had said, when Jason pulled another question out of thin air.

"Can we have Jack?"

Getting in the truck, she shot him a look. "I don't think so, honey. We have enough animals, and he's used to living inside. Besides, I think Betsy's family will probably take Jack in."

"Poor dog," Jason said, gazing out the window. She blinked back the tears misting in her eyes and tried to concentrate on getting to the church.

After the service had started, when Carny had almost given up on Logan's attending the funeral, he walked into the church, head down and shoulders slumped. She saw him slip into the back pew and look toward the coffin at the front of the church. Jack lay curled next to it, still unwilling to leave his master's side. The other mourners had told Carny how Betsy'd tried to get Jack out of the church for the funeral, but he'd growled at her, so she'd left him alone.

Carny couldn't help playing the facts over in her mind. Had she been wrong about Logan? Would he really have given back a check for a hundred thousand dollars if he were, indeed, a con artist? She couldn't imagine a scenario in which her father, no matter how attached he got to someone, would give back a hundred grand.

Logan had seemed truly shaken by Slade's death, and the tears she'd seen in his eyes when he'd stood at the coffin had been real. She knew she wasn't wrong about that. But she'd been sure she wasn't wrong about his being a fraud, either. Now she was just confused.

Jason snuggled closer, leaning his head against her as dear old friends stood and told stories about Slade. The barber would have enjoyed it. It was a shame that people waited until you were gone to say good things about you.

When the service ended, the crowd spilled from the church and headed to the small cemetery next door, where all the members of the congregation were buried when they died.

Carny saw Logan slip out of the crowd and hang on the outskirts, waiting for everyone to go by. Something about his forlorn posture moved her, and quietly, she went toward him. "You okay, Brisco?"

He nodded. "Yeah. Fine."

"Are you coming?"

Logan turned as the church's side door opened and the pallbearers brought out the coffin. Jack followed them.

"Yeah, I'm coming."

Jason reached up for his hand, and Logan hesitated, then took it. Together, the three of them walked to the grave site.

Logan kept his eyes on Jack as he followed the casket to the tent set up over the freshly dug grave.

Jack whimpered as the pallbearers lowered the coffin into the grave. He lay with his chin on the dirt, his eyes trained on the coffin, until the closing prayer came to an end and the crowd broke up. Logan couldn't have said why that sight touched him so, but an unspeakable despair, rooted deep in his heart, came over him. Struggling with the tears that were so foreign to him, Logan let go of Jason's hand and went to the dog.

Stooping, he said, "It'll be all right, boy." He scratched behind the dog's floppy ear, and Jack looked up at him with moist, soulful eyes. Logan stayed there, stroking Jack and talking softly to him, until the last of the guests had offered condolences to Betsy and her family and only a few stragglers remained behind. Among them were Jason and Carny, who offered to take Betsy's children for the night so she could rest.

"No, I think it would be better if they were home," Betsy was saying. "But I appreciate it, Carny. I really do." Wiping her eyes, she turned to Logan, sitting beside the dog.

"I don't know how I'm going to get him away from here," she said. "He almost bit me earlier. And we can't keep him. John's allergic to dogs."

Logan didn't stop his reassuring stroking as he asked, "What are your options?"

"Honestly," Betsy said, "we're considering having him put to sleep. He's old, and he was so attached to Daddy . . ."

Logan stood up. "He's not that old. He's just confused right now, Betsy. He doesn't understand."

"I realize that," she said, "but we can't just let him hang around in the graveyard. I honestly don't know what else to do."

Logan looked down at the dog, who still

gazed down at the coffin. "I'll take him," he said.

"What?" Betsy's eyes lit up. "You would do that?"

He glanced from Betsy to Carny, who looked even more confused than she had when he'd given back the money. "Yes," he said. "Jack seems to like me. And I've always wanted a dog."

Carny's eyes narrowed. "Logan, are you sure? You're not exactly set up for a dog."

And what'll you do with Jack when you skip town? Logan asked himself. But that didn't seem to matter right now. There were times in a person's life when logic had to be overruled. This was one of them.

"Jack's easy to take care of," he said. "He's housebroken, polite, and he'll just go with me everywhere I go. Like he did with Slade."

But that dog will undermine everything you need to do, young man! he could almost hear Montague shouting. *How can you run, blend into the background, change identities? The authorities will catch you just by identifying the dog!*

None of that mattered as he reached down and scooped Jack up in his arms. Jack whimpered and looked back at the grave, but he didn't struggle as Logan carried him to his car.

Seventeen

Carny pulled her motorcycle into Logan's motel parking lot, pulled off her helmet, and straightened her hair.

She didn't like being confused. It disturbed her, and it blurred the lines and grayed all the colors. It made her feel unbearably vulnerable.

But these new developments with Logan had thrown her. How could a con artist give back a hundred thousand dollars that no one even knew he had? How could he take up the care of a grieving dog, when he had to stay on the run?

In the hours since the funeral, the remote possibility that Carny could have been wrong about Logan had tiptoed through her mind, then finally taken center stage, forcing her to come face-to-face with it. No matter what else he was, Logan Brisco was a man with a heart, as well as a conscience.

He didn't answer immediately after she

knocked. Just when she was about to give up, the door opened.

The room was dark, lit only by a small lamp in one corner. She felt like an intruder. "Carny," he said, clearly surprised.

"Did I wake you up?" she asked.

He ran his fingers through his hair. "No. I was just reading. Jack was asleep in my lap, and it took me a minute to move him."

She came into the room and saw Jack, curled up on the bed, looking up at her with sad, sleepy eyes. "Is he all right?"

"He will be. We've kind of been bonding."

She smiled and turned back to him. With his face half in shadow, half in light, he looked almost compassionate, and almost as vulnerable as she felt. "You know, you're blowing all my theories about you. I hate it when that happens."

He breathed a laugh. "Well, I guess something good came out of all this." He went to clear the books off a chair so she could sit down. "Where's Jason?"

"He's at Nathan's. I had to go over to Betsy's to take her some casseroles I made. She's going to have a lot of company for the next few days."

"That was sweet."

"Yeah, well, that's what you do in Serenity when there's a death in the family. You don't know what to say, so you bring them food. Anyway, she asked me to send all this stuff over to you."

She handed him the bag, and he reached into it.

"It's just Jack's food and the blanket he likes to sleep on, and his bowl. Familiar things . . . to make the transition a little easier."

Logan took the bag and set it down on the table. "I fed him a hamburger for supper. He ate some of it, but he didn't have much appetite." Dropping into his chair, he rubbed his face.

"A lot of responsibility, isn't it?" she said softly. "I mean, after being alone for so long, suddenly having to worry about someone else."

She could see that he was in a reflective mood, and his guard was down. Why that fascinated and attracted her, she wasn't sure.

"A few years ago, I knew a fourteen-year-old kid who had no home, no place to go, and no money except what he could make hustling pool," he said softly. "And someone came along, at just the right moment, someone who had every reason to keep going and not look back. But he stopped and took that fourteen-year-old kid in, made him his partner, and taught him to believe he was somebody. You know who that kid was?"

"You," she said without a doubt.

"Yeah. And if Montague Shelton could encumber himself with a fourteen-year-old runaway, then I can take care of an orphaned dog."

For a moment, Carny couldn't think of a reply. His eyes were weary and defeated.

"Tell me about your parents," he said suddenly.

She couldn't tell if he was changing the subject, or if it was connected. "What do you want to know?"

"Are they still living? Do you see them? Talk to them?"

"Yes, on all three," she said. "I may have wanted to escape their lifestyle, but they're still my parents."

"Do they approve of your becoming an upstanding citizen?"

"I'm not sure they believe I have," she said with a rueful smile. "I think they're a little doubtful that things will work out for me."

"Do they love you?"

Her smile faded. "Of course they do. I'm their daughter."

"Lots of parents don't love their children."

"Well, mine do. I'm their only child. There

was never any question that they loved me."

"Then why did you leave?"

Sighing, she got up and walked across the room, then turned back to him. "We came to Serenity, and set up next to this little church. It was really cold one Sunday morning, so I went in to get warm. And what I heard there changed my life."

"What did you hear?"

"That to Jesus, I'm not just the inconvenient daughter of petty thieves. I could be the child of a king. They told me I could be forgiven for everything I'd ever done. That I could have peace." She blew out a laugh. "That's when I started to dream . . . that I could have a real home, and real friends, that I could stay in one place, and belong there, and raise my children to belong. When Abe came along, he said all the right things. He seemed like a man who cared about the same things, and could give me those things. So I married him and stayed in Serenity. The marriage turned out to be a bad idea, but staying in Serenity was just right."

"I envy you," he said.

"Why? You can do the same thing."

"Not really. I'll always be an outsider."

"It doesn't take a lot to be an insider in Serenity," she said. "They're very accepting people. You've already seen that."

Sliding down in his seat, he leaned his head back. "Do you ever miss it, Carny? Traveling, I mean? Do you ever miss the gypsy life?"

"Never. I spent too many years wishing for a backyard where I could plant a tree and watch it grow. The first year I had my house, I planted three trees in the yard. In a few years, they'll be big enough to climb."

"But what about your husband? Being a widow wasn't part of your plan."

She sighed. "No, it wasn't. But you know how it goes. You make lemonade."

Again, that contemplative silence filled the room, and she wondered what he was thinking. Her eyes roved around the room and landed on the books he had stacked on the table. She scanned the titles; they all had to do with amusement parks.

"Why all the reading?" she asked.

"Just trying to anticipate any problems that might come up," he said. "It's kind of like comparing notes with others. I was particularly interested in seeing how other parks have affected the communities around them."

Again, she was at a loss. His interest indicated that he was sincere, that he wasn't a fraud, that he had every intention of building a park.

But her instincts said otherwise.

As if he could read her conflicting thoughts in her expression, he asked, "What are you thinking?"

She sat back down. "Oh . . . I was just thinking that my parents have good hearts. My father used to have a miniature horse he exhibited in a freak show, and he sometimes let it in our trailer when it was cold out. And lots of times I've seen him give a kid a free teddy bear for his girlfriend, just to help him earn points with her."

"What's your point?" he asked, as if he knew that it somehow related to him.

"My point, Brisco, is that compassion doesn't necessarily preclude fraudulent behavior. A con artist can save a cat from a burning building one minute, then turn around and rob someone blind in the next minute, without one stirring of conscience. That you may have a good heart doesn't mean that you're a good person."

"It doesn't mean I'm a bad one, either."

"No, it doesn't," she said. "And there's the problem. I'm having trouble deciding which you are."

"Maybe you just need more data," he suggested quietly.

"Maybe so," she said with a smile. She

202

stood up. "Well, I have to go now. I have to get Jason to bed."

He got up and walked her to the door and paused a moment before opening it for her. "I like you like this," he said.

"Like what?"

"Sweet, soft, gentle . . . even if you are still suspicious."

She didn't like the warmth burning on her face. "I've got to go now. You are coming to the lesson tomorrow, aren't you? It'll be the first one in the cockpit."

"Jack and I will be there," he said.

"Jack's already taken the course," she said. "I taught Slade two years ago. Jack has enough hours in the air to get his own license." Then, winking, she said, "See you later."

As she walked out to her bike, she felt him watching her, and her face warmed again. She didn't look back until she was on the motorcycle, pulling out of her space.

Logan was leaning on the rail above her, watching as she drove out of sight.

EIGHTEEN

The dilemma that plagued Logan was getting harder and harder to resolve. It was time to move on. The problem was, he didn't want to leave.

This had never happened to him before. In fact, he wouldn't have believed it was possible. Oh, there had been times over the years when he'd grown fond of a woman, enjoyed her company, and regretted leaving her. But this was different.

Enough of that. His problem was that he hadn't made enough of a score yet. He just had to refocus. He needed to step up the promotion of the park. Go in for one last sweep of the town, get the money out of any remaining townspeople likely to give it to him. But to do that, he needed something new to tell them. Some new morsel of hope to seal the deal. He needed a gimmick.

As he thought, his fingers absently flicked the remote control of the television, skipping past channel after channel, until finally he came to the country music video station. Dolly Parton sat in a bar with some of her music cronies, singing "Romeo." Logan had been to her park in Pigeon Forge, Tennessee, two years ago, and he'd thought then that someone with more imagination could have done a better job of planning it. But it didn't matter, since it was her name that drew crowds.

And suddenly it came to him. Why hadn't he thought of it before? That was what Serenity needed for its park. A star who could be a partial investor, and whose name would draw millions, not just from Texas but from all over the country.

He watched the next video flash on the screen, an old one featuring Roland Thunder, the winner of five Country Music Awards last year. This video was made long before he became famous as the country/rock star who was also a NASCAR champion. Forbes had listed him as one of the richest men in America last year.

Logan doubted he could convince everyone that Thunder had agreed to put his name on the park, not this early in the game. But he *could* tell them that Roland was considering his involvement. The mere possibility would have people lining up outside Logan's door to give him more money, and those who already had would dig deeper.

Logan brainstormed possible names for the park. Roland Land came to mind . . . No, that wouldn't work. Roland Park . . . Thunder Park. Not good enough. But maybe . . . Thunder Road, like the Springsteen song Roland had covered and put back on the charts. Yes, he could see it now. Would the town buy it?

As Jack got off the bed and came to lie at his feet, Logan reached down to stroke his coat. The truth was, Logan wasn't having much fun figuring out new ways to fleece the town. It had become a chore instead of a challenge. A lonely job. A job he'd rather not have, but one he was stuck in, because he'd already dug himself so deep.

In a job like his, there was no turning back. He'd made his own prison, and no one else could set him free.

NINETEEN

News spread like a forest fire the next day, starting in the diner where Logan and Jack ate breakfast, and making its way through the barbershop and the beauty salon, down through the drugstore and printer's, across to the hardware store, and up to the post office and florist. Roland Thunder was considering investing in the park and putting his name on it.

Carny heard it first from Lahoma at the Clippety Doo Dah, when she brought Lahoma the delivery she'd picked up for her in Dallas that morning. "Who told you this?" she asked.

"Well, Logan. He's been telling everybody. Roland Thunder is gonna come for the opening and give a special concert for all the investors, and folks are sayin' he might even build a house here and live here part of the year! Can you imagine it, Carny? Roland Thunder in Serenity?"

"No, actually," Carny said. "I can't imagine it."

"Well, it's gonna happen. And I'll be a part of it. I've got an appointment with Logan this afternoon. I'm gonna get a piece of *this* action. Have you invested yet?"

"Of course not," she said. "I'm still not convinced it's legitimate."

"Oh, Carny," Tea Ann Campbell said from under the dryer. "When will you stop suspectin' him? He's the nicest man I've ever met. How can you watch him traipsing around town with that dog and not just know he's pure as the driven snow?"

Carny didn't argue. No one in town would buy her objections anymore. Logan had convinced them. And the truth was, she was starting to wonder herself.

But Roland Thunder? Something about that didn't ring true. Where would Logan have gotten a connection like that?

She left the beauty shop and started up the street to the hardware store to make another delivery while she turned the new information over in her mind. As she passed the barbershop, she saw Logan and Jack chatting with Cecil, to whom Slade had left the shop.

Slowing her step, she looked at the dog, sitting where he had always sat, though his head was tipped and his ears were cocked, as if he waited for Slade to come in at any moment and take him home.

The men in the shop looked up when she came in. "Hey, guys."

"Hey, Carny," Cecil said.

Logan grinned that big, irreverent grin. "Well, look who's here, Jack."

She bent to pet the dog. "How's he doing?"

"About as well as you could expect. He's a little confused. A little sad."

"Do you think it was a good idea to bring him here?"

Logan shrugged. "I don't know, but I figure a little familiarity never hurt anybody."

"Maybe." She straightened up, and sliding her hands into the pockets of her khaki shorts, said, "So what's this I hear about Roland Thunder?"

Logan looked at the others, apparently waiting for someone else to answer, then said, "Well, it's not a done deal yet. But we're close."

"We've even got a name for the park," Cecil said. "Thunder Road."

"Thunder Road? Don't you think that's a little silly?"

Logan laughed. "Hey, if he's willing to

invest millions of dollars, we'll name it anything he wants."

"And he really suggested Thunder Road?"

"Well . . . no," Logan said. "Actually, that was sort of my idea. I haven't run it by him yet. But he's ninety percent committed, and I'm giving Serenity a few more days to invest. It's not too late to throw some in, Carny."

"I don't think so, Brisco. How do you know Roland Thunder?"

"I don't know him," he said. "One of my investors, a bank down near Houston, does business with him, and he was looking for some new ventures. It was actually his idea. He got the idea from Dollywood. My investor decided to hook him up with us."

"So, do you have a contract?"

Undaunted, he shook his head. "Nope. None of this is a done deal. It all depends on my getting enough enthusiasm here to convince my employers and bigger investors that Serenity's the place to build it. Thunder can't sign anything until they know for sure there's going to be a park."

It all sounded so pat, so logical, yet there wasn't anything anywhere that could be verified as authentic — it was all based on Logan's word. Logan had just appeared here out of nowhere, his company had never returned Carny's calls to verify his employment, and no one in Serenity knew yet who the major investors were. Meanwhile, this man was taking money from her friends like there was no tomorrow.

"What if it all falls through?" she asked. "Do the investors really get their money back?"

"Of course."

"With interest?"

He laughed. "No, not with interest. It's a risk, and I've told everybody that. They won't lose their money, but if the park falls through, they won't make any, either."

To Carny's disappointment, this wasn't the same man she had seen, ruffled and vulnerable, in his motel room last night. He was on stage now, all charm and salesmanship, the man with all the answers.

"You sure you don't want to come in with us, Carny?" Cecil asked. "You stand to gain more than any of us in Serenity. You'll have to expand the airport, and you could make a killing."

"Not interested," she said, going to the door. "I didn't come to Serenity to get rich."

"Well no, but wouldn't it be nice if you did?"

"It's kind of a moot point, isn't it, Brisco?" she asked over her shoulder as she left the barbershop. And she knew, even as she walked away, that he watched her.

Driving home, she couldn't shake the feeling that he had almost counted her among his marks. He had almost persuaded her, yesterday, that he was legitimate. He had almost made her think he was an honest man.

But he'd had on his con man mask today, that charismatic smile that hid the poison. She really didn't know much about him, despite her research. And all she'd learned last night was that he'd met a man when he was fourteen . . .

Montague! That was the man's name. And his last name . . . Montague . . . Montague Shelton! When his guard was down, when he hadn't been covering up or putting on, when he'd only been himself, he'd revealed that name. Quickly, she turned her truck around and revved it, heading for the sheriff's office to dig a little deeper into Logan Brisco's past.

Joey Malone was Carny's primary connection at the sheriff's office, though she knew everyone there. Two of the six deputies had been past suitors whom she had finally shaken off, politely but firmly. Joey was the only survivor among them, and he was clearly pleased that she had decided to pay him a visit.

"I need a favor," she said, when he'd bought her a Coke from the machine and offered her a seat at his desk. "I know you can help me."

He smiled. "I'll do anything you ask, Carny, you know that. Unless it's illegal."

"No, it's not," she said. "I want you to run a name through your computers. See if he has a record, any arrests, anything you could tell me."

"I can do that," he said. "Who is it?"

"Montague Shelton," she said. "I don't know if that's his real name. Would his aliases be registered?"

"Maybe, if the FBI or somebody ever had reason to investigate him. What's the deal? Is he one of your dad's carnies?"

"No, no," she said quickly. "This has nothing to do with my father. Actually, it's a long story."

Joey punched a few keys on his computer. "Let's see," he said, waiting for it to come up. "Montague Shelton . . ."

In a moment, the screen filled with data, and Joey stared at it, fascinated. "Wow. Look at that. Had charges under three aliases, plus his real name. Maurice Hinton, Shelton Ainsworth, and Sidney Moore. Died sixteen years ago."

She stood behind Joey and scanned the screen. "Are those arrests?"

"Yeah," Joey said, moving the cursor down. "Had one conviction in 1983 for mail fraud. Served six months."

"Mail fraud," she repeated. "That's a con artist's crime, huh?"

"Could be. Another conviction in 1985, for passing counterfeit checks. Only served three months that time."

Both of those convictions would have been before he had taken Logan in. "Does it say anything about a partner?" she asked. "Any accessories to his crimes?"

He scanned the rest of the report and shook his head. "No, nothing. There is something else here, though. Apparently, between the time he got out of prison the last time and the time he died, there were twenty-four warrants out for his arrest."

"Twenty-four?" she asked. "Where?"

"All over the states," he said. "The charges range from theft by swindle to counterfeiting. Looks like he managed to evade the authorities until he died."

For some reason she couldn't name, Carny felt as if a fist had just punched through her stomach. Those were the years when Logan would have been with Shelton.

And if Shelton had been involved in swindling, then Logan had been a part of it too.

And that meant she wasn't wrong about him.

"Are you sure there's no mention of anyone else in these arrest warrants?" she asked. "Maybe even a child? A teenage boy?"

"Nothing," he said. "The FBI file might have something a little more detailed."

"Joey, could you get that?" she asked. "It's real important."

He frowned. "Why? Who is this guy?"

She sighed and glanced around, making sure no one overheard them. "I think he was someone real close to Logan. In fact, he might have been his mentor. If I'm right, that gives us a big clue to Logan's credibility. Please, Joey. Can you do this for me?"

He sat back in his chair and stared at Carny. "I'll do my best, but I should tell you. I ran a check on Logan myself, just because you were so upset about him at the meeting. Turns out, he has no priors. None at all."

"That only means he's never been caught," she said, getting to her feet. "And that may not be his real name. Call me when you get the file, Joey. And try to hurry. Serenity might be running out of time. If he leaves and takes all that money with him, we might never be able to find him again."

"You're assuming an awful lot, Carny."

She looked at him sharply. "Are you going to help me or not?"

"Yeah, I'll help you," he said. "Just don't get your hopes up. And I gotta tell you, I hope to God you're wrong. My dad just cashed in his IRA and invested it with Brisco. And my uncle's taking out a second mortgage on his house."

Closing her eyes, she whispered, "Why is everyone so stupid?"

"Because they want it to be true. It would be such a good thing for Serenity if he can do what he says he can."

TWENTY

Logan wished that this whole thing wasn't a scam. As he stood in the assembly hall of the elementary school and looked out at the bright, clean, hopeful faces of those children who expected him to change their world into something magical, he hated himself. Serenity already had magic, but he'd made them long for more. When the principal had asked him to come talk to the children again about the school project related to the park, he'd almost said no. But he had to commit. Either he would see this scam through, or he would take off. Since he wasn't ready to go, he made himself accept the invitation.

"So what I'm proposing," he went on, standing and pacing across the stage with Jack close on his heels, "is that you children help me by drawing pictures, writing down ideas, brainstorming, if you will, until you come up with wonderful, outrageous ideas of the kinds of rides you'd like to see in the park. We're going for originality, and the more fantastic the better."

He saw Jason's hand go up in the middle of the auditorium. "Yes, Jason," he said.

Jason smiled, puffed up with pride that Logan knew him by name. "Do you want the rides to have something to do with Roland Thunder?"

"They can," he said, "but they don't have to. I'm looking for ideas that we can develop, things that no one else has, that will draw people from all over to our park."

Another hand went up. "Yes?"

"What if a kid wants to invest?"

Logan hesitated. "Well, now, every little bit helps, sure, but I think ideas are more what I'm trying to get from you."

"But if we have some money, and we give it to you, would we be partners too?"

"I'd only take your money if your parents let me know they're okay with it," he said. "But yes, everybody who invests is a partner."

"And would we get free passes?"

"Every one of you who comes up with an idea that we use will get free passes," he said. "I guarantee it. You don't have to give me your allowance."

"But we can if we want?" someone else asked. "And then, when the park starts making lots of money, we'll make money too, won't we?"

"Theoretically, yes," Logan said, "but like I told you, I'd rather have your ideas."

The bell rang, saving him from any more questions about investments, and he breathed a sigh of relief as the children were dismissed. He shook the principal's hand and thanked him for allowing him to come again. Then he felt someone tap his side.

Jason stood behind him, his eyes wide and admiring, and when Logan stooped down to the child's eye level, Jason said, "That was good, Logan. And I have lots of ideas."

"That's great, Jason," he said, "but you know, it's too bad we can't reproduce your fishing hole and offer it as a part of the park. That was the most fun I've had in years."

"We can go again! How about today?"

"Isn't your mom expecting you home?"

"No," he said. "I'm going home with Nathan today, because she had a couple of flights she had to make. You could come over, and we could all three go!"

He straightened and watched the children dispersing from the auditorium. He really had no reason not to go with Jason. He had nothing to do until the children went home and worked on their parents. Tomorrow was the day he expected to sweep up and prepare for his getaway. Between the enthusiasm of the kids and adding Thunder's name to the park, very few citizens would be able to resist.

"Besides, you told me you could help me with my math. I'm having a little trouble with my addition. I could bring my book, and we could work on it while we fish."

Logan smiled. This kid might have a future as a con artist. That persuasive nature must run in the family. "All right," he said finally. "Let me go change, and Jack and I'll meet you at Nathan's in half an hour. How does that sound?"

"Great!" Jason said, jumping down from the stage and heading out of the auditorium. "See you in a little while. We're gonna catch a zillion fish today!"

Nathan and Jason were armed with bait, poles, and math books when Logan got to the Trents' house. Taking his share of the load, he went with the two boys and Jack through the woods, around the lake, to the special, private area where he and Jason had fished the other day.

While Nathan watched their poles, patiently waiting for one of the lines to get a bite, Logan looked over Jason's homework. "Ah, here's what you've done wrong," he said, pulling a pencil out of his pocket. "You haven't carried the one."

"I don't understand about carrying the numbers," the boy said.

Patiently, Logan explained how it was done. Rapt, Jason listened. When he thought he understood, Jason attempted a problem himself, and his eyes lit up with pride when he got it right.

"I've got it now. My friend Caleb in fifth grade has to do fractions. I'll hate that."

"Yep. Understanding the least common denominator is a whole new thing."

Jason thought a moment. "So when Mom says that the park will reduce us all to the least common denominator, is she talking about fractions?"

Logan chuckled. "She means that the bad people will bring the good people down, instead of the good ones bringing the bad ones up. But she shouldn't worry, because there won't be any bad people here. We'll keep them all out."

"Anyway, if they did come, I think bad people can turn good, don't you?" Jason asked.

"I couldn't have put it better myself, Jason. And if there's ever a place where a bad person could turn good, it's got to be Serenity."

The words left him feeling surprisingly melancholy. Was it really possible for someone like him to change? No, he thought. He was in too deep.

They fished until they'd caught more fish than they wanted to carry home, and then they pitched Jason's baseball until it was time for Logan to make his way back.

"Your mom worked me in for a lesson at five thirty," he said.

Jason wasn't ready to leave. "You go on, and we'll stay here for a while longer. And remember, this place is secret, okay?"

"All right, kiddo." Logan picked up a stick for Jack to fetch as they made their way back through the woods. "See you later."

"Tomorrow?" Jason asked hopefully.

Logan laughed. "Yeah, okay. Tomorrow. And I want to see that math paper again. See if you can have all those problems corrected by then."

"Piece o' cake," Jason said. "And don't rile Mom, okay? I don't want her coming home in a bad mood."

Logan couldn't help laughing as he walked back through the trees.

TWENTY-ONE

Leaning against Logan's car fender, Carny watched Logan and Jack emerge from the woods behind the Trents' house. She saw the look of guilt that passed across his face when he saw her. "Where's my son?" she asked.

"With Nathan — down at the lake fishing."

"Have you been with him?" She already knew the answer. Her flight had been canceled, so she'd come home early. When she'd come next door to pick up Jason, she'd discovered the truth.

"Yeah, we did a little fishing," he admitted.

"You've got a lot of nerve," she said through her teeth.

He sighed and slumped against the car. "What exactly is wrong with my going fishing with your son?"

"First, you didn't ask my permission. And

223

second, I warned you to stay away from him."

"Look, Jason invited me," he said. "He's a hard kid to reject. He looks up to me, God knows why, and I can't help responding to that, because I don't think anyone else ever has."

"Give me a break," she said, her face warming. "Every kid in town looks up to you. I heard about your little assembly at school today. You're the pied piper, for heaven's sake."

He turned away. "That's different. That's business. Jason looks up to me for different reasons." He brought his gaze back to hers, and for a moment, she almost believed she saw sincerity there. "He seems to be hungry for a father figure."

Those words enraged her, and she blinked back the tears that only came when she was livid. "He has me, and he has this town. There are men all around him who love him. His grandfather, our neighbors, our friends, coaches . . . that's a whole lot more than a lot of little boys have."

"Tell me about it."

"Don't feed me that, Brisco. You had a man in your life. A very dominant influence."

He frowned. "And who would that be?"

"Montague Shelton," she said, throwing up her chin. "I can just imagine what he taught you."

For the first time since she'd met him, she saw fury in his eyes. "What are you talking about?"

"I'm talking about your friend, the grifter. I'm talking about his two convictions for fraud and counterfeiting, and the twenty-four warrants out for his arrest when he died."

Compressing his lips, he said, "And what conclusion has that brought you to, Carny?"

"That I've been right all along," she said. "That you're nothing but a low-life swindler."

"Let me tell you something about Montague Shelton," Logan said, his eyes blazing as he stepped closer to her. "He was the only person in my entire life who cared what happened to me. He was a good man."

"You think taking someone's life savings is something good people do?" she asked. "You think he was better than most other crooks because he didn't pull a gun on his victims?"

"People can recover from temporary financial setbacks."

"Yeah," she said with a bitter laugh. "If they're willing to work two jobs and never retire and sell everything they own to buy food! You don't get it, do you?"

"All right, so he was a con artist. So are your parents. You can't assume that I'm one any more than I can assume you are."

"Hey, I live here. I work here. I'm raising my son here. You're the one who blew into town with nothing but a smile and an idea."

"It's a good idea, Carny, and you know it. And I may have had a questionable upbringing, but that doesn't mean I don't get the chance to settle down myself! I'm no different from you. You should just be glad that when you came to Serenity, no one here judged and accused you the way you've judged and accused me!"

The fervor in his words confused her. He had a point — she had departed from the ways of her family, even though dishonesty had been drilled into her all her life. It wasn't so far fetched to think that he, too, could have chosen a cleaner path.

She let out a heavy sigh. "If I'm wrong about you, Brisco, I'm sorry."

"Wow, that's some apology."

"Yeah, well, I'm not prepared to go any further than that."

He studied her. "All right. That's fair."

They stood quietly for a long moment. Then he asked, "Does this mean you're canceling my lesson for today? I was looking forward to getting into the cockpit."

She shrugged. "Meet me at the hangar. You've already paid, after all."

Carny left him standing, got into her pickup, and slammed the door. And as she pulled out of her driveway, she told herself that she was losing her mind. There was no reason on God's green earth that she should trust him. Yet, somehow, she almost did.

The lesson in the plane was fraught with tension, making the cockpit seem even tinier than it was. Carny's words were clipped and to the point. In previous lessons, she had tested Logan's knowledge of the plane's controls, navigational equipment, and check sheets, all of which they'd covered in ground school. Now, they took the plane up so that he could apply what she had taught him.

"Not bad," Carny was forced to admit, watching him turn the plane and circle back over her hangar. "You have a good feel for this."

"I told you I'm a quick study."

She refrained from saying that all con artists were quick studies. He'd seemed genuinely hurt, earlier, by the fact that she kept accusing him, and by her derogatory comments about his friend. His pensive, quiet attitude confused her. There was real sincerity in his eyes. Authentic vulnerability.

"Tell me something," she said into her headset. "When you and Jason were fishing, what did you talk about? The park?"

"No," he said. "We talked about fishing, and I helped him with his addition, and we had an interesting talk about 'least common denominators.' "

She glanced at him, noting the slight grin. Jason must have repeated something she'd said. "You helped him with his math? Why didn't he ask me?"

"I don't know," he said. "But I'm good at math, and I think I explained it so he can understand. He was going to take it home and work on it and bring it back for me to look at tomorrow. We planned to go fishing again."

"No need — I'll check his work," she said.

She talked Logan through the approach and landing, and both of them were quiet until the plane was on the ground.

As the plane taxied to the tarmac, Logan spoke again. "Look, about this thing with Jason. I honestly wasn't trying to go behind your back. It's just that I'd never been fishing before, believe it or not, and the first time I went with him I enjoyed it so much that I couldn't wait to do it again."

Her head snapped toward him. "The first time? This wasn't the first time?"

He sighed. "No. There was one other time. You thought he was with Nathan, but I went instead. Carny, mostly we sit and fish and don't say anything. He cut me in on something fun that I hadn't experienced before. He's a great kid, and I like being around him. But obviously it upsets you. I won't do it anymore."

She cut off the engine, and for a moment they sat still, neither speaking. "You have to understand, Brisco. I want to protect my son. That's why I never went back to the carnival. That's why I kept him here in Serenity."

"I don't blame you," he said, imagining what it must have been like for Jason to have a mother like her. "He's the most precious possession God's given you."

Another long moment passed, and she whispered, "That sounds funny coming from you. I didn't have you pegged for someone who believes in God."

He stared out the cockpit window for a moment, wrestling with the question. "I used to. My mother used to say prayers with me, take me to Sunday school. But that was a long time ago. Then I lived with a family who went to church but lived like the devil.

As you grow older, you start questioning the logic in believing."

"Whether you believe or not doesn't change God's existence."

"I know," he whispered. "I think I really do believe, whether I consciously want to or not. I'm just not so sure God believes in me."

"You might be surprised," she said. "I was picking pockets when I was seven years old. Helping to fix games when I was ten. I used to feel like I had too much baggage to ever turn around. But then I found out that he's even a shepherd over the black sheep."

Logan smiled softly, and his eyes sought hers. "I don't think I've ever heard it put quite like that. Still trying to convert me, Carny?"

"Heavens, no," she said. "I'd never believe it if you did convert."

"That's right," he said with a chuckle. "You'd figure it was a part of a con."

Silence settled over them again. Finally, she sighed. "Look, Brisco. I guess it wouldn't hurt for you to go fishing with Jason now and then. As hard as it is for me to admit, I guess he needs that."

Logan stared at her, surprised and touched at the tiny step she'd taken toward accepting him. "Thank you, Carny," he said.

"I promise I won't do anything to hurt him."

She opened the cockpit door and got out, the stiffness of her posture indicating that the conversation was over. Only then did Logan realize how much the concession had cost her. But it had cost him as well.

As she walked back into the office, he stood still in the middle of the hangar. There wasn't much that he liked about himself right now. He had almost succeeded in earning her trust, knowing all the while that he intended to betray it.

TWENTY-TWO

When Logan drove up to Carny's house the next afternoon, Jason was waiting for him, armed with two fishing poles and a bucket of bait. Out of his pocket stuck a fat envelope, and his shirttail was half out of his pants. His face had grown more freckled from time in the sun, and Logan smiled at the sight of him.

"Logan, I've got something for you!" he said, running to the car and dragging one of the poles in the dirt. "Something really great."

Logan got out and took the poles from Jason as Jack hopped down from the front seat. "What? Tell me."

"Our investment." The boy stopped to breathe. "At school, everybody brought their investment, and they gave it all to me —"

"Whoa," Logan said, bending down and getting eye level with him. "Start over. What do you mean 'everybody brought their investment'?"

"I mean, the kids. The teachers didn't know, because we thought they might not like it. But they each brought what they had to me. I've got three hundred dollars here. Is that enough, Logan? Can you go back to those people now and get them to start building the park?"

Logan straightened slowly and took the envelope from Jason. "Three hundred dollars? Where did everybody get it?"

"Allowances, birthday money, piggy banks. I had sixty dollars that was last year's birthday money and the money in my stocking last Christmas, and another sixteen dollars and fourteen cents in my piggy bank. And don't worry. I made a list of all the investors and how much they gave, so when we get rich, you'll know who gets what. That's how you do it, isn't it?"

"Yeah," Logan said quietly. "That's how, all right. But I was serious when I said I wasn't trying to get money from the children. I just wanted ideas. And I'll have to check with all the parents."

"We know. And the teachers are collecting the ideas, 'cause there's so many. But isn't this great, Logan, about the money? Aren't you happy?"

"Yeah, sure," Logan said, trying to sound enthusiastic. "It's great. Really."

"Is it enough? 'Cause we could probably raise some more, if we had more time. We were thinking we could have a bake sale or wash cars."

"No," Logan said. "This'll be fine. It's real close."

Jason's eyes danced. "Are we gonna be rich, Logan?"

Logan hesitated. "You know, Jason, being rich isn't always about money. You already are richer than you know, what with your mother and all the people who love you, and this great town you get to grow up in. Money isn't going to make you happier."

"Sure it is, because you can buy lots of cool stuff," the boy said. "You know what's the first thing I'm gonna buy? One of those pretty red dresses like they have in the window of Miss Mabel's Boutique, for my mom, so she can get a husband."

Logan laughed in spite of himself. "I don't think your mom is too worried about finding a husband."

"Then he has to find her," he said, "and I think that red dress is just the thing that'll lure 'em. Come on. The fish are really biting today. I just know it!"

Logan stood for a moment as Jason ran

off ahead of him and disappeared into the trees. This afternoon wasn't going to be as carefree as Logan had expected.

It didn't pay to have a conscience, Montague had always told him. And all afternoon, as Logan talked and played and fished with the little boy who trusted him, he discovered how true that statement was.

His conscience, which he'd always managed to carefully ignore, had begun to rear its ugly head with amazing frequency lately. Even Jack seemed to look at him with shame-filled eyes, as if to say he knew what Logan was up to and didn't want any part of it.

Stupid. That was what he was. He was stupid to get involved with Carny Sullivan's son. He was stupid to take on the care of a dog. He was stupid to have stayed this long.

They caught half a dozen fish, but Logan couldn't shake his melancholy mood. When he was ready to go, Jason wasn't ready to quit fishing yet, so Logan said goodbye and walked pensively back to his car. He had to do something, and fast. He was sinking so deep that, if he didn't act now, he might never get out.

Driving back to the motel, he made the decision that it was time. He would take what he'd already gotten — more than he'd expected when he first concocted this scheme — and get out of town. But the thought gave him little comfort. Reaching for the dog that lay curled on the seat next to him, he said, "So, Jack. How would you like to see the world?"

The dog gave him a blank look, and Logan stroked his soft coat and thought about how difficult it would be to travel now. Jack would complicate Logan's life drastically.

But he couldn't leave Jack behind. Logan knew what it was to be alone and confused. He understood abandonment and grief. No one, until Montague, had cared what happened to him. Nurturing Jack meant, in some small way, nurturing the child in Logan who had had no one. It was silly, he thought, and some shrink would probably have a field day with it, but there it was, nonetheless.

He pulled into the motel parking lot, and Jack followed him up to their room. It still smelled of must and stale cigarette smoke from the previous occupants. He had fantasized more than once of buying a little house in Serenity, putting a few pieces of furniture in it, and actually unpacking his bag for a while, but his practical side had told him how ridiculous that would be.

Locking the door, he pulled out his bag, rolled up his clothes, gathered all of his toiletries. Then he rounded up all the paperwork and log sheets that he'd kept, all the notes he'd taken on building a real park, and all the books he'd studied about it. He was definitely leaving here with more than he'd come with, breaking another of Montague's rules.

He would have to move fast. He needed to get out of the country before the people of Serenity realized they'd been had. Maybe Costa Rica. Even with extra baggage and a dog, he'd probably be all right there.

After boxing up his computer and printer, he made one last check of everything in the room. Satisfied that he'd packed it all, he sat down at the table to count the cash he'd gotten from the citizens of Serenity. It was enough to live off for a couple of years, while he kept a low profile wherever he wound up, just long enough for the Feds to stop looking for him. There was no doubt that the moment Serenity realized he'd run out on them, Carny would have the FBI on his case.

He pulled the fat envelope Jason had given him out of his pocket, dumped out the three hundred dollars in coins and dollar bills. At the front of the stack of money, he found a page in Jason's crude handwriting, listing the investors by first names only, and the amounts they had contributed.

Are we gonna be rich, Logan? The boy's words echoed through his mind, and he tried to imagine what Jason's innocent little face would look like when he learned that he'd lost all his friends' money, and that Logan had been nothing more than a crook.

He searched his mind for the rationalizations that usually came so easily. Jason needed to learn this lesson. It might save him a wad of money later in life. He needed to realize that he shouldn't trust someone so readily. He needed to understand that crooks come in all shapes and sizes, and that they needn't look scruffy or questionable to stab you in the back.

But none of those rationalizations worked. Jason would be worse for these lessons, not better. That was why Carny had chosen to raise him in Serenity, after all. She was trying to protect her son in a way she had not been protected.

And what would she think? That she'd been right? That Logan was nothing more than a two-bit thief with an expensive smile? That the tiny bit of trust he'd begun to cultivate in her was proof of her weakness? Would she ever trust a man again?

He didn't like the sudden black hole that had formed in his heart, and he couldn't stop the disturbing questions that kept racing through his mind. Finally he made out a new envelope and addressed it to Jason. He stuffed the children's money into it, along with the list, and sealed it.

Then he began to harden himself enough to leave the town behind forever.

TWENTY-THREE

The evidence was indisputable.

Carny gaped at the broken piggy bank on Jason's desk, its pieces left scattered over the wooden top as if he'd been distracted by something else. The bank had been almost full after she'd made him return the money to it, yet there was no sign of the money now.

She told herself to stay calm, that there was probably an innocent explanation. He'd probably forsaken the four-wheeler he'd been saving for and decided to buy a pair of skates or a new fishing pole instead. The fact that he'd done it without consulting her, thus breaking a major rule in their household, disturbed her even more.

As the sun was beginning to go down, she went looking for him and found him in the woods on his way back from the lake, carrying the string of fish he'd caught and talking to himself. He was alone, a fact that relieved her somewhat, though she was sure she'd seen Logan's car parked nearby earlier.

"Jason!" she called.

He spotted her and, smiling, picked up his step until he was running toward her. "Mom, we caught six. Logan let me keep all of them."

"I need to talk to you," she said. "In the house."

He looked up at her with saucer-shaped eyes. "What's wrong?"

"Come on, Jason. In the house."

"Is it about Logan?" he asked, walking as fast as he could to keep up with her. "You said we could fish together. Don't you remember?"

"I remember," she said, almost feeling sorry for him. She opened the screen door and held it for him as he went in. "Put the fish in the sink. You can help me clean them later."

He did as she said, then washed his hands and turned back to her. "What is it, Mom?"

"Jason," she said, pulling out a chair and sitting down so she could face him eye to eye. "I want to ask you something, and I want you to tell me the truth. Where's the money that was in your piggy bank?"

He immediately glanced away. "I'm sorry

I broke it, Mom, but it was taking so long to shake it out, that I finally just whacked it. I know I was supposed to ask you."

"Jason, where is it?"

"Well, I decided I didn't need a four-wheeler. There are more important things."

An overwhelming feeling of injustice washed over her, and she felt her heart tightening. "What things?"

"Well, you know how you're always teaching me to save. Some things are just like saving . . . only they make you more money later."

She knew then where the money was, and why he was trying so hard to avoid answering her. Closing her eyes, she whispered, "Jason, did you give that money to Logan?"

He was silent for too long, and when she finally opened her eyes, she saw him staring stubbornly at her.

"Jason, I asked you a question. Did you give that money to Logan?"

"Yes," he said through tight lips. "And the money I had under my mattress too. Last year's birthday money and my Christmas money. But so did all the other kids at school. We raised three hundred dollars. We're gonna be rich, Mom!"

Instantly, she shot to her feet, almost knocking over the chair. "And he took it?

He actually took the money from little children?"

"Well, why wouldn't he? We want to be partners too. We're gonna be VIPs, Mom."

"No, you're not!" she shouted. "You're not going to be anything, because I'm getting your money back tonight! And if he won't give it to me, I'll press charges and have him thrown in jail!"

"No, Mom! You can't do that! I want him to have it! All the kids want him to!"

"How much of it was yours, Jason? Exactly how much?"

"Seventy-six dollars," he said. "But I don't want it back. If you get it, I'll find a way to give it back to him. It's not your money. It's mine!"

Carny was livid. "Go to your room! Now!"

He kicked the coffee table, then headed to his room, slamming the door. She followed him and threw the door open. "Now you stay here until I tell you to come out!" she shouted. "And while you're in here, you can clean up that broken bank!"

"You're so mean!" he yelled. "No wonder you don't have a husband!"

The words stung, as if he'd said he hated her. Carny slammed the door again, collapsed against it, and before she could control herself, tears assaulted her, and she covered her mouth as the sobs rose to her throat. Logan Brisco was not only destroying her child's innocence, he was causing a huge rift in her relationship with Jason. A rift that hadn't been there before.

Logan had to be stopped.

Pulling herself together, she ran to the phone and called her in-laws. They answered on the third ring.

"Hello?"

"Bev, I need you. Can you come over for a little while and watch Jason while I go out?"

Bev hesitated. "Carny, are you crying, honey?"

"Can you come or not? It's urgent."

"Yes, of course. We'll be right over. Are you all right?"

"I will be," she said, her voice quavering. "Please . . . just hurry."

She hung up the phone, then sat down at the kitchen table and covered her face. Jason had never in his life talked to her the way he had today. Their conflicts had been few and far between, and the ones they'd had were minor. His words cut her more deeply than she could have predicted, and that she'd been made into the bad guy made her furious.

How could Logan take money from the

kids? She'd been so foolish to trust him enough to let him alone with her son. That made her just as gullible as the rest of the town.

She heard the car drive up in the driveway, and she got up and met her in-laws at the door. "Jason's in his room," she said. "He's grounded, so don't let him out."

"Carny, what's happened?" J.R. asked, taking her by the shoulders. "I've never seen you like this."

Carny realized that, even when Abe had abandoned her, she had never let her in-laws see her cry. "Jason gave Logan all his money, J.R. Seventy-six dollars, and Logan took it. I know you think he's legit, but a man with any integrity would not take money from babies! I'm going to get it back, and Jason doesn't like it."

Bev looked at J.R., and finally, he nodded. "Whatever you need to do, Carny. Logan shouldn't have taken it without your permission."

"And he knew how I felt about it," she said. "He knew!"

Wiping her eyes, she grabbed her keys. "Let me just tell Jason you're here, and then I'll go."

She went back to Jason's door and flung it open. "Jason, your grandparents —"

Her voice dropped as she realized her son was gone. The window was open, and the curtains flapped in the breeze.

"Jason!" By then, her in-laws were right behind her. In a mad panic, she pushed past them and rushed back through the house for the door. "Jason!" she screamed. "Jason, you get back in here right now!"

When there was no answer, she ran across the lot separating her from the Trents and banged on the door.

Janice answered it right away. "Carny, what's wrong?"

"Where's Jason?" she asked breathlessly. "Is he over here?"

"No," she said. "Nathan's doing his home-work. We haven't seen Jason since earlier today."

"Are you sure?" Carny asked. "I've got to find him. He can't have gone very far."

She ran into the woods behind the house. She heard Janice calling from behind her. "Carny, don't go back in there. It's dark! He wouldn't go there after dark!"

Still, Carny ran through the brush, be-tween trees, calling as she ran, until she reached the lake. "Jason! Jason, please come home. It's not safe for you to be out here when it's dark. We can talk about this!"

Silence. She listened for the sound of a

crackling leaf, a breaking limb. All she heard was an occasional cricket or the rumble of a bullfrog. "Jason, please!"

Two flashlights came from the direction of the house, and soon David Trent and J.R. joined her. "We looked in our storage room and in the tent in the backyard, Carny," David said. "He's not there."

"And we searched the house," J.R. told her, coming up behind David. "Carny, where do you think he is?"

"I don't know," she said, "but keep looking around the lake. I'm calling the police! And then I'm going to see Logan Brisco."

TWENTY-FOUR

Logan checked his watch and decided it was too late for UPS to do a pickup, but he still had time to get his boxed equipment to the FedEx Store before they closed at eight. Setting his bag on the bed, he dialed the closest airport, which was an hour away in Odessa, to get departure times. There was a flight to Los Angeles around midnight, so he booked it.

The insistent knock at his door was unexpected, and for a moment, he sat still, unwilling to answer it.

But the knock continued, and finally, he cracked the door open just enough to see Carny. He stood in the opening so that she couldn't see into the room.

Her face was alive with fury, and her eyes were red. "Where's Jason?" she demanded.

"Jason? Didn't he come home?"

"Of course he came home!" she said through clenched teeth. "And then he left again. Where is he, Brisco?"

"Carny, I don't know!"

With more force than he would have expected from her, she shoved him back from the door and pushed her way inside. "Jason!" she called.

"He's not here!" He tried to stand between her and the bags on the bed, but it was too late.

She stopped, stunned, and looked from the bed to Logan and back again. "Going somewhere?" she asked, fresh tears filling her eyes.

"Yes . . . no! Carny, why are you looking for Jason? What's wrong?"

"You!" Grabbing his bag with both hands, she flung it off the bed. Jack jumped up from the floor, startled. "You're what's wrong! You took money from my baby, turned him against me after you promised you'd never hurt him, and now he's gone . . . and you . . . you're getting ready to leave, aren't you? Just like I said! Only I didn't want it to be true!"

Logan took her by the shoulders and turned her around. "What do you mean, he's gone? Where did he go?"

"He ran away, you scumbag!" She shook his hands off. "Who knows where he'll go! And it's dark, and he's so little!" Her voice broke, and she lost herself to sobs, a sight that Logan was quite sure few people had ever witnessed.

"I didn't ask for the kids' money, Carny, and I wasn't going to keep it," he said softly. He went to his coat and fished the fat envelope with Jason's name on it out of his pocket. "It's all there. Every cent the kids gave me."

Wiping away her angry tears, she looked up at him. "And what about the adults, Brisco? Are you giving theirs back too? Before you flee into the night?"

He turned away. She saw right through him, to all the dark, ugly places that had never seemed dark or ugly until he'd come to Serenity.

"No, I didn't think so," she said. "I'd hoped I was wrong about you. You had so much potential." She headed back to the door.

"Carny, wait!"

"I can't. I have to find my son!" she cried.

The door slammed, and Logan stood for a moment, reeling from the impact of her words. She had wanted to trust him, that woman who'd had so many reasons not to trust. And he had just given her one more.

He turned to Jack, who sat on the floor, whimpering. And as he looked at the bed, where his whole life was packed neatly away in one bag, a briefcase, and a couple of boxes, he realized that he couldn't leave town.

Not yet.

Grabbing the keys to his car, he said, "Stay here, Jack. There's something I have to do."

Logan found Jason in the first place he looked. He was in his secret spot at the lake, a place Logan knew the boy had never been to at night, a place that seemed more ominous than peaceful with the moonlight playing through the trees and the shadows dancing beneath them.

At first, Logan saw only the soft mound on the fallen log, but when he got closer, he realized it was a sleeping bag, opened up and draped over the boy, not to keep the warmth in, for it was May and not very cold, but probably to keep out those things he feared the most. The things he hadn't thought about when he'd resolved to run away. But little boys never thought anything would hurt them, least of all the grown men they counted as their friends.

Logan stepped closer, and in a quiet voice said, "Jason?"

Startled, the boy looked out from under

the sleeping bag. "Oh, Logan," he said, catching his breath. "You scared me. I thought you were a mean animal."

"Sorry," he said, sitting down on the log next to him. "But you shouldn't be out here at night by yourself."

"I'm not going back."

Logan looked at the boy staring off into the lake, his features stubborn and angry, but still so innocent. "Why not?"

"Because my mother treats me like a kid."

"Your mother happens to be worried sick about you. She came to me crying, Jason. Do you want to make your mother cry?"

Jason didn't answer for a moment, and finally, he asked, "What did she say?"

"She was looking for you. Everybody's looking for you. Jason, running away is no answer. Why don't we go back, and let her —"

"No!" he said. "If you came out here to talk me into that, then you can leave. I'm not scared to stay here by myself."

Logan sighed. "I know you're not. Look, what do you plan to do? Spend the night on this log? What about tomorrow? What will you eat?"

"I'll fish," he said. "I'll start a campfire and cook it myself, and live like Huck Finn, without anybody telling me what I can do with my money."

"Jason, your mother was right about the money. I never should have taken it from you. I gave it back. Your mother has it."

"See?" the boy said, throwing off the sleeping bag and standing up to face him. "I knew she would do that! She's ruining everything!"

"She's trying to protect you, Jason."

"Well, I don't need protecting. I can make my own decisions."

For a moment, Logan stared quietly at the boy, knowing that nothing he said right now was going to make any difference. "All right," he said finally. "I won't try to talk you into going back. But I hope that sleeping bag will fit two, because I'm staying here with you."

Jason gaped at him. "What?"

"You heard me. I'm not making you go back, but I won't leave you here, either."

"What about Jack? You gonna leave him alone all night?"

"He'll be all right."

Jason looked confused. "Yeah, well, you can stay tonight, but tomorrow, I'm taking off, and you can't come. I don't need anybody slowing me down."

Logan would have found Jason's words amusing, except that he remembered making the same decision himself when he was fourteen. "It's lonely out there, Jason."

"I don't care."

He patted the log, urging the boy to sit down, and finally, Jason did. Logan put his arm around him and pulled him against him. Weary from the battle, Jason laid his head against Logan's chest. "Jason, I know how you feel, buddy. I really do."

"No, you don't."

"Listen to me, Jase. Listen real close, because I'm gonna tell you a story, and I'm only gonna tell it once. It's not easy to tell, and I've never told it before. Are you man enough to keep it to yourself?"

Jason pulled back and looked up at him. "Sure I am."

Logan hoped the boy couldn't see the mist in his eyes as he cleared his throat. "Once there was a little boy who lived with his mother, and she was the most wonderful person alive. He didn't know his father, but it didn't really matter, because his mother gave him so much love that nothing seemed to be missing."

Jason pulled back slightly and looked down, and Logan knew that he thought he was talking about him. "Did she keep him from giving his own money for really important things?"

Logan set a finger on the boy's lips, shushing him. "This little boy was only five, and money was the furthest thing from his mind. He liked to be read to and he liked singing songs with her and he loved bedtime, because that was when she tucked him in, and they cuddled while they said their prayers."

He hadn't expected the memories to be so painful, and he found his mouth going dry as he got the words out. Jason was quiet now, listening.

"The little boy stayed with a babysitter while his mother went to work, and every day she came just before suppertime and picked him up. But one day, she didn't come."

"Why not?" Jason whispered.

"The little boy didn't know. He waited and waited, and finally the baby-sitter fed him, and then she told him that he would be staying with her that night."

Logan's voice wavered, and he stopped and waited for a moment, trying to rein in the emotions he had never voiced before. But the words had to come out. "He kept thinking that she'd be there soon, but the next day, she didn't come. He waited and waited, sitting by the door most of the day, watching out the window, but his mother never came.

"Finally, a social worker came to the babysitter's house, and she took the little boy. She told him they were going to find him a new home."

"Why?" Jason asked.

"He didn't know. All he knew was that, when his mother came back for him, she wouldn't be able to find him. They put him in a home with people he didn't know, people who didn't have much patience with him, and he sat by the window most of the time, staring out, waiting for his mother to come. But she never came."

Jason's eyes were moist as he considered that for a moment. "Because she didn't know where he was?"

"That's what the little boy thought," Logan said, taking a deep breath. "That little boy got real angry, and he threw a lot of fits, so the family he was with didn't want him anymore. They wound up moving him from one foster home to another. For a long time, he kept waiting for his mother to come get him. But then he couldn't remember how she looked . . . what she smelled like . . . When he was ten years old, he was sitting in the social worker's office one day, waiting for her to assign him to a new home, when he saw his file. He opened it and learned that his mother was dead."

"Dead? When did she die?"

"That first day she didn't come home, when he was five." He cleared his tight throat. "That was the worst day of his life, when he found out the truth."

Jason stared up at him, horrified. "Did anybody ever adopt him?"

"No one ever did," Logan said. "The file described him as 'a precocious, angry child, prone to trouble.' All his life, all he wanted was to have a real family, where someone loved him, where he could count on people, where he was important. He didn't care if he got to make his own decisions or if he got to spend his own money, and he didn't even care if it was a poor family. He just wanted to belong somewhere. But that never happened, so one day, when he was about fourteen, he decided he was old enough to be on his own, and he ran away."

"Just like me."

"Not exactly like you," Logan said. "He was older than you, and he was running *to* something. He was looking for a place to belong. You already have a place to belong."

Jason considered that for a moment. "What happened to him? He was all right, wasn't he? On his own, I mean?"

"No, Jason, he wasn't. He was very lonely,

and he did dishonest things to make a living. He lost whatever childhood he had left, and he never really found what he was looking for."

Captivated, Jason gazed up at Logan with sad eyes.

"Jason, do you know what that little boy's name was?"

He shook his head.

"It was Logan Brisco. That little boy was me."

Jason caught his breath, and stared at Logan with a new reverence. "Really?"

Logan swallowed the emotion in his voice. "Yeah, really. And you know what? If I'd had one person who loved me like your mom loves you, my whole life would have turned out differently."

As he held the little boy's gaze, he saw the tears forming in Jason's eyes. They dropped over his lashes, and Logan pulled him against himself and held him while he cried.

After a moment, Jason looked up at him. "Logan, I want to go home."

TWENTY-FIVE

When Carny ran to embrace Jason, her face brought back a fantasy that Logan had had all his life. It was of someone — anyone — running to him with that look of pure love and unconditional belonging.

He watched as she clung frantically to the boy, tears streaming down her face. Then, pulling back, she made a lame attempt to look angry. "Jason, I could kill you for pulling such a stunt. Don't you ever do that again!"

"I'm sorry, Mom."

She crushed him back against her and held him tighter. "Where were you?"

Jason couldn't seem to answer, so Logan stepped in. "He was at his secret place at the lake."

"I looked at the lake, Jason! And Grandpa and David — didn't you hear us calling?"

"Yeah, I heard," Jason said. "But I didn't want you to find me."

She wiped her eyes and stood up, looking down at him. "Jason, I love you. Don't you know that?"

"Yeah, I know, Mom," he said weakly. "I love you too."

"And you won't ever run away again, will you?"

"No, I promise."

She looked around at Nathan's parents and her in-laws. "You hear that, everybody? He promised."

Laughing with relief, she called the police to tell them all was well. The Trents said good night, and the Sullivans herded the weary child to his room to get ready for bed. Carny watched until he was out of sight, then turned back to Logan. "Thank you," she whispered.

"Don't mention it."

Their eyes locked for a long moment, and finally, he said, "I'm sorry I caused all this trouble."

She gave a mirthless laugh. "I honestly thought you'd be halfway to Mexico by now."

He didn't know what to say. There was no point in trying to hide anything from her. "I'm not going anywhere, Carny."

"I saw the suitcase and boxes, Brisco."

"That doesn't mean anything." He was

quiet for a moment, thinking of all the things he wanted to say. But she wouldn't believe any of them. Finally, he said, "You'd better get to bed. We have an early lesson tomorrow. I think I'll be able to take off with no problem, but I need some help learning how to land."

Understanding flickered in her eyes, and she said, "I'm not sure you're ready, Brisco."

"Sometimes it's just easier to glide. But sooner or later, a man has to come down. I just need help learning how."

Logan walked back to his rented car on the street near the trees beside Nathan's house. As he drove away, he wondered if she believed that he'd still be in town tomorrow morning.

What would happen if he told the townspeople that King Enterprises had decided to pull the plug on the park — that they wouldn't be building it anywhere? He could give all the money back. He hadn't spent much yet. Then he could stay here in town, get a real job, buy a house, get to know Carny better.

No, it wasn't that simple. Someone would learn the truth. Carny was already sniffing it out, with what she'd learned about Montague. There was no way he could stay here indefinitely without the truth coming out.

It wasn't that he feared the authorities. If he gave the money back, no law would have been broken. But he hated the thought of Carny learning for sure that he was a crook. He couldn't belong in a place where people knew who he really was — even if he stopped being that person.

He pulled back into the Welcome Inn's parking lot, then sat in his dark car and looked up at the night sky. "God, I don't know if you're there or not. Maybe you don't listen to grifters. Can't say I blame you. But if it's true that you can change people, then maybe you could change me." His voice broke, and he pressed his head on his steering wheel. "If only these people could accept a man like me the way they accepted Carny."

He stopped himself, feeling ridiculous. What was he doing? Praying? Did he really think he could just start playing the part of a decent citizen and make it stick?

He went back up to his room. Jack greeted him at the door, glad to see him, and Logan realized that the dog had finally stopped waiting for Slade. He depended on Logan now. In some small way, that was a victory. There *was* someone who cared whether he ever saw him again. There was someone who needed him. Even if it was a dog.

Squatting, Logan petted the animal, and Jack licked his face. "Did you miss me, boy? I don't think anybody has ever missed me before." He stood and opened the door again. "You need to go out? Come on."

Together, they walked down the stairs and across the parking lot to the cluster of trees where Jack had been doing his business. As the dog sniffed around for the perfect place, Logan talked to him quietly.

"Jack, if a guy was going to make good on a promise and do something he'd never really intended to do, where would he start?"

The dog gave him a sidelong glance, then kept sniffing the trees. "I mean, if I built the park for real, then I wouldn't be a fraud. And it would help the town. It really could pull them out of their slump. But where to start?"

No answer came, and he felt the weight of Serenity on his chest. Maybe it was stupid. Maybe it was ludicrous to think that he could actually build the park and stay here in Serenity, with everyone believing he was exactly who he said he was.

When Jack finished, they went back in, and the dog sat on the bed and watched him as he unpacked his bags. "I have to approach it like a con artist," he said. "Look at all the possibilities, as far-fetched as they may be. I've done impossible things before, and I've persuaded people to do outrageous things. Why couldn't I convince the bankers to actually do this?"

King Enterprises was his own company, complete with a business license and address at a P.O. box inside a UPS store. Its phone number had a recorded greeting that made the place sound legit. But what if it *became* legit?

As he talked to the dog, ideas began to whirl through his head. He *could* do it, if he just planned it out carefully enough. It didn't matter that he had lied about there being other investors, or that he'd never tried to communicate with Roland Thunder, or that he didn't even know who owned the land he was proposing to build the park on. He could find a way to make good on those claims after the fact. He could do it now.

Plans poured through his mind as the night grew older. He worked through the night, making timelines, checking facts. And as dawn brought the first rays of sunlight through his window, he felt better than he'd felt in a long time.

The challenge breathed new life into him. He was ready to pull the biggest con of his life. The one that wasn't a con at all.

TWENTY-SIX

Carny was almost surprised to see Logan when he pulled up at the hangar the next morning. Even though he had helped her find Jason, and despite that quiet, vulnerable moment last night, she half expected that he had disappeared in the dead of night.

Yet here he was, with Jack at his heels, ready for his lesson as if it were any other day in Serenity.

"How's Jason this morning?" Logan asked as he entered the office.

She smiled. "Fine. I was going to keep him home from school, since he didn't get a lot of sleep last night, but he wanted to go."

"Good," he said. "I'm glad he's okay."

It was only then that she noticed he was holding something behind his back. "What's that? What are you hiding?"

With an awkward grin, he brought the wrapped box around and handed it to her. "It's for you. I hope I got the right size."

"For me?" She looked almost distressed as she took it. "Logan, you shouldn't have gotten me —"

"No, it's really from Jason," he said. "Sort of. Open it and I'll explain."

She opened the box and pulled out the red dress that had been on the mannequin in the window of Miss Mabel's Boutique for the past two weeks. She had noticed it, but she would never have bought it for herself. It was too expensive, for one thing, and it would definitely draw attention — something that made her uncomfortable. Still, she tried to smile. "It's . . . beautiful. But . . . how could it be from Jason?"

Logan leaned against her desk, smiling. "Yesterday when Jason gave me the money, he told me what he would do with his earnings. He said the first thing he'd buy was that dress in Miss Mabel's window, so that you could wear it and find a husband."

Carny almost choked. *"What?"*

Logan chuckled. "Yep. That's what he said. He wanted you to look nice so you could find a husband."

Flabbergasted, she dropped the dress back into the box. "I hope you told him that I'm not in the market for a husband."

"I told him I had that feeling. He said it didn't matter, that the dress would make husband candidates find you."

She moaned and dropped into her chair. "That child."

"It was sweet," Logan said. "And this morning I thought it was kind of sad that Jason wasn't going to earn that money now. I hated to think of you going through the rest of your life without finding a husband, so I thought I'd go ahead and get it as soon as they opened. Time's a-wasting."

Twisting her lips to keep from laughing, Carny threw the dress at him and hit him in the face.

"Hey, now!" Laughing, Logan caught it and shook it out. "It really is gorgeous, Carny. I think you should wear it."

"It's not me," she said. "But thanks, anyway. You can take it back now."

"Oh, no," he said. "I insist that you keep it. Your son has excellent taste, even if his motives are a little questionable."

She took the dress back and sighed. "Where on earth would I wear this?"

His smile grew more serious. "Guess someone will just have to take you out someplace fancy."

"I'm not the fancy type."

"Oh, but I think you are," he said. "There's a beautiful French restaurant in Houston, and it would do that dress justice."

"Well, Houston's a long way from here."

"Not by plane."

She laughed. "Right. We're supposed to hop in the plane and jaunt down to Houston for one dinner? I don't think so."

"A woman who drives a Harley can't be spontaneous enough to do that?"

She regarded him soberly. "I like adventure, but I have Jason to think of and a business to run."

"What if it coincided with business?" he asked.

She smiled at his persistence. "How could it?"

"Easy. I hire you to fly me to Houston, and then Dallas, and later to Austin, where I have to meet with some of the bankers who want to talk to me about investing in the park. While we're there, I take you to dinner . . . in that red dress."

His mention of his investors took the amusement out of the moment. She folded the dress and laid it back in the box. "Come on, Logan. We both know there aren't any investors. And I'm not interested in flying your getaway plane."

"Getaway plane?" he asked, throwing his hand over his heart. "I'm hurt. Carny, you'll know my every move. We'll get hotel rooms next door to each other, so you can hear me if I skip out. And I'll have to leave Jack with somebody while I'm meeting with my team. He can stay with you, sort of as collateral."

She hesitated, wanting to believe him. "Logan, are you forgetting that I saw the packed suitcases last night?"

"You never gave me the chance to explain."

"Explain what? You were on your way out of town."

"Yes, but why? It was for this trip, but I was planning to go by car. Your reaction made me realize what people might think if I just disappeared like that. So I'll keep my room here, leave all my stuff, and one of Serenity's most upstanding citizens will fly me wherever I need to go and keep an eye on me while I'm there."

For a moment, she only stared at him, wondering if he could, indeed, be trusted.

"Come on, Carny. I have to meet with these people. It's very important. I'm offering you the chance to make sure I don't run out with the money."

"All right," she said, finally. "I'll do it. But it's going to cost you."

"I never doubted that."

"When do we leave?"

"I was thinking about Monday. That should give us time to get all our ducks in a row. And we won't have to miss the church picnic Saturday."

She stared at him for a long moment. "Okay," she said, finally. "I'll make sure that time is free."

"And don't forget the dress," he said.

She held his gaze for a second longer than she should have. "Thanks, Brisco. For the dress, and for Jason . . ."

Logan shrugged. Their eyes locked, eloquent with words that shouldn't be spoken.

"I guess we should go out to the plane now. You wanted me to teach you how to land, didn't you?"

Logan smiled and followed her out.

TWENTY-SEVEN

Carny stepped into the sheriff's office, a slow-moving, quiet place, where a handful of men in uniform sat with their feet up on their desks, reading the paper, talking on the phone, and waiting for a call to come in so they'd have something to do. Joey sat at his desk in the corner, intent on a *Newsweek* article he was reading.

"Hey, Joey," she said, startling him.

He jumped to his feet. "Carny. I thought you weren't coming until later."

"You got me so curious on the phone," she said, "I had to come find out."

"Yeah, well, we got the FBI file back on that fellow." He set the magazine down and reached for the folder at the corner of his desk.

"Montague Shelton," she said. "Was there any mention of Logan?"

"Not by name." He sat back down and flipped through the file. "But there was something interesting. Several accounts say that Shelton traveled with a companion. Some said it was a teenage boy, others claimed it was a man in his twenties. The common description was that he was tall — around six-two. But each description has different hair color, different ages, beard, no beard, mustache, no mustache. Shelton's sidekick went by Mark Sanders, Larry Jenkins, Skip Parker, and Lawrence Cartland. Who knows if it's all the same guy? Could be different people."

Carny leaned forward, reading over his shoulder. "Look at this. One of their victims, a wealthy lady who gave them ten thousand dollars to invest in a real-estate venture, described the younger man as having 'a charming, friendly grin, rather nice looking, brown hair, blue eyes, and a demeanor that made you trust him instantly.' "

Joey looked up at her. "Sounds like she still liked him, even after he suckered her. Does that sound like anyone we know?"

Carny studied the report, frowning. "It could describe any number of people."

Joey looked surprised. "The only one like that around here is Logan. The smile, the eyes, the hair, the fast talking."

"Yeah, but it could be two different people." She flipped through the pages in the file, stopping at one full of pictures. Most had been taken by video cameras at banks and automated teller machines, but there was no way to identify either of the men, for they were obviously wearing disguises. "How long ago *was* all this?"

"At least fifteen years," Joey said. "When Shelton died, they must have closed the file."

"And they never looked for the other guy?"

"Oh, they convicted a guy named Lawrence Cartland, but it couldn't have been Logan, because that guy was convicted and sentenced to fifteen years. He would still be serving. Might get out early for good behavior or work off some of his time, but not that much."

"Besides," she said, "Logan really did graduate from college during that time, and I talked to people who worked with him at A&R Marketing."

Joey looked puzzled, and she understood his confusion. She was the one who'd urged him to investigate Logan in the first place, convinced that Logan was a crook. Now she was arguing against it. Why? Because, she admitted to herself, she didn't want to believe Logan was a two-bit thief. She thought about the things Logan had told her the other night, when she had confronted him about Montague. What if he had been telling the truth, and his con-artist history had died with Montague Shelton? What if he'd been on the level ever since? She, of all people, had to believe that people could change.

"Carny, I'm thinking about sending a picture of Logan to the FBI, so they can check with other scam victims to see if they can identify him."

"No," Carny said quickly. "I don't think that would be right."

He looked at her as if she were crazy. "Why? You're defending him, aren't you? I don't get it."

"No, it's just that . . . I'm having my doubts now. And I'd hate to start some big FBI investigation on him if he's changed."

His jaw dropped. "I thought you didn't believe the deal was really going to happen. What's up?"

She sighed. "He gave back Slade's check. He could have kept it but he handed it over to Slade's daughter. And last night, it was Logan who brought Jason home. Logan didn't have to look for him, but he did. The dog confuses me a little too. Why would a con man take on the responsibility of a dog? It doesn't make sense if he constantly has to skip town and doesn't want to be identified. And then there's the trip he's scheduled for next week. He has meetings, he says, with his big investors in Houston, and he's hiring me to fly him."

Joey's face changed. "You're falling for him, aren't you?"

Carny gasped. "No! Of course not! How could you even suggest that?"

"If he's a swindler, Carny, then he's a good one. If he can make you believe in him, then he can fool anyone."

"Maybe he's not fooling us, Joey. Maybe this is all for real."

"Do you really think so?"

She paused for a long moment, trying to decide. Who was she kidding? There were still doubts in her mind. "No, not really. Go ahead and send the picture in. I guess it couldn't hurt too much to find out."

"All right," Joey said, pleased. "Now all I have to do is get one. I've asked around — nobody seems to have the man's picture. But it shouldn't be hard to get one."

"What about his driver's license picture? Can't you pull that up?"

"I tried. Haven't been able to find one in his name. Do you know what state it would be in?"

"Alabama or Virginia, maybe?"

"Nope. Checked both."

"Well, you could pull him over for a traffic violation. He'd have to show you his license then."

"I've followed him already, but the man never speeds."

"You don't have to wait till he does."

"Yeah, I do. The mayor invested, and he asked the sheriff not to harass him. He was afraid he'd choose another town."

"Then take a picture of him on your phone."

"Yeah, I'll try that."

As Carny left the station, a sense of dread washed over her. It suddenly occurred to her that she didn't want to know who Logan Brisco really was. She liked the illusion he had painted in her mind. The one where he was just a nice guy with a big idea and a talent for persuasion. The guy who would take her out to dinner someplace worthy of a red dress.

Jason seemed pensive that night at supper. Worried that he was still angry at her, Carny took his hand and made him look at her. "What's wrong, Jase? Let's talk."

He shrugged. "Nothing. I was just thinking about Logan. It's sad about his mom."

"What about her?"

"Well, he told me he loved her and she died when he was five. Mom, no one told him, and for all those years, he just waited and waited for her to come get him. He didn't know what happened to her."

Carny didn't like the uncomfortably sympathetic feeling grabbing hold of her. "That is sad."

"He only found out she was dead when he saw it in his file. Did you know he grew up in foster homes?"

"Yeah," she said. "I heard something about that."

"Mom? I think Logan's lonely, don't you? Oh, he makes friends real easy, but I think deep down he's real lonely."

"That's why he took Jack."

"It is?"

"It surprised me. He travels a lot, you know, and a dog will make it harder. But he felt some kind of bond with Jack." She smiled softly and patted her son's hand. "It doesn't matter. You're sweet to worry about Logan."

"I still don't think he's a bad man," Jason said.

Carny sighed. "Maybe you're right, Jason. Maybe he's good, after all."

TWENTY-EIGHT

That night, Carny got a phone call from her parents.

"Honey, wait till we tell you. You won't believe it!"

"What?"

"We made a huge score last week. Your father's a genius. Course we had to leave Arizona real fast."

She groaned. "Where are you now? Prison?"

"Durango," Lila said. "Anyway, it looks like your father and I might be able to retire by the end of the year. And guess where we want to settle down!"

Her heart plummeted. "Where?"

"Serenity! Won't that be a hoot? All of us together again? Cooking up who knows what! And I'll get to see that little grandbaby of ours whenever I want! And once that amusement park is open, we can set up some of our flat stores in it."

Don't panic, she told herself. They'd never really come here to set up their rigged booths. It was just a whim.

Her father took the phone. "Honey, what's the progress on the park? I think we need to be in on the planning stages, if we're going to get involved."

"Mama, Pop, it could be years before the park is built, if ever. Besides, you'd hate it in Serenity. It's boring and dull and nothing ever happens. All we do is work and go to church. I'm telling you, you wouldn't last a month."

"Well, if it's so boring, why do you live there? Our Carny wouldn't settle for a life of humdrum. No, siree. If it can satisfy you, it can satisfy us."

She was getting a headache. "Besides, I don't think they're planning the kind of rides and booths you have. They're shooting for all new, original ideas. And there won't be any games or freak shows. And they're doing complete background checks before they'll hire anyone." She was making it up as she went along, but she was desperate. "Mama, if you and Pop apply, they'll find out your history. Besides, they all know my background, so they'd know yours the minute you introduced yourselves."

"Details," her mother said. "Your father

will work all that out."

She rubbed her temple. "Mama, I hear Jason coughing. I need to check on him. Can I talk to Ruth real quick first?"

"Sure, honey. The days are going fast. Before you know it, we'll be right there in Serenity! 'Bye."

Carny let out a heavy sigh as Ruth came to the line. "Carny?"

"You've got to talk them out of this, Ruth. They can't come here."

"I know."

"Really. They'd never fit in. I mean, the people here are innocent and trusting. Mama and Pop would take advantage of them. I couldn't take it!"

Ruth hesitated for a moment. "Well, frankly, Carny, I was thinking about coming too. At least for a while."

Carny sighed again. "Don't get me wrong, Ruth. I love you, and I'd love to have you here. I love Mama and Pop too. If only they weren't always looking for an easy mark." She wanted to cry. "Do you think they could ever change?"

"It would be about as easy as me dropping three hundred pounds."

"Do I need to worry? I mean, do you think they might actually come?"

"Maybe, maybe not."

"Well, I'll just have to talk them out of it. Man, they should put a badge on me here. I feel like I'm single-handedly keeping Serenity clean. I never expected it to be this hard!"

That night, as she tried to sleep, Carny kept dreaming about Logan picking pockets at a huge amusement park with rides that looked like crude children's drawings, her parents selling Chemo Tonic, guaranteed to fend off all types of cancer, as well as gout, gallstones, and toothaches, and Ruth sitting in all her glory while people paid to stare and laugh at her.

One thing was certain. If all this came to pass, Serenity would never again live up to its own name.

TWENTY-NINE

Like the town dance, the church picnic was another excuse for the people of Serenity to get together. The music of High Five was nearly obscured by laughter and talking. The air was rich with the scents of apple pie, grilled hamburgers, fried catfish, and a pig roasting in a barrel grill. Across the lawn, a group prepared for the three-legged race, while pony rides went on at the south side. On the east side of the church stood a crane with the name "Bouncin' Bungees" on it. A short bungee cord hung from it, waiting for its first victim.

As Logan got out of his SUV and started across the church lawn with Jack beside him, he experienced that odd feeling of familiarity and belonging again. These were people who made him smile, people he enjoyed, people who welcomed him.

"Hey, Logan!"

He saw Jason running toward him. "Will

you run the three-legged race with me, please? Mom was going to, but they talked her into bungee jumping. They're about to start! Hurry!"

"Well . . ." Before he could protest, Jason grabbed his hand and dragged him toward the race, yelling for them to wait for him. And as they tied Jason's little leg against his, he looked toward the crane, wishing he were there instead. He might have known Carny would be among the first to jump. You could take the woman out of the wild, but you could never take the wild out of the woman. Something about that pleased him.

The whistle blew, and before he was ready, Jason took off, pulling Logan with him.

"Whoa, hold on!" Logan shouted. "We have to do this together."

"Hurry, Logan! Nathan and his dad are getting ahead of us."

Logan eyed David and Nathan just ahead of them. "Okay. Left, right, left, right . . . good. Come on, we can do it." When they had their legs moving together, he shouted to David, "What's the matter, old man? Can't you go any faster than that?"

"Come on, Nathan!" David shouted. "Let's make 'em eat our dust!"

Soon the two teams had left all the others behind. Neck and neck with Logan and Jason, the Trents battled to get ahead. Logan and Jason put everything they had into the final stretch of the race and made it over the finish line a nose ahead of the Trents. Whooping like a kid, Logan hopped around with Jason. But they had stopped too soon, just beyond the finish line, and suddenly the rest of the racers stampeded them.

Logan tried to run left, and Jason went right, and within seconds they were on the ground, laughing and trying to break free as the others fell on top of them.

Everyone seemed to be drowning in laughter as Logan untied them and got to his feet.

"Way to go, Logan!" someone shouted.

"That was great, Jason! You've found your calling!"

Logan ruffled Jason's hair, glad he'd had a part in putting that pride on the boy's face.

Carny hadn't jumped yet when Logan made his way over to the crane and pushed through the crowd forming at the bottom. It was a long way up to the platform where they hooked her to the cord, and his stomach flipped at the thought of her falling that far.

"That girl is Grade-A crazy," Lahoma muttered.

"I hope they hook her up right."

"Can't we stop this before someone gets killed?"

"She'll be all right," Logan said. "Carny's tough."

The crowd grew deathly quiet, except for the music and laughter on the other side of the church, as Carny stepped to the edge of the platform. "Are you guys ready?" she shouted down, without a hint of fear in her voice.

A chorus of discouragement was the crowd's reply, but Carny only laughed. Then, counting to three in a loud voice, she hurled herself head first off the side of the platform and fell seventy-five feet, bounced back fifty, and yo-yoed back and forth, hanging from her feet for what seemed forever.

When she finally stopped bouncing and hung upside down, Logan ran to stand under her as the crane lowered her to the ground. "How was it?" he called up.

"Fantastic!" she said, breathless. The crane slowly brought her down. "Now get me down so I can do it again."

He hesitated. "I don't know, Carny. Actually, being tied up by your feet and hung upside down becomes you. It makes you seem more . . . vulnerable. Puts color in your face too. I think I like it."

"Brisco, let me down!"

"Not until you agree to let me go with you on the next jump."

"You mean, you and me together?" she asked, her face turning even more crimson.

"Yep. Right now."

She flashed him a wicked grin. "Okay, Brisco. You're on."

Grabbing her around the hips with one arm, he unhooked her feet with the other and flipped her down to the ground.

Like an acrobat at the end of a glorious stunt, Carny raised her arms, inviting applause. "You should all try it. It was such a rush! Come on, Lahoma! Brother Tommy, you can do it!"

Lahoma backed away, and Brother Tommy only laughed. "I'll wait until God intends for me to fly."

"Oh, you coward," she teased. "It's a piece of cake. Like stepping off a curb."

Jason ran forward and shouted, "I will, Mom! I'll go!"

The crowd laughed.

"Sorry, Jason. You have to be eighteen. That's the rule."

"Aw, I never get to have any fun."

"I know," she said. "You're such a deprived child." Turning to Logan, she smiled her biggest smile. "So are you ready,

Brisco?"

He bowed and swept a hand to the ladder. "After you, m'lady."

Flushed with excitement, Carny stepped up the ladder.

"Have you done this before?" he asked, coming up behind her.

She looked down at him. "No, but I've ridden plenty of roller coasters. I love them. I love the feeling of being completely out of control, staring danger right in the face, unable to do anything but ride it out."

"I would have guessed that about you."

She laughed. "Doesn't take a psychoanalyst."

"But you live such a quiet, risk-free life. I mean, except for the planes and the motorcycle."

"Balance, Brisco. That's the key. I have balance. Now let's go look death in the face and spit at it! Whoa!"

Logan laughed, but as he got to the top of the ladder and peered down, he realized this wasn't really that funny. "Uh . . . maybe it would be better if we went separately, instead of together. You can go first."

"Not a chance, Brisco!" she said. "A deal's a deal."

"Yeah, but it was supposed to scare *you,* not *me!*"

Carny laughed. "Just forget that it's a hundred feet to the ground, and that if something goes wrong and the cord snaps or comes unhooked, you'll die at the moment of impact. Unless, of course, you land in just the right way, and then you might live long enough to have a few minutes of the worst suffering of your life. Forget all that, and just think about how much fun it is!"

"Gee, Carny, you're just full of comforting thoughts, aren't you?"

"Actually, it's real safe, Brisco. I checked out everything carefully before I jumped."

"Right," he said, feeling a little sick. "And you're an expert. You'd know if something was going to snap."

"I'd feel it in my gut," she said. "And I don't feel it about me. You, on the other hand . . . Nah, it's probably safe."

He shot her a somber look, and laughing with delight, she said, "I'm kidding! Are you coming or not?"

"Yeah," he said. "Let's do it."

They put on a harness that strapped them together, back to back, then the crew hooked them to the bungee cord. As they stood at the edge of the platform, preparing to jump, Logan tried not to look down.

"How did you talk me into this?"

"You talked *me* into it," she said. "Now, at the count of five —"

"Five, nothing," he said, taking her hand. "We're going now!"

And before Carny could prepare herself, Logan had jumped, pulling her with him.

She screamed all the way down, and when they reached the bottom, he began to laugh hysterically as they bounced back up. For several moments they bounced and bobbed, laughing like children.

A crew member came to let them down, and from the crowd, he heard someone shout, "Hey, Logan!"

He glanced up and saw Joey aiming a camera. Quickly, he spun, putting his back to the camera.

"Hey," Joey said. "You messed up my picture. Turn around."

The crew member let Logan down, and he hit the ground running. "Wait. Jason's calling me. Catch me later."

Carny's laughter died as she watched him disappear. Shooting Joey a look, she said quietly, "I think I heard Jason too. Try him again in a minute."

"I will," Joey said, lowering his voice. "Try to hem him in when you eat. I'll get him then."

■ ■ ■ ■

But Logan kept close watch on Joey and his camera for the rest of the day and managed to avoid him. When it seemed that he couldn't avoid the camera any longer, he decided to slip away from the picnic.

He hated leaving early, and as he and Jack went back to the musky-smelling room at the motel, he realized how soul-tired he was of running. But he still had a lot to do before he could stop. He'd already deposited enough money into his account to cover the bad checks he'd written. He'd been on the phone for days making appointments in Houston for next week. If he didn't have big investors now, he'd certainly have them by the time he came back. That is, if someone like Joey Malone didn't get the Feds on his trail before he had the chance to try.

Clyde Keppler's hot-air balloon floated over their heads as they ate, but instead of looking up, Carny kept scanning the crowd for Logan. Where had he gone? One minute, he'd been standing in a cluster of people, campaigning about the park like a politician who reveled in the chance to get so many constituents together in one place, and the next minute he was gone.

"Mom, did you see Logan leave?" Jason asked her.

She looked down at her son and, with her thumb, dabbed the barbecue sauce smeared across his face.

"No. Did he leave?"

"I guess so. I haven't seen him in a while."

"Why would he?" she asked, frowning. "He was having a good time."

"I think he didn't want his picture took," Jason said. "Mr. Joey kinda made him mad."

"So he just left?"

"I guess," he said with a shrug. "I don't know why. It's not like he's ugly. I'd like to have a picture of him."

"Then I'll get you one," she said with greater resolve than she'd had before. "Next week when I fly him to Houston, I'll get a picture of him then."

"Will you wear the red dress?" Jason asked, lifting his brows.

"I might," she said. "If I go someplace nice enough to wear it."

"Oh, you will," Jason said. "Logan's gonna take you someplace real nice. He said he hoped you had some dancing shoes."

Carny tried not to smile. "Yes, well, Logan says lots of things."

"He means them all," Jason said, biting into his roasted pork again. "You'll see."

THIRTY

The air was thick with tension as Carny and Logan took off Monday morning for Houston. Logan seemed preoccupied and pensive, and Carny couldn't help wondering if this trip was proof of his legitimacy or just another con to get him out of town quickly.

While he'd loaded his bag into the cargo area of the plane, Carny had peeked into the appointment book he'd brought with him and laid on the seat. He did have appointments with bankers penciled in. Either he was really going to talk to them about the park, or he was going to rob several banks. Gloomily, she realized that the former would have surprised her more than the latter.

"So what's this trip all about?" she asked him when they'd reached their desired altitude and were cruising south.

"Just an update meeting for the investors and potential investors," he said. He pulled a calculator out of his pocket and began recomputing numbers that were listed on a computer printout.

"Are you going to see Roland Thunder?"

"Don't know yet," he said. "We'll see."

Carny didn't believe for a minute that Roland Thunder had anything to do with this. It was ludicrous. Yet . . .

Logan seemed so serious, so intent on his work, preparing for his meetings. He wouldn't take this so far if it was nothing but a con, would he? He would have just walked away with the cash he'd collected.

Trying to break the tension and still get some information out of him, she decided to make her own confession. Adjusting her microphone, she said, "I talked to my folks the other day. They want to retire from the carnival and settle in Serenity."

Logan looked up. "Is that good or bad?" he said into his headset.

She sighed. "I'm ashamed to say it, but I think it's bad. Don't get me wrong. I love my parents. I really do. But they don't belong in Serenity."

"Because of their past?"

"No," she said, "because of their present. Their lifestyle isn't exactly compatible with small-town life. Besides, they want a piece of the park. They want to set up some booths and rides and run them."

"And you think that would be a bad idea?"

She hesitated. "Brisco, the only way a park like this could work is if we can preserve the integrity and hometown sweetness of Serenity. As much as I love my parents, I don't think we can do that if they come here with their entourage of carnies and try to run the show."

"You're right," he said. "We'll have to be strict about who's involved in the park. In fact, we should probably have a park commissioner to ride herd on that."

"Good idea."

He looked at her then, grinning. "Do I detect a hint of faith in you? Are you starting to believe I'm not a liar?"

She sighed. "I don't know what I believe." She glanced over at him. "So what am I supposed to do while you're meeting with the bankers?"

"Stay in the cockpit and keep the plane running," he said with a wry grin.

She smirked. "I knew this was the getaway plane."

He laughed. "That was a joke, Carny. Actually, you can do whatever you want. Stay in your room with Jack, or go shopping, or go sightseeing, or you could even come with me."

The last suggestion wasn't one she'd expected. "Really? Come with you?"

"Sure," he said. "Of course, you couldn't actually come into the meetings with me, since these are mostly old boys, and I'll have better luck with them if I'm alone. But you could wait in the waiting area, if you want. I did tell you you could keep an eye on me, after all."

Carny thought for a moment, then decided to call his bluff. "All right. I'll do it."

"Good." He went back to studying his notes. "I'll just leave Jack in the hotel room."

The fact that he didn't object or try to find some way out of it, surprised her again. This was getting too confusing. How was she supposed to figure him out, if he kept acting normal? She'd based her whole perception of him on his being a swindler. If he wasn't one, then she didn't quite know how to feel about him.

She'd get her mind back on track with the camera, she thought. She'd try to take his picture, and he wouldn't let her. That would remind her that he was a crook. It would reinforce, yet again, what she already knew.

Somehow, she needed to hang on to that belief, because trusting him meant that she'd eventually have to deal with the feelings she'd been trying to deny — the feelings that had the potential to hurt her even more than his duplicity might have.

Logan got them adjoining suites at the St. Regis Hotel in Houston, a luxury hotel that made Carny wonder who was paying for it — the big investors from the banks, or the small ones in Serenity. He told her to take an hour or so to relax while he made some phone calls. He would come get her for lunch, and then they would go to his first appointment.

As she waited, she prayed that she wasn't being set up for disaster.

The first call Logan made was to a limousine service, from which he ordered a chauffeured Rolls-Royce to pick up Carny and him at two o'clock to transport them to the first bank. It had worked for him before, when he'd opened accounts with bad checks, taken out loans under the guise of a wealthy New York businessman, and perpetrated more than a few cons of bankers. The first impression was the most important, and when the bankers saw him drive up in a chauffeured limo and walk in dressed like a Wall Street tycoon, they immediately believed he was someone whose business they wanted. The rest was just a matter of persuasion.

He then called all the bankers he'd made appointments with, confirming that they would see him and reaffirming the fact that he was shopping for investors, but that he was choosy about who he went into partnership with. That, he hoped, would set the tone of urgency and of competition. Nothing made a banker want a client more than the possibility that he may not be able to have him.

After the phone calls, he sat staring at Jack, who looked a little queasy and tired after the flight. "That was nothing, boy," he said softly. "The real ride's about to start."

Could he really pull this off? Getting real investors would take all the talent he had as a con artist. That it was for a legitimate venture wouldn't matter. His powers of persuasion would still be sorely tested. He'd have to pit one bank against another, drop lots of names, and look uncommitted to whatever bank he was visiting at the time. And it would all be done in the name of the town of Serenity.

He'd done his homework. He knew the age of every banker he had targeted, how long they'd been running that bank, what other banks they'd worked for, where they'd gone to school, whether they were married, their spouses' names, how many children they had, what big ventures they had funded . . .

But he didn't plan to use that information today. The background was just so that he could read them more accurately, judge them, gauge them. It was only so he could determine what kind of pitch they would respond to.

He hoped Carny wouldn't throw a wrench into his plans. Even though she would be waiting in the lobby, one wrong move on her part could blow his cover. One wrong word from either of them, and he wouldn't be able to make these investors give him the time of day.

When he stopped by her room, he was pleasantly surprised at the way she had transformed herself. As if she realized the importance of the meetings, she had twisted her hair up and donned a little yellow suit that looked expensive enough to suit the bankers, though he suspected it had come from the sale rack at Miss Mabel's. Her high heels emphasized her shape and made her look sophisticated. She looked the perfect match for a man who could afford a chauffeured Rolls. He relaxed, reassured. It was all going to work out as fantastically as the scam would have, if he'd gone through with it.

"You look perfect," he said, stepping into her room.

"You don't look so bad yourself." She reached into her bag for the camera she'd brought, and waited for him to blanch. "Smile and let me get a picture."

Logan grinned his best grin and allowed her to flash three pictures right in a row. "Now, are you finished?" he asked. "We've got a lunch reservation."

She set the camera down, apparently pleased. "Sure, I'm ready." She followed him out, locking the door behind her.

She hadn't expected to eat a five-course meal in the hotel's fanciest restaurant, but Logan's tastes were evidently more opulent than her own. Not certain whether it was his investors or the citizens of Serenity who were financing this trip, Carny ordered only a salad and glass of iced tea.

"Aren't you hungrier than that?" he asked as she eyed the steak the waiter had brought him.

"Not hungry enough to pay what that steak costs."

He laughed. "What do you care? I'm paying for it."

"With what?" she asked. "My in-laws'

money, or the Trents', or Brother Tommy's?"

He sighed. "You'll never give up, will you? For your information, I'm using my own money for this."

She smiled then. "Oh . . . well, in that case, what do they have that's really expensive?"

When she'd ordered, he slid back his chair. "Well, then, if you'll excuse me for a minute, I'm going to find the men's room. Don't eat my lunch while I'm gone."

Smiling, she watched him walk out of the restaurant and wondered if the restroom had windows. Any minute now he was going to escape and leave her holding the bag for lunch.

No, she was being silly. Logan wasn't going anywhere, except to the restroom. Maybe it was time she ignored her suspicious instincts and just enjoyed this. After all, he *had* let her take his picture. He wouldn't have stood there and let her take it so easily if he'd had anything to hide.

Sighing, she finished her salad. Things might be on the level, after all.

Logan bypassed the men's room and rushed to the elevator, rode up to their floor, and trotted up the hall. When he'd checked in, he had gotten the desk clerk to give him two keycards for each room, just in case he needed to get into hers for something like this. Fishing hers out of his pocket, he opened her door and slipped inside.

The camera was sitting right where she'd left it. Deftly, he clicked through the digital images and deleted the ones of himself. Then he put the camera back exactly where he had found it.

Chances were that she wouldn't know she'd lost the pictures until they were back in Serenity. Hopefully, she'd think it was her own error.

Smiling, he slipped out of her room, hopped the elevator, and cut back across the lobby to the restaurant, where Carny was waiting.

THIRTY-ONE

They had just finished dessert when the maître d' approached their table. "Excuse me, Mr. Brisco? Your limousine is here."

"Thank you," Logan said, laying down a couple of bills. "This should cover the check and the tip." It paid to make an impression. Word got around.

"Thank you, sir."

Carny was quiet until the maître d' disappeared. "Did he say your *limousine?*"

"Yes," Logan said, getting up. "Ever ridden in one?"

"Well . . . no, not really." She followed him across the lobby and out the front door, but the expression on her face told him she was more concerned than impressed.

A chauffeur waited beside a gold Rolls-Royce, and upon seeing Logan, he opened the back door for them. "Good afternoon, Mr. Brisco."

"Hello." Logan shook the chauffeur's

hand. "We're going to see Mr. Gastineau at MidSouth Bank on Congress Street."

Carny hesitated before getting in. "Logan, are you sure . . . ?"

"Get in, Carny," he whispered. "The man's waiting."

Clumsily, she slid onto the seat and made room for Logan. "Who sent this?"

"The banker I'm working with," he said. "And please, if you meet him, don't say anything about the limo. He sees me as a successful executive of King Enterprises. We don't want him to think we're not used to this kind of treatment."

Why had he lied to her? he wondered, looking out the window as the chauffeur got in. He could just as easily have told her the truth — that he'd hired the limo himself to look important when he drove up at the bank. But he didn't want her to think he was a phony.

As the thought came into his mind, he knew that it was absurd. Of course he was a phony. Everything about him was phony.

It probably hadn't been smart to bring her along, he thought as the limo pulled away from the hotel. But proving to her that he was legit was almost more important than *making* himself legit.

He made himself comfortable and

grinned. "So what do you think?"

She feigned nonchalance. "It's nice, for a Rolls."

He laughed aloud, and the chauffeur glanced into the rearview mirror.

"So who's your first victim?" she asked.

He shook his head. "They're not victims, they're investors. I have to convince them that Serenity is the right place for this park."

"And why are you so sure it is?"

"Because the town needs it. And because wherever we build it, I'm going to have to live there. And Serenity is where I want to live. And because I think it'll make my investors a killing."

She looked out the window. "Will you know from this trip whether they'll approve the Serenity site or not?"

"Maybe," he said. "I hope so. If these bankers join us, the rest of the group is sure to see that Serenity is the place."

"And what if they don't?" She brought her gaze back to him. "What if they tell you that isn't what they had in mind? Will you give back all the money you've collected from Serenity?"

"They won't say that," he said. "The amount I've already raised speaks volumes about Serenity's level of commitment to the project. That's the kind of community they're looking for."

"You didn't answer my question. If they don't, will you give the money back?"

He faced her directly. "All right, Carny. If they decide not to build the park there, yes, I'll give the money back, just like I've told you before. I'll have to, won't I?"

She didn't answer, but again looked out toward the street.

The limousine turned onto Congress Street, and ahead, Logan saw the MidSouth sign on a black marble-and-glass building. Just as he remembered, the first floor was showcased in glass. Perfect, he thought. The officers of the bank would see him riding up in the limo, and if his hunch was right, he'd be greeted at the door by someone who mattered, and he'd be noticed by everyone who could see the street.

Montague would be proud.

Then he'd employ every sales technique Montague had ever taught him, and give the bankers a pitch that would make them salivate. He had done it before.

He got his briefcase, checked the contents, then snapped it shut as the chauffeur pulled to the curb. Carny reached for her door handle, but Logan stopped her. "Let him," he said, as the chauffeur got out and came around to open the door.

As Carny stepped out, Logan was pleased to see that people along the sidewalk were watching them, waiting to see what celebrity or billionaire would be making an appearance today. Through the bank's glass wall, the secretaries peered curiously out at them as well. Good. Just the effect he'd wanted.

He asked the driver to wait for them. Setting his hand on the small of Carny's back, he escorted her in.

They had scarcely reached the door when a man in a suit opened it for them.

"Good afternoon, sir," he said, shaking Logan's hand. "I'm Andrew Seal."

"Good afternoon," Logan said. "Logan Brisco, and this is Miss Sullivan. I have an appointment to see Mr. Gastineau."

"Yes, of course, Mr. Brisco," the man said. "Miss Sullivan. I'll take you up myself."

All the way up, Mr. Seal talked about the weather in Houston and questioned Logan about the length of his stay.

They stepped off the elevator into a plush lobby with secretaries working quietly along the perimeter. Mr. Seal escorted them to the bank president's office and asked them to have a seat while he alerted Mr. Gastineau that they were here.

They took the elegant sofa against the wall. "What do you think so far?" he asked with a grin.

Carny smiled. "It's okay, if you like having your feet kissed. And you do like it, don't you, Brisco?"

He chuckled. "Doesn't everybody?"

"No, actually," she said. "It makes me very uncomfortable. Makes me feel like a fraud."

"Well, don't worry. Gastineau isn't a foot-kisser. When I go in, you just wait here. And be patient. It could be a long meeting. If you decide to leave, you can take the limo. I'll call the chauffeur when I'm ready to be picked up."

She smiled. "I'll stay here, Brisco."

"Still afraid I'll break and run?"

She laughed softly. "Well, I don't think you can easily escape from a twentieth-floor window, so I feel pretty secure here."

"As long as you're in the same building?"

"Something like that," she said.

THIRTY-TWO

A few minutes later, while Carny waited in the anteroom outside, Logan made himself comfortable in the chair across from Gastineau, an overweight, balding man who carried his extra pounds with a polished dignity. As unassuming as he seemed, though, Logan had done enough homework to know that he was as shrewd as they came. His name carried a lot of weight in Texas financial circles, and if Logan could nail him, the other bankers would be more likely to hear him out. "I have two reasons for wanting to meet with you today, Mr. Gastineau," Logan said. "One is to open an account in your bank. I'd like to start with a half million dollars, and within the month, I'll deposit a million more." That, he hoped, was the amount he'd raise in Serenity when the last holdouts came aboard.

Gastineau cleared his throat and immediately pulled out the necessary paperwork. "Certainly, Mr. Brisco. Will this be a transfer from another bank?"

"I have a cashier's check," Logan said.

"Wonderful," the man said. He took the check Logan gave him, made the necessary notations, then took off his glasses and sat back. "And do you want this account in your name?"

"I'll be the only signatory on the account for now," Logan said, "but I want the account to be in the name of the town of Serenity, Texas."

"You want it in the name of a town?"

"Yes," Logan said. "The town of Serenity is in the process of raising money for a huge amusement park we're planning to build in that area. We're working on trying to get Roland Thunder involved, and if we do, his name will be connected with it much like Dolly Parton is connected to Dollywood in Pigeon Forge. The money I'm depositing is just a portion of the cash the citizens of Serenity are investing. And we're hoping you will have the foresight to see what a tremendous investment this is."

Gastineau listened carefully. "An amusement park. In this economy?"

"Yes, precisely *because* of this economy," Logan said, plowing past the doubt in the man's voice. Digging into his briefcase, he said, "I've brought you my business plan, my projected costs for the venture, projected profits over the next ten years, comparisons with other parks across the United States . . ." He paused, and chuckled slightly. "Actually, Mr. Gastineau, I should probably go over one thing at a time with you. We'll start with the projected profits, so you can see what an opportunity this is for you."

He handed Gastineau the booklet he'd designed on his computer, then taken to Julia Peabody to print and bind. Sitting back, he opened his own copy.

"You say other banks in the Houston area have agreed to invest?" Gastineau asked.

"You're the first I've offered it to," Logan admitted. "I'm meeting with Alex Green at First Trust Bank this afternoon, and tomorrow with John Van Landingham at South Federal. I also have several bankers in Dallas and Austin I'm meeting with. It's an opportunity you don't want to miss, Mr. Gastineau. The profit margin is very high. And as icing on the cake, it'll create hundreds of jobs in a town that really needs them."

Frowning, Gastineau opened the booklet and zeroed in on the numbers. "Interesting," he muttered, and Logan grinned.

As Logan embarked on the rest of his spiel, he had Gastineau hanging on every word.

One down, a dozen to go, he told himself. If he could just keep the con going long enough, he'd be legit before he knew it. And then all of his lies would turn to truth.

When an hour and a half had passed and Logan still hadn't come out, Carny was beginning to regret waiting. She considered sending the secretary in to make sure he hadn't slipped out some back door, but then she told herself that was ludicrous.

When the door finally opened and Logan came out, laughing with the bank president as if they were old friends, she breathed a sigh of relief.

"I'll call you at the hotel and let you know what time my board of directors plans to meet, Logan. I'd very much like you to be there yourself."

"I'll make it a point," Logan said. "And if you think of any questions in the meantime . . ."

"I'll certainly call."

Carny got to her feet, and the older man smiled. "I'm so sorry we kept your lovely wife waiting for so long."

"This isn't my wife, sir. This is Ms. Sullivan. She's my pilot."

"Pilot!" Gastineau said. "Well, I never would have guessed!"

Carny smiled and shook his hand. "It's nice to meet you, Mr. Gastineau."

He took her hand in both his own. "Forgive me for keeping Logan so long."

"That's all right," she said.

Gastineau saw them to the elevator, and when the doors closed, she expected Logan to let out a long sigh. But instead of being drained, he seemed energized. She fixed her gaze on him. "Well, how did it go?"

"It looks good," Logan said. "I'm meeting with his board of directors tomorrow."

"Will they make the decision about where to put the park?"

"They might. But I'm expecting to have to fly everyone to Serenity and show them the site before there's a final decision. How many people can your plane accommodate?"

"Six comfortably in my Baron, but if we needed to we could rent Hugh Berkstrom's Learjet. I'm certified for it. I sometimes fly it when his regular pilot isn't available."

"That'll work," he said.

The chauffeur was still waiting when they reached the car, and as Carny got in, she couldn't help the confusion taking hold of her. She was almost getting excited about the prospect of getting the park under way.

Logan could convince a tiger that it was a zebra. And she was beginning to wonder if that was exactly what he was doing to her.

THIRTY-THREE

Logan was secretly relieved that Carny opted to go back to the hotel while he met with the second banker that afternoon. It didn't pay to have her around too much when he was wheeling and dealing. One inconsistency could blow everything, and he had no doubt that she was mentally recording every word that was spoken. Maybe the scene with Gastineau had been just what she needed to convince her.

If it had, the scene with Alex Green, the president of First Trust Bank, would have sent that faith tumbling down.

Logan looked out the window as the sun began to set and told himself he could relax now. There was no harm done.

But he hadn't been so sure of that when he'd driven up in the limo, gotten out, and told the bank officer who greeted him that he had an appointment with Mr. Green.

Mr. Green had turned out to be a woman.

If Carny had heard him make that slip after he'd told her he knew all these bankers, it would have been a dead giveaway. Fortunately, Ms. Green never had to know about the mistake, and neither did Carny.

But Alex Green had been as difficult to deal with as he'd expected Mr. Gastineau to be. Logan had ramped his charm up full tilt, but if it affected her, he couldn't tell. He'd showcased his intelligence, citing figures and statistics and comparative analyses of other parks. Her continued reluctance became an even bigger challenge, and he found himself nursing the same kind of adrenaline burst that he felt when he pulled off a particularly challenging scam.

By the end of his interview, he had persuaded her to come to Serenity to tour the area so she could decide for herself whether her bank's money would be well spent there. She had finally agreed, and as he left, instead of feeling energized by the success, he was exhausted.

He paid the driver for the day's use of the limo, plus a tip, then went up to his room and collapsed on his bed. He couldn't believe how much harder it was to pull off the truth — albeit with a few variations — than to pull off pure fiction. How could that be? Hadn't enough been at stake before, when he feared getting caught and sent to prison?

The difference, he told himself, was that there was more than prison at stake now. If he succeeded, he'd be a hero in the little town he'd come to care so much for. Carny would trust him entirely. Jason would continue to look up to him. And he would still be treated as though he belonged.

All he had to do was accomplish the impossible, make no mistakes, and perform a couple of miracles.

After shedding his coat and tie, he went to Carny's room.

"Tough day, huh?" she said with a smile.

"Yeah, but it was worth it." Jack inched around Carny as Logan came in, and Logan stooped down to pet him. "Hey, boy. You've probably been wondering where I was, haven't you? You didn't think I left you, did you?"

The dog licked his face and neck, and Logan laughed. "I think he's getting used to me, don't you?"

"Yeah. Slade would feel real good knowing he's happy." Closing the door, she turned back to him. "I walked him a few minutes ago. So how did it go?"

Logan got to his feet and handed her the bottle of wine he'd been carrying. "I stopped on the way back and bought us a bottle of wine. Sort of a pre-celebration celebration."

"What does that mean?"

"It means that we're getting real close to having something to celebrate."

She went to the wet bar in the corner of her room and found a corkscrew. Deftly, she peeled the foil off the cork, dug the corkscrew in, and pulled the cork out. "So when do we know for sure?"

"Could be weeks," he said. "I have lots more meetings. But you and I need to put our heads together tonight and decide exactly when we can come back to pick up Gastineau and some of the others on his board and take them to Serenity. Then we'll plan another day to take Ms. Green and her people. Are you up to this?"

She poured wine into a glass. "Depends. Are you paying me?"

"Of course. Although I was hoping to combine some of these trips with my flight lessons, so I can log some hours. Can that be done?"

"Sure," she said. "As long as an instructor's along."

Smiling, he took the wineglass and waited for her to pour herself one, but instead she stuffed the cork back into the bottle. "Aren't you drinking with me?"

"I don't drink."

"Well, you sure opened the bottle like a pro."

"I have lots of experience at things I don't do anymore," she said, going to the couch that sat in front of the huge picture window overlooking the city.

He sat down next to her. "A little glass of wine won't hurt."

She smiled and pulled back her hair. "Maybe not, but I don't need it. I have lots of fun without it."

"Don't you ever just want to relax? Sip a glass of wine, put your feet up?"

"With my background, Brisco, there's a fine line between relaxing and running amok."

"What does that mean?"

"It means that with a little juice, I could either sleep for ten hours or do a trapeze act on the power lines. It could go either way."

"So you have a problem with alcohol?"

She shook her head. "I'm a woman of extremes. Of course, if I don't drink, I don't have a problem."

Disappointed, he swirled the wine in his glass and watched it slosh against the sides. "I was just hoping we could have a toast together."

Her laughter shot through to a place in his heart that wasn't frequently visited. "I know what you're up to. You were hoping to get me drunk so I'd pass out, and you could steal my plane."

He grinned. "You got me."

"Yep, the jig's up, Brisco. Not gonna work on me."

He went to the sink and dumped out the wine. "All right. If you don't drink, I won't either."

When he turned back, he saw the guarded pleasure on her face. Their eyes met, but she quickly looked at her feet. "I think Jack needs to go out again," she said.

He looked at the dog lying on the carpet. It was clear he wasn't dying to go out. "What's the matter, Carny?" he asked with a smile. "Afraid to be alone in here with me?"

"Hey, it was your idea to bring the dog." She got her key card.

He smiled and opened the door. "Come on, Jack. Carny and I are going to walk you whether you need it or not. My mere proximity in this suite is scaring her to death."

Carny slapped his chest, and he grabbed her hand and pulled her out. Jack followed them to the elevator.

"I'm not scared of you, Brisco."

"Oh yeah, you are." He kept smiling as they got on the elevator. "And truth be known, maybe you should be."

He had finally rendered her speechless. They reached the first floor, and she followed him out to the pool area. Jack headed for a cluster of trees at the back corner.

Carny took off her sandal and dipped her foot in the pool. He watched her with longing in his heart. "So, let me ask you something," he said finally. "If you had never nursed this tremendous doubt about me, if you believed who I said I was, if you thought I might have a shred of decency . . . would there be any chance for us?"

She looked unabashedly into his eyes. "To do what?"

He grunted, which made her smile. "To get involved. To have a relationship. To get to know each other better."

"Is this how you sweet-talk all the notches on your briefcase?"

"Every one," he said, his gaze dropping to her lips. "But you know, there haven't been any ladies on my radar in Serenity. Not that there haven't been opportunities. I just haven't taken them."

"And why not, pray tell?"

"Maybe I had my eye on first prize," he whispered. "My heart wouldn't let me settle for less." With the admission, he felt as scared as he had on that bungee cord.

"And what does your heart have to do with it?"

Was she teasing him? "Everything," he said. "Believe it or not, Carny, with me there's a lot of heart involved."

She laughed, and to his surprise, he felt hurt. "You don't believe I have a heart?"

Her grin faded then as she considered that for a moment, and her eyes softened infinitesimally. "Yeah, Brisco. I know you have a heart. I'm just not sure you know what to do with it."

Maybe she was right. Maybe he didn't know what to do with it. He'd never really had the chance to learn. "I told you, I'm a quick study," he whispered.

She swallowed, and her gaze fell to his lips. "Yes, you are," she said. "I just wish I knew how much you needed to learn."

"A lot," he assured her, as serious as he'd ever been. "I need to learn a lot. About love. Commitment. Friendship. But I don't give up easily."

"Guess we have that in common." Her hand came up to touch his face.

That simple touch beckoned him in a stronger way than he'd ever been beckoned before, and before he had the good sense to stop himself, his lips were hovering over hers, offering her the chance to pull away or knock him to his knees. But she didn't move.

He wasn't sure if it was he or she who breached the final millimeters between their lips, but when they came together, it was a dual effort. Her hand came around to the nape of his neck, up through his hair. He lost himself for that moment.

Carny felt weak as she melted further into the kiss, as though her heart would collapse, as though her breathing would stop, as though all sense and logic would abandon her. She had felt something close to this on her father's roller coaster once . . . the one that had later jumped the track in a trial run and crashed into the dunking booth. And that was just what she feared would happen now.

Slowly, she broke the kiss. "Well, Brisco," she whispered, her forehead still pressed against his, "I can see that's one area that you don't need to learn about."

He smiled. "Another thing we have in common."

His lips touched hers again, and for a moment, she let herself fall into the warmth of his kiss, the security and commitment of his embrace. But she was no fool. They were miles apart in their value system. He wasn't a believer in God, and she couldn't see herself in a relationship with anyone who didn't share her faith and care about the things she cared about. He was wrong for her on so many levels.

Again, she broke the kiss, and pressed her hand on his chest. "I have expertise in other areas, Brisco. Like getting involved with the wrong men."

"What makes you so sure I'm the wrong man?"

"Because I still don't entirely trust you. Because I still question every move you make. Because I don't really know who you are. And what I do know scares me."

"I'm whoever you want me to be," he said. "I'm whatever you need."

"That's what I'm afraid of," she said softly. She turned and saw Jack plodding back toward them. "I don't want a custom-tailored man, Brisco. How can I trust a chameleon?"

"A chameleon?" he repeated. "You think I'm a chameleon?"

"You change according to your environment. One minute you're the good ole boy shooting the breeze in the barbershop, the next you're riding in a chauffeured Rolls and going to meetings with bank executives."

"So I can relate to all types of people. Is that a crime?"

"No, of course not."

"Then what's the problem?"

"The problem," she said, thinking hard, since she wasn't entirely sure what the problem was, "well, the problem is . . . the problem is that I was dead sure you were a con artist. Dead sure. And then the dog, and Slade . . . and Jason . . . and today I saw you with those people, only . . . I'm still not sure it all rings true. I'm still not sure I trust you."

He looked genuinely hurt as he bent to scratch Jack's ear. "So you still don't believe I'm legitimately trying to help Serenity?"

She turned over the things in her mind that she did believe. "I think I believe that you're trying to build the park," she said, "although I'm not absolutely sure that you're as far along as you say. I think I believe that you genuinely like the people in my town, and that you'd like to help them."

"You think you believe?" he asked. "Thanks, Carny. Thanks a lot. And what about you? What do you *think* you believe about the way I feel about you?"

"I think I believe that you're attracted to

me," she said. "No, I take that back. You're obviously attracted to me. But that may partially be because of the challenge I represent. I don't think you've been rejected by many women in your life."

She could see that she'd hit a nerve, and his face reddened. "You missed your calling, Carny. You should have stayed in the carnival as a fortune-teller."

"You know as well as I do that the biggest talent a good con artist has is the talent to read people. I was raised learning to read people, Brisco, and I think you were too. After a while, you start noticing details about people, expressions, words they use. Slowly, your mind works out the puzzle, until you've got all the pieces in place, and you know how that person feels, how they think, how they'd react . . ."

"And what about the margin for error?"

"Yes," she said. "There is that. But I haven't often been wrong. And neither have you."

His eyes were soft, sweet, as he stepped closer. "I don't want to hurt you, Carny. I really, really do like you."

A gentle smile crept across her lips. "Believe it or not, Brisco, I really, really like you too. And there's a part of me that really hopes you're genuine."

For a moment, he couldn't answer, as though he'd never had a better endorsement, or a more touching affirmation. Finally, he managed to smile.

Carny only smiled back. "So are you gonna feed me or what?"

"Sure," he said. "I'm taking you to Bon Ami, like I promised. You did bring the red dress, didn't you?"

"You bet I did. Jason insisted."

"Yeah, Jason and me . . . we've got a strategy."

"A strategy for what?" she asked with a laugh.

"For finding you a husband," he said, going to the door. "Whether you want one or not."

Carny hit him in the stomach as they led Jack inside.

THIRTY-FOUR

"This reminds me of the restaurant where Ricky Ricardo used to sing in *I Love Lucy* reruns," Carny said when they'd been seated at their table in what looked like an old-world opera house.

Logan admired the woman across from him rather than their surroundings. "Have I told you that Jason knew what he was doing when he picked out that dress for you?"

Feigning disgust, she looked at her watch. "Well, I've had it on for almost an hour now, and I haven't had any proposals yet. This husband-hunting isn't all it's cracked up to be." She shifted in her seat, as if uncomfortable with his admiration. "Changing the subject — I've been thinking about my parents, and their threat to come to Serenity. What if they actually do it? What if they try to horn their way into the plans for the park?"

He thought for a moment. "Well, no offense, Carny, but I don't think they fit the profile of the kind of employees I had in mind."

She seemed relieved. "And what if they were to invest a big hunk of money?"

He stared at her for another moment, realizing that a week ago he might have taken it. But that was before the park was legitimate . . . before he decided to turn his lies into truth. "I wouldn't take it."

A slow smile spread across her face. "Thank goodness."

He frowned. "What do you mean?"

"I was testing you," she said. "And miraculously, you passed."

"Why? Your parents aren't really coming?"

"Oh, they're definitely talking about it." She shifted in her seat. "You see, Brisco, even if the park is real, I'm still against it. I think it'll change Serenity. But if it's what the rest of the town wants, all I can do is try to make sure Serenity isn't violated by it."

"I realize that," he said. "Which is why I've been thinking about a specific role for you in the park."

"Oh, no. I don't want anything to do with it."

"You might want this," he said. "I was thinking of making you the park commissioner. You could actually be in charge of maintaining the park's integrity. Making sure you only have honest people working there, with only honest attractions, and that the park represents the best and cleanest . . . and sweetest aspects of Serenity."

Her expression didn't change noticeably. "That would make me a direct adversary of yours. As you built the park, I'd be second-guessing every step of it."

"Aren't we already? Frankly, I'm settling into the role."

"You've got to be kidding. It would be like shooting yourself in the foot."

"No, it would be like making sure I didn't overlook anything. I'll be busy, Carny, and things will get past me. I can't think of anyone in the town who'd be better suited to sniffing out corruption. If I recommended you to the mayor, I'm sure he'd appoint you."

She sat back and considered it. "But what about my airport?"

"That's up to you," he said. "You could keep running it, or turn it over to someone else to run. I'm not kidding about our expanding the airport. It's got to be done."

"That would take years and millions of dollars, Brisco. The kind of traffic you're talking about would require a towered airport and longer runways."

"Yours can already handle commercial-sized planes."

"There's a difference between a Learjet and a jetliner. And a difference between a municipal airport and a private one."

"I'm just saying either you'll upgrade it, or someone else will build one in another place, and they'll be the ones to get rich. If I were you, I'd be the one to do it."

"I'm not interested in being rich, Brisco. My parents have chased money all their lives, and it hasn't gotten them anywhere."

"I think you have stronger values, Carny. You could handle money, if you had it. You wouldn't gamble it away on schemes and scams. And you'd have something to leave Jason."

"I'm leaving Jason plenty," she said. "Values, security, peace of mind, and memories of a happy childhood. Don't you realize how valuable those things are?"

For a moment, his eyes grew serious, and he looked down at his food. "Actually, I do."

She seemed to read his thoughts. "Me too," she whispered.

The pianist started to play, lending an oddly romantic background to the conversation that had little to do with romance. "We're so much alike, Carny. A lot more

331

than you like to think."

"I know."

Their eyes locked in a startling merge of emotions. Finally, Logan whispered, "Will you dance with me? You look too pretty not to be seen on the dance floor."

Her smile was more satisfying than all the scams he'd ever pulled off, and getting to his feet, he took her hand and pulled her with him.

He didn't know the tune the pianist played, and it didn't matter. As if she'd always been his partner, as if he'd learned to dance with her, they moved across the dance floor with grace and finesse.

In the anonymity among the other dancers, they weren't adversaries at all, but two people aware of the locked chambers of each other's soul. Two people who were reaching an understanding.

He looked down at her, stricken by how beautiful she was, how special, how delicate. But she was also tough, like him . . . a survivor. A striver. A reacher. There wasn't much in Carny's life that would stand in the way of her getting the kind of life she wanted. Not even Logan.

He didn't know if it was the music or the way she felt in his arms that compelled him to lower his lips to hers, but before he knew it, they had stopped dancing and stood motionless in the center of the dance floor, and he was kissing her again.

Carny seemed to free-fall into that kiss.

The song ended as their kiss broke, and Logan led her back to their table. As hard as he tried to get through the rest of the meal with his thoughts intact, he found that it was too late.

He had fallen hard, and he wasn't sure he would survive it.

Country music spilled from the club in the hotel when the cab brought them back.

"Do you like country music?" he asked.

She shrugged. "Sometimes. Do you?"

"Sometimes," he chuckled. "I saw you two-stepping like a champ at the town dance, but truthfully, I would have pegged you for the Led Zeppelin type." Taking her hand, he said, "Come on. Let's go in."

He pulled her into the club, and they took a table at the back and looked across the crowd of people to the singer on the stage, doing his own rendition of a Clint Black song.

"He's pretty good," Logan said.

Nodding, Carny scanned the faces in the crowd, the way she'd always done as a child in the carnival. Her gaze landed on a man just coming in the door, a man with a cowboy hat and sunglasses. For a moment, the glasses snagged her attention, and she wondered why anyone would wear shades into a dark nightclub.

He slipped into the shadows near their table and seemed to scan the place for an empty table. But she and Logan had gotten the last one.

Suddenly she recognized him. "Eric Hart."

"No, that's a Clint Black song," Logan said.

"No, Brisco," she whispered. "Right there. That guy in the glasses. It's Eric Hart."

Logan looked up, squinting in disbelief. "It looks like him, but it can't be him. What would he be doing here all by himself? He's one of the biggest stars in country music."

"I don't know, but it's him. Look how he stands. Look at that tattoo on his hand. That's Eric Hart! He's looking for a place to sit."

Before she knew it, Logan had shot out of his chair and was shaking hands with the star. She watched, astonished and a little embarrassed, as he pointed to their table, then came back with Eric.

Carny stood up as they reached the table. "Eric, I'd like you to meet Carny Sullivan. Carny, Eric Hart."

"Nice to meet you, ma'am. I hope I'm not intruding. Logan invited me to sit with you."

"Of course," she said, shooting Logan an incredulous look. "Do you two know each other?"

Eric laughed. "No, but I've got a feeling Logan doesn't meet too many strangers." He leaned forward and, in a low voice, said, "I'm surprised y'all recognized me. I was hoping to be discreet."

"Oh, we won't call any attention to you," she assured him as he motioned to the waitress to bring him a drink. "What brings you to town?"

"Concert tomorrow night," he said. "I like to get to town early, just to relax before all the madness starts."

The band launched into a cover of one of Eric's tunes, "Dreamscape." Chuckling, he glanced back at the band. "Hey, that singer's better than I am."

Carny and Logan laughed with him as the song played on.

An hour later, Logan and Eric were deep in a conversation about the park, and Carny realized with chagrin that Logan was making a sales pitch to the star. That riled her. It wasn't right, violating the man's privacy to hit on him for money.

"We've been looking for a star to name

the park after. You know, kind of like Dolly-wood. You're just the caliber we're looking for."

With a forced smile, Carny nudged Logan. Had he forgotten about Roland Thunder? Logan set his eyes on the ceiling and waved his hand as if creating a banner. "I can see it now. Hartland."

"Hartland?" Carny repeated, resisting the urge to stick her finger down her throat.

But Eric didn't seem to find the idea silly. "I like it," he said. "An amusement park. Hmm. I never thought of that before. What kind of investment would I have to make?"

That's it, Carny thought. *Here's where he nails him for the money.*

"Well, that would be negotiable. The profit margin for you would be tremendous, because there would be licensing involved. The gift shops would be full of items related to Eric Hart and your better-known songs, and some of the rides could go along with your themes. It may work out that we don't need any investment at all from you, if you agree to let us merchandise your name, in return for shares of the park."

"Merchandising, huh?" Eric asked. "This is sounding better all the time. How long will you be in Houston?"

"We'll be leaving the day after tomorrow,"

Logan said.

"Perfect. Can you meet with my agent and me tomorrow? Say, ten o'clock?"

"Sure," Logan said.

"I'm in the penthouse here." Fishing through his hip pocket, he pulled out a card. "Here's the phone number so you can get through. Call before you come up, and I'll make sure you don't have any trouble getting in."

"All right," Logan said, shaking Eric's hand. He stood up, looking at Carny. "You ready to go, Carny?"

"Yeah, it's getting late," she said. "It was great meeting you, Eric."

"You, too," he said. "We might be seeing a lot more of each other."

As they left the club and went inside and across the hotel, Carny gave Logan a curious look. "How about that?"

"Talk about being in the right place at the right time." The elevator doors opened, and they stepped in. "Do you realize what it could do for us if we could get a commitment from him? The investors would be calling *us!*"

"I thought the investors *were* calling you. And what about Roland Thunder, and all that Thunder Road stuff? And the fact that the park would be bigger than Disney and put parks like Six Flags to shame?"

"Optimism," Logan said. "Roland Thunder was always just a possibility; I may never have landed him. And now that I've met Eric, why not go with him? He's a bird in the hand. I just never dreamed we'd have a shot at him."

"Hartland," she said as the doors opened. She stepped off. "Sounds a little corny, don't you think?"

"Dollywood isn't corny? Opryland isn't corny? Even Disneyland is named after Walt Disney."

They came to her door, and as she stuck her key card in the slot, he braced his hand above her head. She stopped and looked up at him.

When his lips grazed hers, she closed her eyes, her heart pounding out its erratic rhythm. Finally, she touched his chest and broke the contact of their lips. "You're an interesting man, Logan Brisco."

"Does that mean you're interested?"

"It means I'm intrigued," she whispered.

"Then surely you could let your guard down a little, just for tonight. Let me come in."

"Oh, no," she whispered. "The fact that I'm intrigued only makes me want to raise my guard higher."

"You still don't trust me?"

She smiled. "I think the problem is that I don't really trust myself. You were right when you said that before, Logan. There's too much at stake."

Then, pressing another kiss on his jaw, she went in and closed the door behind her.

THIRTY-FIVE

The next morning as they flew back to Serenity, Logan's eyes were bright. Eric Hart's interest had breathed even more life into his plans for the park, and despite herself, Carny was beginning to catch the vision.

"I need a lawyer," he said into his mike.

"For what?" she asked.

"Someone to represent the park. We'll need to start drawing up contracts soon."

"Well, there are two lawyers in Serenity. Alan Robard is probably your best bet."

"I know Alan. I'll call him."

"Doesn't King Enterprises have their own attorneys?"

He was silent for a moment.

"Logan?" she prodded.

He didn't look at her as he answered. "Yeah, about that. Turns out that King has reneged on the idea of building a park anywhere."

"What?"

"Don't crash!" he said, grabbing the yoke.

"I wasn't going to crash." She tried to refocus her thoughts on flying the plane.

"It's okay. I gave them my resignation and told them I wanted to go ahead with the plans myself."

"Logan, doesn't that change everything?"

"Not really. I was the one raising the money, and I hadn't turned any of it over to them yet. Once the new investors come to Serenity, I'll explain it to them. Their relationship is with me, not with King Enterprises."

She let that information sink in. King Enterprises had never returned her calls. "When did this happen?"

He sighed. "I've been getting hints of it for the past few days. Finally had to face the writing on the wall this morning. But it's okay. We can still do all of it."

She tried to breathe. Would he have admitted this if it was all a scam?

"So has Eric made a commitment?" she asked.

"He's that far from it," he said, holding up his thumb and forefinger. "He's coming to Serenity next week, but it's top secret, so don't tell anybody."

"And are the bankers top secret too?"

"I'd rather they were, until everything is nailed down."

Something about the secrecy disturbed her. "You told us that Roland Thunder was almost committed, but he really wasn't, was he?"

"Well, not totally."

"So you were lying."

"Not lying. I never claimed it was a done deal. Think of it as a card game, Carny. You've got some cards showing, and some hidden."

"But your deck is stacked."

He shot her an annoyed look. "What's your point?"

"My point is that I think you used Thunder's name to get others to invest. And then you used those investments to impress the bankers. Then you used the bankers to impress Eric Hart. And eventually, it has a snowball effect, but you aren't absolutely sure of any of the players, so you have to juggle it all very carefully."

"So what's wrong with my having faith in my juggling abilities? Carny, I've been juggling for a long time. I know how to make deals. I do it better than anyone I know."

"What other deals have you put together?"

He hesitated. "Lots of them, okay?"

She kept her eyes on her instruments.

"Name some."

"I put together several big real-estate deals along the east coast. And I helped with the buyout of a major hospital in Kentucky."

"What was the name of it?"

Aggravated, he glared at her. "What's your point? Do you think I made up Gastineau and his bank? Do you think Eric Hart was just some actor I planted in that bar to convince you I'm aboveboard?"

"I think that you're not above using dishonesty to reach a real goal."

He shifted in his seat and adjusted his microphone. "It's not easy putting together an endeavor like this, Carny. Not just anyone could do it. It takes a lot of wheeling and dealing, and you can't go into a bank empty-handed and expect them to invest. You have to have other commitments from other investors. You have to have a plan."

"It sounds an awful lot like what my parents do."

"Don't be such a cynic," Logan said. "There's a difference. Your parents take the money and run. If I do my job right, everybody who invests gets rich. I'm the man who has to convince everybody. It's a good thing they're not all as hard to convince as you. The bottom line is that nobody's going to get hurt."

"Are you sure about that?"

He met her eyes then. "Yeah, Carny, I am. I'm real sure. I need for you to believe me."

For a moment, she only stared out the window, wishing . . . *hoping* that it was true. She wanted to believe, despite the doubts still whispering in her mind.

Over the next few days, Carny transported planeloads of bankers back and forth between Houston and Serenity, with Logan flying most of the time and logging his flight hours. She listened to the conversations over the headsets on the flights, and was amazed at how prepared Logan was to answer all their questions.

And when Eric Hart made his discreet flight into Serenity in his own plane, she realized that this might just turn into reality.

And Logan Brisco might be here to stay.

Carny had been home for a week before Joey reminded her of the picture she was supposed to have gotten in Houston.

"I got it," she told him on the phone. "He stood right there like it was no big deal and let me take the picture."

"Email it to me," Joey said. "I need to get to work on this right away."

She hesitated. "Joey, I really think I was

wrong about him. He really is working on the park. It just looks too real to be a scam."

"Hey, are you wimping out on me?"

"No," she said. "I just . . . I feel guilty going behind his back trying to dig up dirt . . . if he does happen to be legitimate."

"You're really hung up on him, aren't you? He's worked his magic on you too."

"No," she said, though she knew her voice wasn't as adamant as she would have liked. "I'm just getting to know him better."

"And you trust him now?"

"I'm trusting him more," she said.

"Well, for that little flicker of doubt you still have in the back of your mind, and for mine, could you just send me that picture?"

"Yeah. I'll do it as soon as I get home."

There was a long pause. "You don't really want to know if he's a crook anymore, do you?"

"I want you to tell me what you find out," she said softly. "But I don't think there's a person in this town who wants to believe that Logan Brisco's a crook."

As soon as Carny got home from work, she shoved her camera's memory card into her computer to email Joey the picture. But it wasn't there.

She flicked through the images, but there

was nothing of Brisco. How had that happened?

Her mind reeled through the possibilities as she called Joey back. It was just too coincidental. Yet it *was* a coincidence. It had to be, because the alternative was something she didn't want to consider.

"Was Logan ever near your camera?" Joey asked her when she reported back to him.

"No, never. I must have just made a mistake. But I'll try again. Jason's birthday party is this weekend. I'll be taking pictures of the kids, and I'm going to see if Logan will come. I'll get him then."

That evening, while Jason played at Nathan's, she went to the Welcome Inn to extend the invitation. She could have called, but she wanted to see him. Whether she wanted to admit it or not, he was getting under her skin.

Logan looked tired when he answered the knock on his door, but his eyes lit up when he saw that it was Carny. "I was just thinking about you," he said.

The greeting was like melting wax warming through her. "I came by to invite you to Jason's birthday party. He'll be eight on Saturday."

Something changed in Logan's eyes, and she would have sworn that he was profoundly moved by her invitation.

"Really?" he asked. "You want me there?"

"I wouldn't invite you if I didn't," she said. "And Jason wants you there too. It's at three o'clock."

"I'll be there."

Another poignant moment passed between them, and a look so eloquent that it almost collapsed her. When he stepped closer to her, she didn't back away. He came close enough that she could feel his warmth through his clothes, could breathe his breath as it swept across her lips. "I think you should know something, Carny," he whispered, "only I don't really know how to say it."

"What?"

"Since I was little, my emotions have pretty much been on dim. But ever since I came into Serenity and met you, they've been as bright as I can stand. Maybe brighter. Sometimes it's better to stay on dim. But I don't think this is one of those times."

Her eyes misted over, and when he leaned down and kissed her, she felt her own emotions bypassing bright and heading for explosive. Her mind was beginning to trust, and her heart was beginning to need, and no matter how hard she tried, she couldn't repress her feelings any longer.

That scared her to death. She couldn't be here with him, this exposed, this emotional. Where would it lead?

"I . . . I have to go," she whispered. "Jason's at Nathan's, and I said I wouldn't be gone long."

"You sure? I've missed you since we got back from Houston."

She couldn't return the admission. Not yet.

"It was nice spending so much time with you," he said. "I don't like not seeing you every day."

"You know where I am," she said with a smile. She looked around his hotel room, where stacks of papers covered every surface, and the blueprints for the park lay spread out on the floor. "Looks like you've been busy."

"Yeah, I've been on the phone all week working with engineers, talking to owners of the land I want for the park, getting numbers together for the investors, working everything out."

She told herself again that it was all real, that she wasn't being scammed. "Maybe you need to rent some office space."

"Yeah, I will when I have a minute to breathe."

"So . . . you'll take a minute to breathe on Saturday?"

He grinned down at her. "That's more important than anything else I have going on," he said, stroking her cheek. "I'll see you Saturday."

"Yeah." Her voice cracked, and she cleared her throat. "At three."

Stepping back and taking her unruly emotions with her, she left his motel, suppressing the urge to run as fast as she could, either back to him, or far, far away.

THIRTY-SIX

Logan was the life of Jason's party, and as Carny videotaped his shenanigans with the children, she realized she wouldn't have expected otherwise.

"Do it again, Logan!"

"Throw me!"

"It's my turn, Logan!"

The children's happy voices rang out over the music playing at the picnic table as they jumped on the trampoline Carny had given Jason for his birthday. Without inhibition, Logan bounced on the trampoline, dribbling the kids like basketballs.

Not once had he seemed nervous about the fact that she was taping him — and he wasn't embarrassed about looking foolish — but later when they assembled the children around the picnic table to cut the cake, when she got her camera and began flashing pictures, she noted a touch of apprehension. Logan managed to escape most of the pictures she took, and when she cornered him, he shoved on a pair of big nose glasses she had given as party favors, and evaded the camera once again.

Annoyed, she finally got him alone. "Tell me something, Logan. Why don't you want me to take your picture?"

"Because I'm not very photogenic," he said. "The pupils of my eyes always come out with this demonic red glow. And I have that old superstition about photography stealing your soul."

"That's ridiculous."

"What's the big deal? You got a picture of me in Houston."

"It didn't come out," she said. "I accidentally deleted it."

"Likely story."

"Let me get a picture of you and Jason together now. It would mean a lot to him. All I want to do is put it up in his room."

"Now who's being dishonest?" His amusement faded, and he gave her a sober look that spoke volumes. "You want it so you can check me out. Do you want a fingerprint while you're at it? How about my dental records?"

She set her hand on her hip. "Do you have them?"

"No, Carny. Do you have yours?"

"Well . . . no."

"All right, then." She felt a wall going up between them, and she didn't like it. Finally, he said, "Go ahead. Take the picture. I don't have anything to hide. You've got me all over that videotape."

Backing away, she brought the camera to her eye. "Smile, Logan. Act like you're having fun."

Logan forced a smile, and she flashed a few pictures in a row. Finally, she lowered the camera. "Thank you."

His smile disappeared, and a melancholy seemed to fall over him. For a while, he sat on a lawn chair away from the kids. She didn't like the change, and she kicked herself for bringing it on. Finally, when he got up to help her clean the picnic table of plates and cups, he stopped her and made her look at him. "Tell me something, Carny. You do believe me about the park now, don't you? You don't think I'm going to skip town with all this money anymore."

"You still could," she said. When he sighed, she wanted to take her words back. "But no, I'm not expecting it anymore."

"Then why do you want my picture?"

"I'd just like a keepsake. I take pictures of all my friends. If you don't have anything to hide, then I don't get why you're hiding from the camera."

"I'm just disappointed that you're still trying to see if I'm on the Top Ten Most Wanted list."

She tossed the last of the plates into a garbage bag and put it into her garbage can. "Other people don't worry about pictures, Brisco. You sound worried."

"Carny, what if people held your past against you? Reminded you of it every time you turned around? Never trusted you because they knew what you were before? What if they spent a lot of time digging up your dirt and made lists of all the scams you helped pull off?"

"I'm not doing that."

"Yes, you are, even though you know people can change."

"So you are avoiding having your picture taken?"

He rolled his eyes and threw up his hands. "You know what? Be my guest. Take a picture and send it all over the country. Make billboards of it. Put it on YouTube, if you have nothing better to do with your time."

A football rolled to his feet, and he reached down and scooped it up. "They're calling me," he said, and headed back to the boys.

■ ■ ■ ■

That night when Logan was alone, his mask fell, and the nonchalance he'd feigned about being photographed began to weigh heavily on his mind. He should have known he couldn't stop her attempts to photograph him forever. That was probably the only reason she'd invited him to Jason's party.

And he'd believed it was because she wanted him there.

Jack hopped up onto the bed next to him, and Logan stroked his rich coat. "Don't worry, Jack. Logan Brisco doesn't have a record. But if they match my picture to Lawrence Cartland . . ."

Here he was, on the verge of doing something legitimate, something that he was pulling off with hard work, ingenuity, and the talent that he'd used to the wrong end so many times before. Carny was beginning to trust him, and that was one of the biggest victories in his life. But it was a hollow victory.

If she sent that picture in to the police, and they shared it with the FBI, someone might make the connection. If the FBI heard he was at it again, they'd come after him and blow his cover, ruining the one shot he had at legitimacy. He had already served time for his previous crimes, but if they thought he was committing fraud again, they'd consider it a parole violation.

In the interest of starting an honest life, he considered breaking into Carny's house and deleting the video and pictures again. But that was absurd.

He threw his arm over his eyes and tried to imagine how she would feel if the FBI came to her and told her that she had been right to suspect him. That he'd even served time for his sins?

The times they had shared would seem like another con to her. The conversations they'd shared, the camaraderie, the laughter . . . it would all seem cruel. She deserved so much better.

For the first time in his life, he wished he could erase his past. The time with Montague, when he'd learned how to be a criminal. The people he'd hurt, despite Montague's rules. Those rules — what a joke. The people they'd scammed were people just like these in Serenity. Though Montague assured himself that no one was really getting hurt, they'd always known better. They just wouldn't let themselves think about it.

The fortune the Feds had taken from him when he went to prison had paid restitution to most of those people, but the pain of what the scams had done to their lives was only hitting him now. Seeing those crimes through Carny's eyes made them all seem so much more real. If she learned about his past, she would realize that she'd been right about him all along. She would feel as if she had been fleeced — and why? Because she'd let down her guard. She would hate herself for getting close to him.

She deserved a decent man who could make her proud. Not some ex-con who had deceived her from the start.

Jack slid off the bed and ambled to the door. "Need to go out, boy? All right. I need some air anyway."

Logan opened the door and walked Jack out. The dog needed no leash. He went where he wanted to go, avoiding the streets and staying close to Logan. But having no leash also gave Jack freedom, if he chose to take it. If he wanted to run away, he could.

That was how Logan had been with Montague.

For the first time, he realized that Montague had taken a huge risk in taking in a young runaway. It had broken his own rules, making it more likely that he could be identified. Yes, Montague had reaped the benefits of having Logan helping him. But taking responsibility for a kid was a huge commitment for him.

Truth was, Logan had been scamming people before he'd met Montague, so he couldn't blame his mentor for turning him into a criminal. He'd known right from wrong. He'd voluntarily gone along with Montague's crimes because he liked making money. Like Jack, he could have left at any time. But even before Montague died, it had been a lonely life. Ironic that he'd found a place where he wasn't lonely and wanted to plant roots, but his own sins were going to keep him from it. Carny would find out the truth, and he would lose everything. There would be no redemption in her eyes.

He walked up the street, Jack sniffing and scampering along beside him. He passed the hardware store and the barbershop and Lahoma's hair salon and felt a longing in his soul to do the right thing for those people. He was trying to turn their investments into something that would make life better for them. But it was about to blow to pieces.

He was tired of running. Tired of lying. Tired of faking it.

He reached the church, its steeple illuminated on the dark street. He sat down on a bench near it, watching Jack explore the bushes.

When Carny had come here with Abe Sullivan, had she told people straight out who she'd been? Did they all know of her colorful lifestyle right up front? Or had she felt like he felt tonight? Worried that people would find out and run her out of town?

She talked about being washed clean and forgiven. But was there such a thing available for him? No, of course not.

Jack came and lay down at his feet, but Logan didn't want to go back to the inn just yet. His eyes strayed to the cemetery where Slade Hampton lay. Had Jack forgotten that they'd planted his master in the ground there? Or was he simply aware that Slade wasn't really there, in the ground, that his body was just an empty shell?

He'd seldom considered it before, but as he sat outside the church that taught of redemption, he wondered if it could be true. They had talked about Slade's soul going to heaven. The people in this town seemed to believe it, and as innocent and naive as they were, they weren't stupid.

He looked up at the steeple, then beyond it to the stars sprinkled so beautifully across the sky. The universe was an artist's canvas, so carefully crafted.

"I wish you were real," he said to the sky.

"That you really could wash me clean. That a person like me could really start over and live in this town, and have a woman like Carny, and be a father to a boy like Jason. But there isn't enough water in all the world to wash me clean of the stains on my soul, is there?"

As if in answer to his prayer, he saw a star shoot across the sky. He caught his breath. Was that a sign, sent by a benevolent God who heard his prayer? No, it couldn't be. As much as he wanted it, he knew better. It was just a meteor.

Tears filled his eyes, and he dropped his gaze and leaned forward, elbows on knees, and looked at the sign for Deep Waters Christian Church, illuminated with two spotlights. There was a verse beneath the name, something he hadn't noticed before. He sat up and squinted, reading. "Whoever drinks the water I give him will never thirst. Indeed, the water I give him will become in him a spring of water welling up to eternal life."

Water. He looked back at the sky, struck by the words. Was *that* the water that would wash him clean?

Somehow, deep in his spirit, he knew the answer. He'd been right that there wasn't enough water on all the earth to wash him clean. The water that would wash him clean wasn't earthly water. It was divine.

He memorized the reference — John 4:13. Maybe there was a Bible in his room.

"Come on, Jack," he said. "Let's go back."

His pace was faster, more purposeful, as he headed back to his room.

When Jack was back on his bed, Logan pulled out the bed-table drawer. As he'd expected, he found a Gideon Bible there. He consulted the table of contents, found John, and read in the fourth chapter of a woman who met Jesus beside a well as she was drawing water.

She too was someone stained with sin, yet Jesus had given her hope. He'd given her living water. He hadn't turned away.

Maybe there was hope for Logan too.

Fresh tears assaulted him as he sat beside his bed and spoke directly to the redeemer of his soul. "I'm sorry I'm a cheat and a liar," he whispered. "But since you're my only hope, I'm going to trust that you're real. If you could just wash me clean . . ."

To his amazement, he *did* feel something happening. A lifting of guilt. A cleansing. A lightness in his soul. Tears rolled down his face. It *was* real. His mother had known it when she'd taken him to Sunday School all those years ago. Maybe from her place in heaven, she was bending God's ear, begging him to direct her son. Maybe that was why he'd wound up in Serenity after all.

But believing he was clean wasn't enough. There were things he had to do to make it right. It was time to tell the truth.

THIRTY-SEVEN

The house was lonely without Jason, and Carny lay awake in bed, listening for sounds of the boys in the woods behind their house, camping out with Nathan's father for a combination birthday and "school's out" celebration. But it wasn't the quiet that kept her awake. It was Logan.

He had been wonderful with the children today, and without him, Jason's party wouldn't have been the success it was. The paradox of Logan Brisco puzzled her . . . yet part of her understood him.

The doorbell rang and she jumped out of bed and grabbed her robe. It was probably Jason. He had probably heard a noise, or gotten cold, or suffered one too many mosquito bites.

She hurried into the living room and peered through the window. It wasn't Jason who stood there, but Logan. Her heart jolted. She opened the door. "Logan?"

He looked as serious as she had ever seen him, but he made no attempt to come in. He merely leaned against the door casing with his hands in his pockets. "I couldn't sleep," he said. "I need to talk to you."

Slowly, she stepped back, allowing him in. She closed the door behind him. "Just a minute. Let me go get dressed." She ran back to her bedroom and threw on the clothes she'd had on earlier. *This is it,* she thought. This was the moment when she'd have to deal with the emotional havoc of getting involved with a man like Logan Brisco. "What about?"

His face was somber, and his eyes held no trace of their usual amusement. "I haven't been entirely honest," he said. "I want to change that now."

"I'm listening."

He took her hand, led her to the couch, and sat down beside her. She pulled her knees up, hugged them, protecting herself from whatever was about to come.

"Today, when you took my picture . . . I lied when I said it was okay for you to take it. The truth is, I *was* avoiding it."

Her heart deflated slowly. "Why?"

"I've already told you that I had a checkered past, Carny. Just like you."

"But if you're not a criminal, what does it

matter?"

He sighed and looked down at his hands. They were shaking. "I have been a criminal. I spent years in prison for my crimes."

Every muscle in her body grew rigid. For a moment, horror overcame her, the horror of knowing she had been right, but that she had fallen for him anyway. She got up and went across the room, as far away from him as she could get without walking out entirely. "I . . . I was right about you? About . . . being a con artist? You really were out to fleece my town?"

"Not anymore, Carny," he said quickly. "The banks and Eric Hart and all the numbers are real. I've worked myself half to death trying to work it all out, once I decided to make it right. But I can't lie to you anymore."

She leaned against the wall, her face still twisted, and shook her head. "Why not, Brisco? Why can't you lie to me?"

It was almost a plea that he take back his confession, allow her to slip back into the naiveté of his lies. To let her feel good just a little while longer.

She hated herself for it.

"Carny, where were you the day you realized you couldn't live the kind of life your parents did anymore? Do you remember?"

She didn't want to stroll down memory lane. She wanted to lash out, scream at him, curl up in her bed and cry.

"Please, Carny. I need for you to think about that. Where were you?"

She shook her head. "I don't know . . . I was . . . in some little town in Louisiana. We were driving all night, because they'd almost been caught at something. I don't even remember what."

"And you knew, didn't you, that at some point, you had to jump off the mad merry-go-round you'd been born onto?"

She hugged herself as her eyes glazed over with the memory. "I'd never felt so lonely in my life. Or so scared. Not of getting caught with my parents and going to jail . . . but of trying to stop the cycle. Of escaping it, somehow, when it was all I'd ever known. And then our carnival wound up in Serenity, and I went into a little church, and everything changed . . ."

"I've been scared, too, Carny," he said, his luminous blue eyes glistening in the lamplight. "And the closer I've gotten to you, the more terrified I've been. But I *will* do what I've promised. Tonight, God spoke to me. Not with words, but with this *knowing* in my soul."

Slowly, his words penetrated, and she let

the fragile edges of hope work their way back into her heart. She turned back to him, struck by the sincerity in his eyes.

"I was sitting in front of the church with Jack. There was this shooting star, and then the verse on the sign at the church. About living water. And it was from a passage about this woman who'd been married like four times before, and Jesus told her he could give her living water."

"The woman at the well," she whispered.

"Yes. She was as messed up as I am. Well, maybe not quite as bad, but she had a history, and lots of baggage. And Jesus wasn't repulsed by her. He gave her something no one else could give her."

She took a step toward him. "You read that?"

"Yes." His mouth was shaking. "Back at the hotel. And I talked to God and told him how sorry I was. And I asked him to wash me like he washed you. And he did."

Was this just another con? Had he found the buttons that meant something to her? The ones that could make her believe? Could it be real?

"As soon as I knew I was clean, I also knew I had to tell the truth." He reached out for her, and she crossed the room and took his hand. "Sit down," he said. "I need to tell you everything."

She nodded and let him pull her down next to him. "Go ahead."

"You were right. It started out to be just another scam."

She closed her eyes and brought her hands to her face. "I knew it."

"But now . . . since I've gotten to know the people in the town, I've been trying to make the park happen for real. If I do that, nobody gets hurt. And if I my make my lies into truth, then I haven't committed a crime since prison." He turned around, closing his hand into a fist. "I can see it happening, Carny, just like I said. But . . ."

Her lips tightened. "But what?"

"But it's so much more terrifying, trying to pull off reality. Illusion is a lot easier." He looked her in the eye. "I'm trying to turn my lies into truth, Carny, if that makes any sense. I'm trying as hard as I can."

For the first time since she'd met him, she didn't find a trace of doubt in her mind. "The King Enterprises story. That you resigned. Was that true, or was that made up?"

"I *am* King Enterprises. I have a business license, a telephone number. And as you've seen, a voicemail system. I made up the story about their pulling out, because I was trying to ease you into the truth."

Ease her into it? She didn't have to question that. She understood it perfectly.

"This may be why God led me to Serenity — so I could see what it would be like to have my slate washed clean, and to find someplace where I could actually belong. To be the person I've only pretended to be. Maybe it's just another selfish motive . . . to want what I can get out of this town. But this time it's not money."

She took a deep breath and let his words sink in. "Selfish or not, wanting a second chance and cleansing . . . well, that's honorable, Logan." An unexpected peace fell over her, and despite what he'd told her, despite what she knew about him, despite what some part of her had always known, she felt closer to him than she'd ever felt to anyone in her life.

When she reached out to hold him, he sank down until his forehead was on her shoulder. For the first time since she'd known him, she didn't doubt him. In her soul, she knew his story was true.

"If I go to the church tomorrow, and tell them who I really am . . . if I offer to give all their money back if they want me to . . . do you think there's any chance that they could forgive me? That I could live here in

Serenity, and actually *belong?* Or would the truth make that impossible?"

She sighed. "I don't know. They're not going to like knowing that you pulled the wool over their eyes."

"But they accepted you, didn't they?"

"Yes, but I didn't hide who I was. They knew from the beginning that I was a carny. My name made that clear. I guess in some ways they saw me as a project, somebody they could mentor and help grow. I never lied to them."

The air seemed to go out of him, and his eyes settled on some invisible spot in the air. "Then what would happen if I didn't tell them? If I just went ahead with my plans, and they never knew that it had almost been a scam?"

She shook her head. "No, Logan. You have to come clean. It's the right thing to do. The Bible says that we should have nothing to do with the fruitless deeds of darkness, but that we should expose them."

"But if I lose the chance to settle here, then I lose everything. And I lose you."

"You can't do this for me. You have to do it for your relationship with God. You have to trust that even if I'm out of the picture, even if you have to leave Serenity, following God's will is still the right path for you. Is it worth it to you?"

"Yes, it is."

"I hope so, Logan. If that's real, then I'm not going anywhere. I'll be here for you."

He wiped his moist eyes. "I know it's too soon, that you're still trying to feel your way through this relationship, but in the interest of full disclosure, I have to say that I've fallen in love with you, Carny Sullivan."

She touched his lips, quieting him. "You say that to all the girls, don't you?"

"Honestly, I've never said it before. And that makes me want to change even more. You deserve an honorable man."

He kissed her and she melted into him, her walls fading away and her fear vaporizing. When the kiss broke, she gazed into his eyes. "I'm falling for you too, Brisco."

He grinned like he'd won the lottery. "I never thought I'd hear those words from you." He brought his eyes back to her. "I'll tell the people tomorrow," he said. "I'll go to church early and ask Brother Tommy if I can talk to them during the service. But I have to admit, I'm scared."

She reached up and framed his face with her hands. "Don't be, Logan. He who began a good work in you will be faithful to complete it."

"Is that in the Bible too?" he asked.

"Yes. Philippians 1:6."

"There's a lot of cool stuff in there, isn't there?"

She laughed softly. "Yep. You should read it all."

"I intend to," he said.

THIRTY-EIGHT

Carny awoke early the next morning and spent an hour praying about Logan's confession before the church. When Jason came in from his night of camping, she got him ready for Sunday school.

"Honey, I want to talk to you," she said as he ate his cereal. "This morning, Logan is going to talk to the church. What he says will surprise you and a lot of others, and it might hurt."

"What is it?" he asked.

"I'd rather let him tell it. But after church, we'll talk about it, okay?"

Worry twisted Jason's face. "He's not gonna build the park?"

"It's not that," she said.

"Oh, good. You scared me for a minute."

He finished and ran off to brush his teeth. As she rinsed out his bowl and put it in the dishwasher, Carny wondered if he'd even understand what Logan was going to tell the congregation. It would be an opportunity for explaining God's goodness and his power of redemption. But the confession could be a blow and a disappointment to all those who believed in Logan.

As she walked into the church building a little while later, her heart raced with anticipation. She saw Brother Tommy coming toward her in the hallway, smiling and speaking to everyone he passed. " 'Morning, Carny," he said.

" 'Morning," she said, surprised that he hadn't mentioned anything about Logan. "Brother Tommy? Logan Brisco was coming to talk to you today. Has he been here yet?"

"Nope, haven't seen him," he said.

Disappointed, she took Jason to his class. Logan was probably just running late. He would probably show up any minute. But an hour later, when Sunday School was over, there was still no sign of him.

As she waited for Jason outside his Sunday School class, Doc Carraway ambled by. "Hey Carny. I figured you'd be flying Logan."

She frowned. "What do you mean? Flying him where?"

"Said he was going to Dallas when he checked out this morning."

Her heart plummeted, and for a moment she couldn't find her voice. "Checked out? What do you mean he checked out?"

"He said he was going to be gone several days and that when he comes back he's getting an apartment, so there was no point in keeping the room."

She reached for the wall to steady herself. "Why was he going to Dallas?"

"To meet with his investors."

On Sunday? Without a word?

She put her hands to her face and tried to catch her breath, but the air seemed too thin and her lungs too tight. "Which ones?" she asked. "Which investors? The banks are closed on Sunday."

"I'm just telling you what he said, Carny. He wouldn't have said it if he didn't mean it."

The door opened and the eight-year-olds burst out. She stared into space, letting the reality sink in, and tried to face what she knew to be true.

He wouldn't have said it if he didn't mean it. Wouldn't he? Wasn't saying things without meaning them a way of life for him? What had made her think he'd meant any of what he'd said last night? *I have to say that I've fallen in love with you, Carny Sullivan.* And what had she said in response? *I'm falling for you too, Brisco.* He'd made her believe. That had been his final con in Serenity — getting into her heart. The challenge was over. He'd won.

And then, to top it all off, he'd made that big, intimate confession, feigned a real coming-to-Jesus experience. It was a final kick in the teeth, just to make sure that all the soft, sweet memories were turned into a mockery.

He probably laughed all the way out of town, his pockets filled with the money he'd extorted from the trusting people of Serenity.

She didn't know which she felt in greater portion — despair or rage. She wanted to scream, to cry, to tear something. She wanted to hurt him, to hate him, to *stop* him.

"Mom?"

She looked down at Jason, who stood in front of her, holding a glittery drawing still wet with glue. Vacantly, she took it.

"Mom, are you all right?"

She looked at the church members smiling and milling around in the hallway. For a moment, she thought of telling them all that if they hurried, they might still catch him. She'd told them over and over. But no one would be any more likely to believe her now than they had before.

No one except Joey.

She took Jason into the church and set him down with his grandparents. Then she went out to her car, locked herself in. Trembling, she punched in Joey's cell number. On the fourth ring, he answered.

"Hello?"

"Joey, I was right," she blurted. "He's gone, and he took all the money!"

"Carny?"

"Joey, listen to me. He left this morning in his car. You might be able to stop him."

"Carny, who are you talking about?"

"Logan Brisco!" she shouted.

She heard the noise of the police station behind Joey's voice. "Where did he go?"

Tears assaulted her with brutal force, cracking her voice. "He took off, Joey. Just like I predicted."

"Are you all right?"

"No!" she screamed. "I'm not. I've been had, just like everybody in this town! Joey, please do something!"

"I'll be right over," he said.

"No," she cried. "I'm at church. You're not listening. Don't come here. Go after him!"

After she cut off the phone, sobs took hold of her. How could she have been so stupid?

How could she have allowed herself to get caught in his con? How had she managed to fall in love with someone she had known all along was a liar?

The phone rang, and she caught her breath as a fragile hope sprang inside her. Maybe it was Logan, and maybe he had an explanation . . .

Without even looking at the caller ID, she clicked it on. "Hello?"

"Carny, it's Joey."

Her heart sank like a lead weight, and she hated herself for hoping — even for a moment — that Logan would call.

"Carny, I just texted Doc, and he felt pretty sure that Logan's coming back."

"Then why did he steal out of town early on a Sunday morning, without telling a soul? He told me he'd be at church, that he was going to come clean to the congregation."

"Come clean? He admitted to you that he's a con artist?"

"Yes. He claimed to have had this God experience . . . Oh, it doesn't matter now. Just stop him, Joey!"

"Did you get his picture?"

"I got it. I'll email it to you. Joey, he told me he had been to prison. That he really was a fraud, but that he's changed. That he really intends to build the park."

"Did he say what name he served time under? What state?"

"No." Why hadn't she asked? "Joey, please go after him. You might still catch him."

"Carny, you can't arrest a man for checking out of a motel."

"Fine, Joey," she said through her teeth. "Do nothing. But don't forget I tried to warn you. I tried to warn everybody."

She tossed the phone onto her passenger seat and got out of the car. She paced the row of vehicles, struggling to decide what to do now.

The irony of it happening to her — when she had known better than anyone else — overwhelmed her. How could she live with herself after being so stupid?

She was no smarter than any of the others, and she supposed that was what Logan's bitter lesson had taught her. He had defeated her in the most personal way — by pretending to share her faith in God. And he'd pulled off the ultimate con. He'd made her admit to falling in love.

She sat out in her car until church was over, then flagged Jason down when he came out. Back home, as he ate lunch, she pulled her suitcase out of her closet and began to pack as fast as she could.

She had to get out of here. She had to go where people wouldn't be constantly telling her that she was overreacting, that Logan would never do anything like that, that their money and hearts and souls were safe with him.

After throwing several days' worth of clothes into a bag, she ran back into the kitchen. "Honey, come on," she said. "We've got to pack."

Jason blinked up at her over his sandwich. "For what?"

She led him to his room, yanked open his drawers, and began pulling out clothes. "We're going on a surprise trip."

"A trip where?"

"New Mexico," she said. "We're going to the carnival to see Grandma and Grandpa."

His eyes lit up. "All right!" he shouted. "I haven't seen them in a long time! Can I ride the roller coaster, Mom? I'm big enough this time!"

"We'll talk about it on the plane," she said. "Just hurry."

She wouldn't be able to breathe freely until she was out of this town, where no one could see the disappointment and failure on her face. She wrote a quick note to her in-laws, telling them where she was going, and ran it by their house on the way to the airport, knowing they were at the Kountry Kitchen eating lunch as they did every Sunday.

She would be out of town before they got home.

THIRTY-NINE

A sad melancholy fell over Carny, adding to the rage she was already nursing, when the rental car crested the hill and the carnival came into view, the Ferris wheels and roller coasters looming into the afternoon sky. Scratch, the sword-swallower, whom her parents had sent to pick her up at the airfield, spoke to the gatekeeper, who let them onto the fairgrounds.

"Look, Mom! The double Ferris wheel! Nathan went on one at the state fair and said it got stuck, and he had to sit up there for an hour until his dad climbed the wheel and got him down."

Carny breathed a laugh. "I've told you not to believe everything Nathan tells you."

"I'm not scared, though. Can I ride it?"

"We'll see." Already, the scents of cotton candy, chicken on a stick, fresh taffy, and cinnamon rolls wafted over the area, conjuring up memories of a childhood where almost every meal was eaten with her fingers while walking down the midway, unless it had been a sandwich thrown together in a moving trailer. Still, it smelled of home.

When the guard opened the gate for them, Scratch drove straight back, through the infield thick with trailers, to where her parents' trailer was parked. The jalousies were broken on it, and it needed a good bath, and the awning that came out from the side to create a makeshift porch was torn. On the side were the words DOUGLAS CARNIVALS LIMITED.

"Your folks had a meeting with the sheriff," Scratch told them, getting out. "But they said to wait here. Either that, or you can walk around the park."

"A meeting with the sheriff? Problems?"

Scratch grinned and hiked one eyebrow. "Nothing a little cash won't fix." Lighting a cigar, he gave a phlegmy laugh.

"What about Ruth?"

"She's tutoring some young'uns right now. But Sas and Peg are over in the Tojo Trailer. Everybody else is working."

"Okay. Is there a bathroom somewhere?"

"Closest donnicker's by the House of Apes," Scratch said.

"What's a donnicker?" Jason asked.

"It's the bathroom, Jase," Carny said.

"Only we can go in Grandma and Grandpa's trailer. The donnickers aren't usually very clean."

"After that can we walk around the park? Please, Mom? I'm hungry, and everything smells so good!"

"Sure," Carny said, taking the key that Scratch offered and unlocking her parents' door. "We'll just freshen up, and then I'll see how many carbohydrates and buckets of grease I can pour down you."

"All right!"

She opened the door and Jason dashed in. Over her shoulder, she called, "Thanks, Scratch."

"No problem, Carny," he said. "Good to have you back."

Jason had already found the bathroom, and as Carny stepped into the trailer where she had grown up, she was assaulted by a wave of nostalgia. This was home, such as it was. This was where she'd slept, traveled, studied. This was where she'd dreamed — of finding a way out, of settling down, of having a normal family where her children's days weren't filled with longing and disappointment.

"Wow, Mom. This is great! Is this where you used to live?"

"Sure is," she said quietly.

"But where was your room?"

"I slept here, on the couch bed," she said. "Grandma and Grandpa slept in that little area at the back."

Jason's enthusiasm faltered a degree. "Where were your toys? Where did you play?"

"I didn't keep many toys," she said, "but I read a lot. And there was always the carnival. I could ride anything I wanted. And I got to play in the animal truck."

"The what?"

Smiling, Carny hooked a finger for Jason to follow her back outside. "This way," she said, glad she'd finally thought of one charming thing to show Jason about the carnival.

They walked between trailers to the eighteen-wheeler parked at the fringe and stepped up on the rim of the bed. There, she raised the door, revealing the treasures inside.

"Wow!" Jason cried.

In the truck, thousands of stuffed animals lay in soft mountains. Stuffed dolls and dogs and teddy bears all lay waiting to be taken to the midway as prizes to the marks who paid twenty times what they were worth to win them.

Jason grabbed an armful and, giggling, fell

back onto a downy mountain of stuffed animals. "Whose are these?"

"The carnival's," she said. "These are all the prizes. I used to play here all the time."

"Really, Mom? They let you?"

"Sure did. These things only cost a few cents apiece, but the marks will pay a dollar a shot to win them. By the time they walk away with one, the agents have usually scored forty to fifty dollars."

"What are marks?"

She caught her breath. "I meant . . . customers."

"Why'd you call them marks?"

"Because," she said, deciding not to deceive him or hide the truth. "You see, Jason, not everybody in the carnival is honest. A lot of the people who work here are just trying to find ways to take people's money. And they don't think of them as people . . . or even as customers. They think of them as targets . . . or marks."

"Did you think of them as marks?"

She sighed. "Yeah, I'm afraid I did, back before I knew that God saw everything I did. Before I cared what he thought. I grew up calling them that."

"Was it a bad thing?"

"Yes, it's bad when you just want to trick them and take something from them . . .

something that you haven't earned. It's stealing." She sat down on a pile of teddy bears and leaned back against the wall.

Jason's eyes rounded, and he looked back out the open door of the truck toward the carnival that had seemed so magical to him before. He seemed to be looking at it with new eyes, as if her words had cast a pall over it that made everything look different. Why hadn't she just let him enjoy it?

Tears sprang to her eyes, tears she hadn't expected. Her gaze drifted out of the truck to the midway just beyond the trailers. Coming here was like moving backward, she thought, and yet she'd had to. These were her roots. They were what made her who she was. Everybody needed to backtrack sometimes, if only to remember how far they had come.

Where did Logan go when he'd finished a con? Did he backtrack? Or was he in Tahiti, counting his money and laughing at how he'd finally gotten her trust? Did he award himself extra points because she'd been such a challenge?

Carny glanced back at her son, who seemed lost in thought. She reached for his hand and pulled him closer. "The carnival can be a fun place. Really fun, if you just know what to avoid. I hope I can teach you not to be a mark, Jason. I hope you'll grow up knowing better than to fall for a gaff."

"What's a gaff?"

She'd done it again. "Don't worry about it. There's just something about being home that makes you slip back into your old vocabulary, no matter how hard you worked to lose it." She supposed no matter how far she ran, she couldn't ever completely escape who she was. It was a startling realization. She was more like Logan than she wanted to admit.

She thought of the apostle Paul, cautioning Christians to press forward and not look back. She remembered his words in 1 Corinthians 6:9, and the list of people who would not inherit the kingdom of God. The first time she saw that verse, the words *thieves* and *swindlers* condemned her. But the next verse made a life-changing difference. *And that is what some of you were. But you were washed, you were sanctified, you were justified in the name of the Lord Jesus Christ and by the Spirit of our God.*

She'd been cleansed of her sins. And the fact that Logan had chosen to fake his own cleansing had no bearing on her own relationship with God.

Logan had stolen her heart, but he couldn't steal that.

"Hey, do you think Grandpa would let me have one of these?" Jason asked, holding up a stuffed alligator.

Jason's question shook Carny out of her reverie, and she took a minute to reorient herself. "I'm sure he would."

"But I'd rather win one. That's more fun."

She tried to think of a nice way to tell him that the games were rigged, but decided to let it rest. It was like telling your child there was no Santa Claus. Part of you knew he couldn't go on believing forever, but another part hated to destroy his wonderment. Maybe she still knew some of the agents at the game. Maybe she could get them to let him win something.

"Carny, my baby!" Carny turned at her mother's shriek and saw the little lady with platinum-bleached hair bounding across the infield toward her.

"Mama!" Jumping down from the truck, she intersected with her mother and allowed her to crush her in a hug.

"You look like one of those cultured ladies," her mother said, stepping back and looking her over. "Like you've been spending all your time in a beauty shop getting your nails done. Are you a lady of leisure now, Carny?"

"Of course not, Mama," she said. "You

know I'm a pilot. And I haven't painted my nails in years."

"Then you must be eating healthy. Where's my grandbaby?"

"In the truck. Under a pile of animals. You'll recognize him right away, since he's the only one who's not purple."

"The same place I always found you," her mother said. "Jason? Jason, come here and give your grandma a big hug!"

Jason sprang up and threw out his arms. "Grandma!"

"You're a little man!" her mother cried. "When did you get so big?"

Jason tried to step over the stuffed animals. "Um . . . I don't know."

"How old are you now?" she asked, reaching up to grab him. "Five, six?"

"I'm eight," he said, lifting his chin with indignation. "My birthday was yesterday."

"Eight? My heavens, Carny, has it been that long?"

"Yeah, Mama. It has."

"Well, we have to make up for lost time, then, don't we? Not to mention birthday presents. Come with me, Jason. I'll show you around the park. Maybe even put you to work, if you're interested."

"That'd be great! Can I, Mom?"

Carny touched Lila's arm, stopping her.

"Mama, no. I'll just keep him with me."

"For heaven's sake, Carny, I'm his grandma. What are you afraid of?"

Carny's face warmed, and she wished she didn't have to fight this battle so soon. "You sometimes . . . get distracted. You might forget him."

"I won't forget you, will I, Jason?"

"And I don't want him being put to work."

"Well, for heaven's sake, what did you think I meant? I only thought that maybe he could stand on the bally of the House of Wonders and make like an announcer. How would you like that, Jason? We'll give you a microphone and you can pantomime the recording."

Carny thought of the freak shows inside the House of Wonders. That was where Ruth used to sit for most of her day while people paid to ogle her, and Scratch did his sword-swallowing trick, and Bounce, the contortionist, bent his body into virtual knots. That was where Allesandro, the half-man, half-woman did his act, and where Georgie Jingles practiced his illusion of being half-man, half-horse. It was where Snake disrobed to show the scales he'd had tattooed all over his body, and where Burt set himself on fire.

The exploitation and exhibitionism of the

House of Wonders was one of the worst parts of the carnival, yet it was the stuff that fascinated little boys.

"Please, Mom," Jason said, bouncing. "Let me go!"

"Mama, I promised him I'd take him on the double Ferris wheel. Don't you want to do that, Jase?"

"Sure!" Jason shouted. "Then can I go with Grandma?"

"We'll see," she said, taking his hand.

Her mother set her hands on her hips and looked disgusted.

"Your mother's afraid you'll like it too much and want to be a carny when you grow up," Lila said. "And there wouldn't be a thing in the world wrong with that."

"Jason's going to be president, aren't you, Jase?"

"No," he argued. "I'm going to be an astronaut. Either that or a baseball player."

Carny smiled. "He's given this a lot of thought."

"Or maybe a sultan like Logan!" Jason blurted as an afterthought.

"A what?" Lila asked. "He knows a sultan?"

"No." Carny frowned down at her son. "Do you mean a consultant, Jason?"

"Yeah, that's what I want to be. Somebody

who plans big fun stuff like Logan, and gets everybody to invest."

Carny's smile fell, and her dismal gaze met her mother's. "Well, I guess that's not so far from being a carny, after all."

"Who's this Logan fellow? The amusement park guy? Did you talk to him about us, Carny?"

Before Carny had the chance to answer she heard a familiar voice behind her. Swinging around, she saw her oldest friend, her dearest confidante, her teacher and mentor, and her personal philosopher, riding toward her on a golf cart. "Ruth!"

Letting go of Jason, Carny ran and threw herself into the massive woman's arms. When she'd last seen her, Ruth weighed five hundred pounds, but Carny suspected she was even bigger now. She had long black hair streaked with gray, and the muumuu Ruth wore was the size of a small tent. Her hug was tight and warm, and her body shook as she laughed out loud. "You look beautiful, baby! Look at you."

Carny pulled back and saw that Ruth's eyes were moist. "And the baby . . . is that little Jason?"

Jason stretched to his full height, and extending a hand, he said, "I'm Jason Sullivan."

"You can call me Ruth," Ruth said, pulling him into a hug and sobbing as if she'd found her own long-lost child. "Oh, you feel so good! And Carny, you look gorgeous. Like a fairy princess or something. Oh, lands, it's so good to see you."

Carny couldn't keep the tears from falling. Of all the people she'd grown up with in the carnival, her parents included, Ruth was the one she had missed the most. "Jason, Ruth is the lady I told you about. The one who taught me practically everything I know."

"The computer lady?"

"Yes," Carny said. "She's the one with the computers all over her trailer."

Ruth wiped at her eyes. "Well, that's a switch. I'm usually called the fat lady. That's what I used to be, Jason, in the House of Wonders."

Jason looked embarrassed, as if he didn't know how to respond to that without hurting Ruth's feelings. "Mom talks about you all the time."

"And I talk about her," Ruth said, sniffing. "A day doesn't go by that I don't think about you two."

"Maybe she'll listen to you, Ruth," Lila said. "I was just trying to talk Carny into letting Jason go around with me for a little while, but she's convinced I'm going to turn him into a delinquent."

"We're going on the double Ferris wheel," Carny said, stroking Jason's hair. "Aren't we, Jase?"

"Now, Mom? Can we go now?"

"Sure can." She leaned over and hugged Ruth again. "I'll be back in a little while, and we can catch up, okay?"

"You know where I'll be," Ruth told her. "You hold on to his hand, now. The crowd has gotten rougher than it used to be, and it's easy to get lost around here."

"Good grief," Lila said, waving them off. "It's the same as it's always been, and Carny grew up just fine. Just look at her now." She leaned over and kissed Jason's cheek. "Make her stop by the Ring Toss to see Grandpa Dooley, Jason. He's filling in for the agent there while he takes lunch. He can't wait to see you."

Jason looked ready to erupt. "Now, Mom? Can we go now?"

"All right," Carny said, laughing. Waving back at Ruth and her mother, she let Jason pull her off toward the midway.

Jason's eyes danced with excitement as they got off the Ferris wheel, and he looked up at her as he cried, "Can we go again, Mom?

Please?"

"Later, Jason. There are a lot of other rides."

"You were so lucky when you were little! Did you really get to ride any time you wanted?"

"Pretty much. But it didn't seem so lucky at the time."

"Why? How could you ever want anything else?"

As they passed a trailer selling corn dogs, she caught the scent of rotting garbage. The noise of battling songs at rides across from each other and the voices of people screaming were beginning to give her a headache.

She took Jason's hand as they strolled up the midway. "I wanted the things you have, Jase. A real house with a backyard, friends I could play with, school . . ."

"But those things are boring."

"Only to those who have them." She glanced up the row of game booths and saw a little girl with stringy blonde hair and a dirty face sitting on the steps leading to the booth door. She didn't know the agent — he was probably one of the newer ones — but she recognized the waif-like look on the child's face and knew without a doubt that she was a carny's kid. "See that little girl over there, Jase?"

"Yeah."

"She's probably traveling with the carnival."

"How do you know?"

"The way she's sitting on the steps, like she belongs there. The way her eyes are scanning the crowd. You know what she's thinking, Jason?"

"What?"

"She's thinking about the children she sees. The ones who are holding their parents' hands, like you. The ones who are excited to be here, the ones who see it as a treat. She's wondering what kind of houses they live in, and if they take ballet, and if they play softball. She's wondering if their parents take them to church or how many kids they have in their classes at school. She's wondering if they have birthday parties."

He looked up at her with saucer eyes. "Didn't you ever have birthday parties, Mom?"

"Sometimes some of the carnies would get together and get me a cake and sing "Happy Birthday." But I always had dreams of having lots of little girls over, all dressed in fancy dresses . . ." She felt that longing that she thought she'd discarded long ago. "Only I never knew many little girls."

"But you knew the sword-swallower, and the magician, and the fire guy."

"Yeah, I did," she said, chuckling softly. "I sure did."

"Hey, kid, did your mama put a bowl on your head to cut your hair or did you cut it yourself?"

Jason swung around and saw Tojo the Clown sitting in his dunking booth, targeting him. "Is he talking to me, Mom?"

"I'm afraid so," she said. "His gaff is to insult people until they get so mad they want to pay money to dunk him."

"Can I?"

"Hey, kid, you can't dunk me. You'd have to let go of Mommy's hand first."

Jason dropped her hand as if it had burned him. "I bet I can."

Carny recognized the agent taking the money and passing out baseballs to be thrown at the plate that would dunk Tojo. "Jello? Is that you?"

The old man chuckled. "Carny?" Laughing, he stretched his arms wide, and she hugged him. "Your folks said you'd be coming today. How are you, kid?"

"Great. Jello, this is my son, Jason."

"So are you gonna stand there scratching yourself, kid, or are you gonna make a fool out of yourself with that baseball?" the clown shouted.

Jason eyed the dunking booth. "Mom, I've gotta dunk him."

Carny laughed. "You sure do. Look out, Tojo," she shouted to the clown. "He's pretty good."

"Is that you, Carny?" the clown shouted back. "What swamp did they drag you out of?"

Undaunted by the standard insults she'd heard all her life, she paid Jello for the privilege of drowning the clown, got her three balls, and gave them to Jason. Knowing they were weighted and rarely hit the plate, she said, "Aim high, Jase. These aren't regular balls."

Jason threw the ball with all his might and missed.

"You haven't lost your spark, have you, Carny? Letting your kid take your shots for you?"

"Try again, Jason," she said. "Aim higher this time."

"Hey, Carny, we could use you back in the carnival. They need another dancing girl."

Jason shot and missed again. "You do this one, Mom. Please, we've gotta dunk him."

"Carny, you still haven't caught a husband you can keep?"

She set her chin. "Better hold your breath, Tojo." Taking the ball, she mentally eyed the plate and tried to concentrate.

"You're gonna need a dozen more to get me down, Carny."

"Just one will be fine, Tojo!" she shouted.

With one rip of her arm, she threw the ball, hit the plate, and sent the clown into the water beneath him. Jason jumped up and down, whooping. "You did it, Mom! You did it!"

"Somebody had to." Dusting off her hands, she took Jason's hand again and pulled him away. "See you later, Jello."

"Later, Carny," the old man said, chuckling.

"You can't do it twice," Tojo sputtered, climbing back onto his swing. "I'll bet you can't come back here and do it again."

"I can be conned," Carny said under her breath, "but it takes a lot more than some wet clown shouting insults at me."

Jason looked up at her, confused.

She sighed. It took someone as slick as Logan Brisco, someone who deserved an Oscar for his work, someone who didn't stop until he'd conned everybody in his way. Someone a world smarter than Tojo the Clown, though he didn't have any more scruples.

They came closer to the booth where her father was substituting, and she heard his laughter over the crowd. The sound made her chest tighten. It wasn't his usual laugh — it was his con laugh. The one that drew people in, set them up to be taken.

"There's your grandfather," she said.

Jason tugged her hand. "Let's go talk to him!"

"Not yet," she said, holding back. "Wait until that customer leaves."

They watched while the young man laid down more of his money for a few more rings to toss, missed, and then looked longingly at the stuffed animal he'd been trying to win for his date. "I'm out of money," he said. "You wouldn't take a check, would you?"

Her father seemed to consider that for a moment. "Well, we don't normally, but . . . well, okay. In this case . . ."

Anxiously, the man wrote his check, tore it out, then handed it to Carny's father. "Twenty-five dollars' worth, huh? You're pretty serious about this, aren't you?"

He gave the mark enough rings to win every animal hanging from the ceiling — if only the game wasn't rigged. He tossed all of them, but hit only one on a winning peg.

The young man's date looked crestfallen,

and the athletic boy seemed humiliated as they started to walk away. "Look," Carny's father said, holding up a hand to stop them. "Everybody has a bad day now and then." Taking down a stuffed dog, he tossed it into the man's hands. "And as for the check — don't worry about it." He tore it up and let the pieces fall to the floor at his feet.

"Thanks, sir," the young man said. "I appreciate it."

"Yeah, well, you were probably going to stop payment on it tomorrow, anyway, weren't you?"

With a laugh that said he'd been caught, the man shrugged, handed the dog to his girlfriend, and strolled away.

As Carny and Jason stepped up to the booth, she saw her father pull the real check out of his sleeve and chuckle as he put it in the cash box. The one he'd torn up had been fake.

"Hi, Pop," she said.

He looked up. "Carny! I *thought* you were probably here by now!" He ran out the door of the booth and embraced her. "Have you grown taller?"

"No, Pop, I don't think so."

"Well, you sure haven't put on any weight. Where's the boy?"

"Right here," she said.

"No!" Her father looked down at Jason and shook his head. "That can't be him. This boy's at least ten years old. My grandson couldn't be more than four."

Jason frowned, unsure whether to be flattered or insulted. "I'm eight. My birthday was yesterday."

"Eight! That can't be."

Carny tried not to laugh. "It is, Pop."

"Well, I think maybe we'd better take him over to the age booth and let Morris see if he can guess his age. He's bound to win something. He's big enough to play linebacker for Notre Dame!"

Slowly, Jason began to smile. "I am?"

"Well, practically. Within another year or two, you'll be a number-one draft choice." Taking Jason's hand, he said, "Come with me. I'll show you. If Morris guesses your age, I'll swallow that sword of Scratch's."

Smiling reluctantly, Carny followed them and watched Jason win another stuffed animal for fooling Morris about his age.

Carny tried not to leave Jason's side that day, not because she wanted to ride everything in sight, but because she didn't want to give her parents the opportunity to be alone with him. By the time night had fallen and they'd ridden the roller coaster, Jason was feeling a little woozy, and his feet dragged as he walked.

"Where are we gonna sleep tonight, Mom?"

"With Grandma and Grandpa. It'll be a tight fit, but —"

"In the trailer? That'll be cool." But his voice didn't have its usual fervor. No wonder — he was exhausted, and Carny had to admit that she was as well.

Still, the thoughts that had rustled beneath the surface all day kept flitting through her mind. She hadn't come here to ride the rides and rekindle old memories. She had come home to nurse her wounds. To wrestle with the fact that she, who'd thought she was immune, had been conned.

It wasn't as if she hadn't been warned. Logan had laid his bet at the very beginning. Winner take all. And he had won.

Jason was asleep within five minutes of lying down, and Carny found herself sitting at the table that had served as her dining table, her desk, her dollhouse, her ironing board, and a million other things as she was growing up. Her father sipped a beer he'd gotten before the carnival had closed down, while her mother nursed the customary hot toddy she had every night before bed.

"So tell us how plans for the park are shaping up," her father said, not bothering to keep his voice low for Jason's sake.

"I told you, Pop. It's not going to happen."

"But you didn't say why."

She leaned back in her chair and wished she had never brought up the subject of Logan with her parents. It had never been easy for her to discuss feelings with them. Her father was a stick-to-the-facts kind of guy. His main interest was the bottom line. And the bottom line usually had to do with how much money it could make him.

"He was a grifter, Pop. It was all a scam."

"Hmm." Her father tossed back the last of his beer and set the glass in the same wet ring he'd taken it from. "Too bad. It was a terrific idea. So where'd he go?"

"If I knew that, I'd go get everybody's money back."

"Do you think he's trying it in another town?" her mother asked.

A sick feeling came over her. "I hope not. But I guess he probably is. Unless he's just lying low for a while, waiting until everything blows over. He's smart. He probably left the country. He made enough to live on for a while."

"He must be good. I wish you'd introduced him to us."

Something about her father's attitude

brought back all her old bitterness about their lifestyle. "Why, Pop? So you could get in on the action? Trust me. He would have conned you too."

"I doubt it," Dooley said, chuckling. "You can't con a man who doesn't want to be conned."

Carny leaned forward on the table, facing off with her father. "That's a lie and you know it."

"Carny!" Lila admonished. "Don't call your daddy a liar!"

Carny chuckled, but there was no mirth in the sound. "All these years, you tried to tell me you weren't doing anything to people that they didn't want done. But it isn't true. You both rip people off all day every day, and you have no qualms about it. It's not true that your victims *want* to be conned. They don't deserve it, Mama! People shouldn't be punished for trusting!"

Her parents just stared at her. Finally, her mother said, "What's going on with you, child? You didn't come here just for a visit, did you?"

She sighed, and wished she could unload all her heartache on them. But they'd never cared about them before. "I just needed to retrace my steps."

Her mother took her hand, a rare, affectionate gesture that took Carny by surprise. "Honey, this isn't your home anymore. You've grown so far away from it, you don't even recognize it now. And it seems to me you have nothing but contempt for it."

Carny sniffed and wiped her eyes. "It's funny. No matter how far you go, you've still got one foot tangled up in your roots, like it or not. And that's the foot that'll always trip you up."

"Did you give him money, Carny?" her father asked. "Is that why this Logan character bothers you so?"

She breathed a laugh and wiped her eyes. "No, Pop. I didn't give him money. I did know better than that."

But she couldn't tell her father that what she'd given him was more personal than money.

"Then it shouldn't matter what he took from everybody else. They probably deserved it."

For a moment, she stared at her father, the man to whom she'd been so loyal all her life. "Pop, I've defended you for years and told myself that you did have a conscience. That you weren't just out for yourself. I've even fooled myself into believing you did it for me. To feed your family.

To survive. And I let myself think that about Logan Brisco too. But you know what, Pop? We can con *ourselves* better than anybody. All the alibis and excuses and justifications . . . they're nothing but scams we turn on ourselves."

"You don't believe that, Carny." Her father got up and went to the small refrigerator.

"Yes, I do, Pop. The truth is that *nobody* deserves to have their pride trampled, or their trust destroyed, or their innocence mocked. Nobody deserves to wake up one day and find out that they've been nothing but a sick pawn in a greedy power game!"

"I'm not buying that he didn't con you too," Dooley said. "He stung you somehow, so you came home to take it out on us."

Lila touched his arm to calm him. "It's all right. That's what parents are for."

Carny wanted to laugh, but it wasn't funny. Instead, the tears fell faster. "I didn't come home to take anything out on you. I came because I needed a time-out. But I'm so tired of all the lies, Pop. Aren't you tired of them?"

"I told you we're trying to retire, Carny. We're doing the best we can. We always have."

But that was just another lie.

Wearily, she got up and covered Jason on the little sofa bed she had slept on as a child. Wiping her face, she said, "I'm gonna go say good night to Ruth. I'll be back in a little while."

"We'll have your pallet ready," her mother said quietly, sounding relieved that this uncomfortable conversation was over. Lila had never liked for Carny to make a scene, unless it had been rehearsed.

Outside the trailer, Carny reached into her purse for her phone. She had turned it off in the plane today, as she always did, and after landing she'd decided not to turn it back on. Dreading what she would find, she pushed the power button. Eight messages came up. Three from her in-laws and Joey . . . and one from Logan.

She stopped between trailers and listened to her voice mail.

The first was from J.R. "Carny, what's with the decision to take off without sayin' goodbye? Call us when you can and let us know when you'll be back."

She heard the beep, and Joey's voice came up. "Carny, you didn't send the picture. I still need it. If Logan hasn't broken a law yet, I can't just go after him. But if I can get the picture to the FBI, they might have something on him. Call me."

She sighed. She'd run off without thinking about that stupid picture. But now it would have to wait — it was on her camera at home.

Finally came Logan's voice. "Hey, Carny. Listen, I know I said I'd be in church today, but I got a call this morning and I had to go to Dallas. Call me and I'll tell you about it. I was thinking that maybe spilling my guts isn't the right approach just yet."

She couldn't stand it. Fighting the urge to throw her phone, she deleted the rest of the message and turned the phone off. So he was still at it, wheeling and dealing, with no mention of his supposed change of heart and his newfound commitment to God. Had he forgotten, or was it even true? Had he only told her what she wanted to hear?

His profession of love was a lie too, just another game.

Fuming, Carny trekked across the fairgrounds to where Ruth's motor home was parked. The lights were still on; Ruth was probably on her computer.

She knocked softly, and heard Ruth say, "Come in."

As she stepped through the double doors, specially designed for Ruth's massive frame, Carny felt a truer sense of home. But the trailer didn't look quite the same. Ruth had upgraded with the latest computer equipment. Several recent-model computers were lined up on a long built-in desk against the wall — the same desk where Carny had gotten her education, where she'd spent so many hours as a child, where she'd found someone to confide in, where she'd felt most accepted and welcomed. She wondered if that little girl she'd seen sitting on the steps of the Duck Shoot was one of Ruth's students now. She hoped so. The child probably needed someone like Ruth in her life.

"Hey, baby," Ruth said from the love seat that her huge body filled. "I was hoping you'd stop by. Are you ready to tell me what's bothering you now?"

Carny smiled and wiped the fresh tears under her eyes. "What makes you think anything's bothering me?"

"Oh, I don't know. Those tears mean something. Besides, you wouldn't have brought your baby here if you hadn't really needed to come home."

Carny dropped opposite her onto Ruth's couch and pulled her knees up.

"Your heart is broken, girl," Ruth said. "I can see it. Don't forget, I'm the one whose lap you used to sit on, when you were shorter than a yardstick, crying and not knowing why. But I always knew."

"You did, didn't you, Ruth?"

Ruth chuckled, the sweet sound warming Carny's heart. "Don't blame your folks, child. They do the best they can."

"So they say," she whispered. "But the truth is, they should have never had a child."

"Probably not. But I'm awful glad they did."

Getting up, Carny went to sit on the arm of the love seat and hugged the woman who seemed to grow bigger each year. "I always wished you were my mother," she said.

Ruth laughed. "Imagine me as a mother. Wouldn't that be a hoot?"

"No," Carny said seriously. "Not at all. You were probably the only one I really missed when I left the carnival."

"And I missed you like crazy too," Ruth said, "but I was awfully glad for you. I had big hopes for your happiness. You haven't let me down, have you?"

"No," she said. "I've been happy. Really happy. It's just lately . . ."

"You fell in love with him, didn't you, baby?"

Carny's shoulders slumped. Wearily, she went back to the couch. Resting her elbows on her thighs, she stared at the floor. "Yes, I did. It's got to be one of the stupidest things

I've ever done. Besides marrying Abe."

"I didn't blame you for marrying Abe," Ruth told her. "He was your escape. You were nothing but a child then, but you're grown now. To fall in love with a flimflam man, when you'd found such happiness there with decent folk . . . I don't know, Carny. It doesn't sound like you."

"Of course it doesn't," Carny said. "Ruth, I've thought and thought about this. Did I fall in love with him because he's so much like Pop? Would my subconscious deliberately seek out someone who led the very lifestyle I hated?"

"Maybe you've been bored in that little town, child. There's a lot of gypsy in you. Maybe part of you misses the excitement. Maybe that's what he represented."

Carny found that explanation unsettling. "That would mean I deserved it. That I invited it. Just like Pop said."

"Dooley told you that?"

"Well, not about Brisco. But that's his general contention about all marks. And that's just what I am. Brisco's mark. Only I *didn't* ask for it, Ruth."

"Are you saying that you don't still have a wanderlust? A need for excitement?" When Carny hesitated, Ruth went on, "Then explain the plane you fly, and the bungee-jumping you wrote me about, and the motorcycle you ride around town. I remember you as a little girl, child. I know you."

"But that doesn't mean I haven't put the lies and deceit and all the ugliness behind me, Ruth. And it doesn't mean that I'd go looking for it again. I've made a good life for Jason and me." She got up and walked into the kitchen area, leaned against the counter. "Ruth, everything changed for me in Serenity. I went to church there, and Brother Tommy told me I could start fresh. He made me believe that whatever I'd done and whatever I'd been in the past could be wiped clean." She went back to the couch, and sat facing Ruth. "Everything changed. *I* changed."

"And then you turned into my teacher and told me all about it," Ruth said. "And I changed, too."

"Everybody there loved me, because that's what they do. They love." Her voice broke. "So if I finally had what I'd always wanted, why did Logan make me want more?"

Ruth shook her head. "Something about him made you want to believe. Something inside you needed what he had."

"Then what does that say about me?"

"It says that you're just as human as anybody else, child. And that you're not so tough. That's why people like Dooley and Lila keep getting away with the same scams. They paint pictures of hopes and dreams. They make hard people trust."

Carny leaned forward. "The crazy thing is, when I think of Logan the way he was last night, I don't see signs of the lies I saw before. He sounded so sincere. He told me what he really was, confessed everything. He said he wanted to change. Ruth, he told me he'd prayed . . . that God had washed him clean too. It sounded so real. He was going to confess to the people in church today . . ." Her voice cracked. "But he didn't. He checked out of his motel and left town." The tears made a second assault, and her face warmed as she pressed it into her hands. "Ruth, I really believed him. But it doesn't matter what I believed. He's gone. He's still got their money. I tried to tell everybody, but they wouldn't listen. And why should they, when I was eating out of his hand too?"

She looked up. Ruth held her gaze for a long moment, processing everything she'd told her. "Maybe he'll come back."

"What?"

"If you believed him that much, and if all you say about him is true, I can't help thinking that maybe it's not over. It's just hard for me to believe you could be taken that way, girl. You're a good judge of people. Maybe you weren't wrong about him. Maybe it's not over yet."

Carny sniffed back the pain that threatened to smother her and whispered, "Trust me, it's over. He left a message that he was rethinking telling the town the truth. That's not surrender to God. He's still playing the game. He didn't mean any of it."

"It's hard to change, baby. Maybe he just lost his nerve. Maybe he needs more time to do the right thing."

Carny wouldn't give him more time. She wouldn't be taken again.

Back at her parents' trailer, she tried to get comfortable on her pallet. But Logan's words last night reeled through her mind, keeping her awake. Disappointment in him ached through her, but her disappointment in herself hurt worst of all.

She realized as she lay awake on the floor of the trailer she had been so eager to leave years ago, with her sweet, innocent little boy lying on the bed where she used to sleep, that it didn't matter who she had been. Ruth's affirming words had helped. In the end, it came down to whether she could look herself in the mirror each morning and know that she'd done the best she could.

She was strong, and she had survived before. She'd get over this, just like the town would. It wouldn't be easy, and it would take time for her to heal. But she had too much going for her to let someone like Logan Brisco rob her of her spirit or the joy in her life.

After a sleepless night, dawn invaded the room, lighting the old trailer with gray tones, and Carny asked herself the final question that kept eating at her.

Why couldn't she hate him?

That was the ultimate punch line of his con. That no matter what he did to her, she couldn't hate him. He was the first person since Abe who had made her fall in love. And that part wouldn't be easy to get over.

Jason stirred and turned over. "Mom? Can we ride the roller coaster today?"

Smiling, she told herself she could get by as long as she had Jason. "Sure, honey."

"Can we stay here a long time?"

"Maybe a couple more days," she said. "Until they tear down."

"Really? We don't have to rush back home?"

"No," she whispered. "I'm in no hurry to get back home."

FORTY

They had been with the carnival for three days when Carny began to sense something in her father that she hadn't seen before. It was the integrity of a grandfather, and the dignity of an older and supposedly wiser man, trying to pass some of his experience on to a third generation.

Finally feeling that Jason would be safe with her parents, she allowed them to take him around the carnival as they handled the myriad details that had to be attended to each day before the gates opened. She watched her parents revel in the chance to entertain their grandson, and felt for the first time that the lessons he could learn here might not be all bad.

She also realized that, despite their lifestyle, she loved her parents. And in their own peculiar way, they loved her.

"Do you think a man who lies for a living can ever be trusted?" she asked Ruth as they watched Jason drive her parents off behind the wheel of the golf cart.

"Do you mean Logan?"

"I guess," she said. "Although I was thinking of Pop."

"Oh, come on," Ruth said. "You trust your father. You know he'd never do anything to hurt you or Jason. He does love you, and so does your mother."

"I know," she said. "And that's what makes me wonder about Logan. Do you think that maybe Logan loved me too, in his way?"

"Of course I've never met him," Ruth said, "but I've been giving it a lot of thought. I suspect he did. And leaving probably caused him as much grief as it caused you."

"How do you figure that?"

Ruth shrugged her wide shoulders. "Well, honey, if a man couldn't change, if he only knew the kind of life where you had to cheat and lie to get by, maybe the last thing on earth he'd want to do is fall in love. Maybe that's why he left. Love was about to make him do things he was afraid to do."

Carny fought back the tears threatening her again and said, "He told me I deserved an honorable man.' " Swallowing, she said, "I felt in my soul that he meant it."

"Then I'm sure he did, honey. Maybe he's

more noble than you think."

"But he backed away from his commitment to confess. He went back to his wheeling and dealing."

"Maybe it was too much for him all at once. People with lots of sins stacked up sometimes can't imagine life as a new person."

Later, when Ruth was tutoring a pair of carnival twins, Carny went to the Ferris wheel. She rode it alone, and when it lingered at the top, giving her a view of the world of her childhood — a view that should have made things clear to her — she remembered Logan's words again. *You deserve an honorable man.*

He *had* meant it. She knew he had. And as crooked as he might have been when he'd come to town, something had changed in him. But it wasn't enough.

As the sun set, she wept in her lonesome seat in the double Ferris wheel. She wept for all the dreams she'd had as a child, walking alone down a midway teeming with families. She wept for the broken heart she kept having to mend, even after vowing it would never be exposed again. She wept for the hopes Logan had tricked her into embracing, when she'd known better all along.

"Jesus," she whispered, "you're plenty for

me. Please help me stop wanting things I can't have."

The Ferris wheel came to a stop while the jockey let off some passengers, and she looked down at the lights blinking beneath her. She listened to the clashing sounds of the rock music at the Himalayan, and the twangy country music at the Bucking-Bronco-Bull ride, and the dubbed voice at the House of Wonders. It all reminded her of a childhood full of chaos and longing, where roots weren't allowed to grow and friendships were never planted. A youth where trust was never cultivated, and life was an endless pursuit of something that didn't exist.

That night, when she was back in Ruth's trailer, Carny came to a sudden realization.

"He did give me something I needed," she whispered.

Ruth's fingers stopped on her computer keyboard. "What would that be, baby?"

"He reminded me that I could fall in love. And that I'm not invincible. That, after all these years of standing on my own, of insisting that I didn't need anyone, maybe I really did, after all."

"You don't *need* anyone, Carny. But there's nothing wrong with wanting someone." Ruth turned her body around on the bench she sat on. "Look at me, honey. I weigh more than anybody I've ever met. I can hardly get up to walk across the room. For years, I made a living getting gawked at all day. But at night, when it's late and dark and cold in this trailer, I sometimes wish . . ."

Carny waited, but Ruth didn't seem able to say the words. "What, Ruth? What do you wish?"

Ruth's eyes filled with tears, and she blinked them away. "Oh, baby, I want more for you than I have. And you do have more. You have that little boy. But you should have even more. You deserve so much. And there's not one thing wrong with your wanting someone to hold you at night."

Carny wiped the tear stealing down her face. "It makes me feel weak. It sets me up to fall."

"I don't know what's worse, baby. Never getting off the ground at all, or taking off and falling. Personally, I think I'd choose to make the memories. Maybe there's an ending you haven't predicted yet, child. Maybe your story's ending is a happy one."

"No, Ruth. I don't think so. How can I ever let myself be vulnerable again?"

"I believe you will, Carny. And when you do, it'll be all right."

But Carny wasn't convinced. She went back to her parents' trailer, slid onto the small bed with her son, and held him close as she slept that night.

When a week had passed, and the carnies were tearing down, preparing to head to California, Carny couldn't avoid it any longer. It was time to go back to Serenity. Time to confront the disappointment in the faces of her friends. Time to admit that she'd been as big a fool as they'd been.

They waited until all the rides had been dismembered, until all the booths had been loaded onto their trailers, until there was nothing left but concrete and tar. Finally, Carny saw the wistful look on Jason's young face. "It's all gone," he said softly. "And it happened so fast. Like magic. Only in reverse."

"What do you mean?" she asked.

"The best part came first. And then there was . . . just nothing."

His words were truer and more profound than he knew, and they left an ache in her heart. Yes, the best part did come first, and when it was gone, it left only dust and garbage. But the imprint of it on their minds remained.

FORTY-ONE

Jason was pensive as their plane left the runway later that day. "Mom?"

She glanced at him, smiling at the headset that was too big for his head. "Can I call Logan when we get home, and tell him we're back?"

Carny hadn't spoken of Logan to Jason since they'd left Serenity, and for a moment, she pretended to be intent on flying the plane.

"Mom?"

"No, honey," she said finally. "Logan . . . Logan is gone. He went to Dallas the morning we left."

He gaped at her. "When's he coming back?"

"I don't know." She struggled to find the right words. "It's kind of like the carnival, Jason. The magic comes first —"

"Logan's not like that."

She bit her lip, wishing she could tell him

he was right. But she wouldn't lie to him. "He is, baby. He's just like that."

"He'll be back," Jason said. "He has to. He's my friend."

Carny didn't answer, and again, Jason waited. Tears came to her eyes. "Honey," Carny said, "we may not see Logan again."

He caught his breath, and when she looked at him, she saw anger rather than surprise. "But what about the park?"

"There are things you don't know about Logan. He hasn't been honest about everything."

"No!" He screamed the word into his microphone, almost bursting her eardrums. She'd never seen more rage on her son's face. Not even the night he ran away. "That's not true! Logan wasn't lying. He'll be back! You'll see!"

Swallowing the knot in her throat, she didn't answer.

She watched as Jason looked out the window, hiding the tears pushing into his eyes. When she reached over to touch his hand, he jerked it away.

"You still think he lies," he said into the mike bent in front of his mouth. "After all he's done!"

"Jason —"

"Well, he doesn't!" he shouted. "You'll

see. Logan's gonna do everything he promised!"

For the rest of the trip, Jason cried quietly in his seat, staring out his window. Carny couldn't seem to fight her own tears, and by the time they landed, she was exhausted from the tension in the plane.

When they finally pulled onto the tarmac at Carny's hangar, she touched his arm. "Jason, you know I love you, and I would have done anything to keep you from getting hurt. I'm so sorry."

"You're wrong, Mom," he said. "I know you are."

The moment she killed the engine and the propeller stopped turning, Jason was out the door, running to their truck.

The Texas sun was directly overhead as Carny reached her house. The grass had grown taller than she liked it, since she hadn't mowed it before she left. Next door, she saw Janice out working in her garden. When Janice saw Carny, she abandoned her rake and walked across the empty lot between them. Before she'd even gotten out of the truck, Janice called through the window, "Carny, where have you been? I've been worried about you."

Carny slipped out of the truck. "We went to see my folks. I'm sorry you were worried, but I left J.R. and Bev a note."

She pulled their suitcases out of the back of the truck. She wanted to ask Janice if she'd heard anything from Logan, but she wouldn't let herself, not in front of Jason.

Handing the smaller suitcase to her brooding son, she said, "Take your stuff in, Jason, and I'll call J.R. and Bev to let them know we're back."

"Then I'm going to Nathan's." Jerking up his bag, Jason took it into the house.

"Go ahead and call them," Janice said, breaking into a soft smile. "Then come over and I'll update you on things." She started to walk away, then turned. "I'm so glad you're back. We missed you." Waving, she cut across the yard.

Carny got her suitcase and went into the house just as Jason shot back out. The curtains were still drawn and the lights were out, and it was hot, since she had turned the thermostat off before she'd left.

It was the first time since Carny had bought the house that she hadn't been happy to come home to it.

She set the suitcase down in her living room and looked at the couch, where she'd held Logan and talked about Jesus.

What had Logan been thinking? That she was a fool?

Tears assaulted her again, and she slumped onto the couch. Taking a deep breath and sniffing back her tears, she grabbed the phone and punched out her in-laws' number.

"Hello?"

"Bev, it's me. We're back."

"Carny, why didn't you call? And why didn't you answer your phone?"

"I turned it off Sunday," she said. "Guess I let the battery die after that. I really just didn't want to talk." Carny heard Jason's shouts outside. She stood and looked out the window. He was running, with Nathan on his heels, heading home with a smile on his face the size of Texas.

"It just isn't like you to go off like that," Bev said. "Are your folks all right?"

"Yes, they're fine. Uh . . . Bev, let me call you right back, okay?"

"Carny, I have things to tell you!"

"In just a minute," Carny said.

Hanging up the phone, Carny hurried to the door and caught Jason as he burst in. "Jason, what is it?"

"Mom! It's started! I told you it would!"

"What has?"

"The park!" He tried to catch his breath. "Nathan said there were bulldozers and cranes, and they're clearing all the land!"

"What?" She turned to Nathan, who looked ready to burst. "Nathan, that can't be. Logan left town."

"Yeah, to get more money," Nathan said. "Now Logan's got all the money he needs. Our money, and the bankers', and some other people he got. It's gonna be so great! My dad took me out there to see the work this morning. They've been working for three days."

Carny felt the blood draining from her face. "Are you sure?"

"Positive. Dad said they're clearing all the trees, but the ground-cutting ceremony is next week."

"Ground-cutting? You mean ground*break-ing?*"

"Yeah, that. The governor is coming and everything!"

She brought her hand to her forehead and released a shaky breath. "This is unbelievable."

"I *told* you, Mom! I told you!"

"Get in the truck, Jason," she said, grabbing her keys. "We're going to see."

"All *right!*"

Nathan called home to tell his mom he was going with them, and they climbed into the truck. Carny screeched out of her driveway and drove toward the site.

"Isn't it great, Mom? Logan did just what he said he'd do. Now aren't you sorry for what you —"

"Jason, please!" she snapped. "Just . . . just let me think for a minute. I have to think."

Jason got quiet, and Carny tried to sort out the thoughts spinning through her mind. If what Nathan said was true, then Logan was going ahead with the plans. And that must mean that he'd decided to keep hiding the truth from Serenity. But maybe he really was making good on his promise to build the park. He wouldn't have spent money on land and excavation if he wasn't.

On the other hand, the failure to honor his commitment to come clean spoke volumes. But maybe . . .

No. She couldn't entertain the maybes. There were too many of them. The town could be operating on assumptions, clearing trees on faith. She drove up the highway until she neared the site, then slowed down.

"Mom! Hurry up!"

Swallowing, she forced herself to step on the accelerator again. And as they passed a cluster of trees, she held her breath.

"Mom, look! A bulldozer!"

Jason began bouncing on the seat, and Carny brought her hand to her mouth.

Across the horizon, she saw bulldozers and bush hogs and other machinery clearing the land. Teams of men worked across the site. "This can't be!" she whispered, pulling the car onto the shoulder.

"I told you, Mom! I told you!"

"But . . . where's Logan?"

Jason and Nathan jumped out of the truck. Slowly, Carny got out too. A man with a hard hat and a clipboard stood near them, talking into a walkie-talkie. "Excuse me," she said. "Who do you work for?"

The man took off his hat and wiped his tanned face with the back of his arm. "King Enterprises and the town of Serenity, ma'am. We're clearing for the amusement park."

Still amazed, Carny looked around. "Are you sure? I mean . . . did they pay you? With money?"

The man set the hat back on his head and laughed. "Well, I sure wouldn't be out here in this heat if he hadn't paid a good portion, lady. And MidSouth of Houston and the FSB of Dallas guaranteed the rest. That's good enough for me, ma'am — I've done a lot of work for them before." He looked her over, then glanced back at her truck. "Are you from the zoning board?"

Her breath seemed to come harder, her

brain spun with possibilities, and her heart hammered . . . but whether it was with hope or dread, she wasn't sure. "No. Uh . . . where is Mr. Brisco?"

"Last I heard he was in Dallas. But he's supposed to be flying in sometime today. We have a meeting at three, so it'll have to be pretty soon now."

The fragile hope growing in Carny's heart frightened her as she took the jubilant boys back to Nathan's. She found Janice sweeping her back porch. "Janice, I don't understand why they started clearing the land so soon. What happened?"

Janice leaned the broom against the wall. "Logan called a town meeting Monday night and showed up with Eric Hart. Eric gave a small concert, then told us he was going to partner with us on the park. They actually chose Serenity!"

So it was going to happen. The park was going to be built. And Logan was going to withhold the truth to make it happen. Did he really think that she — ?

"I know you're still worried, Carny. We all know you were right about him."

"Wait. What?"

"After the concert, when Eric left, Logan told us the truth."

Carny narrowed her eyes. "What truth?"

"That he really came here to con us."

Carny almost choked. "He told you that?"

"Yes. He said he fell in love with the town and God got hold of him. He asked our forgiveness."

Carny was dizzy. She reached for a patio chair to steady herself. "He really did that?"

"He did. He had all our cash separated into envelopes and offered to return it to anyone who asked. Some people took their investments back. But the rest of us forgave him and decided to trust him. After all, he didn't have to tell us. People change. We've seen that happen in you, so we knew it could be done. If God can forgive, then we should, too, right? We're setting up a corporation called Serenity Trust, so we'll be partners with the other investors. It's really happening, Carny."

Carny couldn't think. Could it be true? Leaving Jason with Janice, she ran back to her truck and headed for the airstrip. As she drove, she had the dizzying feeling of teetering on the edge of a cliff, waiting to fall off with the slightest breeze. Her heart pounded and her adrenaline surged.

The airport was quiet when she got there, and she went straight to the radio and sat in front of it, wondering who would be flying him in.

"Serenity ground, King Air Zero-Niner Bravo. Anybody there?"

Carny attacked the radio mike. "Serenity to zero-niner Bravo. Who is this?"

She heard a loud whoop. "Carny, is that you? You're back?"

"Brisco?"

"Oh, thank you, God." She heard a long pause, then, "Carny, why did you take off like that? Why haven't you been answering your phone? Didn't you get my messages?"

She slapped her hands over her face, then grabbed the mike again. "I got one . . . part of it. It made me mad so I deleted it. I thought you reneged."

Again, a long pause. "I thought you trusted me."

"I did, until you skipped town!" She carried the mike toward the window, until the cord pulled her back. "Where are you, Brisco?"

"About fifteen miles southeast of Serenity," he said. "Which runway are we using?"

"Runway one-eight," she told him. She let go of the mike, went to the window, and looked southeast. She couldn't see him yet. Not sure whether to laugh or cry, she went back to the mike. "Serenity to . . . whoever you are."

She heard him chuckling. "King Air Zero-niner Bravo."

"What did you do? Steal a jet?"

"I'm in Eric Hart's plane," he said. "He's in big, Carny. All the way in. We're calling the park Hartland."

She laughed and shook her head. "I heard."

"I have a lot to tell you. Are you ready to talk me down? I'm still not sure about these landings."

Collapsing back in her seat, Carny wiped her eyes. Then it occurred to her what he'd said. "Tell me you're not alone in that plane, Brisco."

"Except for Jack," he said. "For some reason, Eric's under the impression that I'm a longtime pilot. So he loaned me the plane for a few days. Only thing is . . . I forgot to tell him my landings are a little shaky, and I haven't yet gotten my paperwork."

Her chest locked. "Are you scamming me again?"

He laughed. "Just a little. I'm with Eric's pilot, who's also a certified instructor. We're completely legit. So what do you think?" he asked. "Fifty bucks says I can land this pup as smooth as butter."

"No bet, Logan," she said. "You've been flying by the seat of your pants all your life. Something tells me you'll land the plane

434

just fine."

She heard him laughing across the radio waves, and hurrying outside, she watched his approach. He had landed smoothly the last few times they'd flown, and she was confident that he could do it. Logan could pull off anything.

It was as if he'd done it a thousand times, and as he came in with the finesse of a veteran pilot, she put her hands on her hips and waited.

Tears flooded her eyes again. Idly, she wondered if she'd ever again be that stoic, free spirit who never cried. So much had changed since Logan blew into her life. She watched him taxi back up her small runway and pull onto the tarmac, and as she wiped her tears, she gave in to the relief and unadulterated joy merging in her heart now. He was here. She could hardly breathe as the plane came to a stop and he opened the door and stepped toward her. Then she couldn't stand still any longer. She broke into a run as he came toward her, and soon he was running too, his face a fragile mask of new, unexplained emotions. He swept her into his arms as they met and crushed her against him.

"Man, you scared me," he said in a fierce whisper. "What if I'd never seen you again?"

She pulled out of his arms and hit his chest. "You left without a word! Just took off! What was I supposed to think? You couldn't have any meetings with bankers on a Sunday, and you hadn't mentioned going the night before. You were going to confess to the church, but you didn't. And you *checked out of the motel!*" She hit him again.

He grabbed her hands to protect himself. "I called you from the road around one that afternoon, after I knew you were home from church. But you were gone, and nobody knew where you were."

"Doc told me —"

"Let me explain. I couldn't sleep that night, Carny, and about four in the morning I got a call from Eric Hart. He said he wanted to see me. He was in Dallas doing a charity concert the night before, and he hadn't gone to bed. He'd been thinking about the park. He asked me to come meet with him before he left for Nashville. And I knew that if I presented his commitment to the town before I confessed, they'd be more likely to believe that I could really do this. I didn't want to wake you up and get you to fly me there on a second's notice, especially with Jason asleep and everything, so I rushed to the Odessa airport and caught the first plane out. But I wouldn't have gone

436

if I'd known you'd think I skipped out on my promises. You could have called."

"I was furious! I didn't want to talk to you. I thought all the God talk was just a farce." Closing her eyes, she leaned her forehead against his chest. All that grief. All that misery. All that soul-searching. And all because she had been so sure he was going to let her down.

"You know, Carny, you're not the only one God can change and make it stick."

She saw the other pilot getting out of the plane, saw Jack bounding down the steps. Before she could answer, Logan kissed her, a desperate, ravenous kiss salty with her tears.

When he pulled back, he whispered, "There's so much I have to tell you."

She grabbed fistfuls of his shirt. "Tell me now."

Wiping her wet cheek with his thumb, he said, "Well, let's start with my fear that I couldn't be the kind of person who wasn't fighting God or conning His people. The past is so powerful, Carny, and when nothing's ever come easy except a scam . . . when the only person who ever cared was a grifter himself . . . when the only accomplishments that amounted to anything were the stings we pulled . . ."

"You start thinking that's who you are, who you'll always be," she whispered. "I know. I've been there."

"And shaking that life loose is the riskiest thing I've ever done. It's scarier than sneaking out of town with a lynch mob on my tail. It's scarier than having your best friend die on you."

His gaze was soft and honest as she stared at him.

His eyes misted over. "But I've really been cleansed. And all of a sudden, the most important thing in the world to me is being the kind of man who pleases God. And God cleared the way, Carny. He gave the townspeople forgiving hearts. They didn't run me out of town. But I never meant to let *you* down. Funny thing is, when I let people down, it's usually planned. This is the first time I've been so desperate not to, and it happened anyway.

"But then I decided that you'd have to come back eventually, and when you did, I'd be here, and I'd spend the rest of my life proving to you that I was different. Even if you didn't want me here, I'd stay, Carny. Because I can do this. I can bring Serenity back with this park. I can make something out of all this. And maybe not now, but someday, God will smile down on me and make you love me."

"It's too late," she whispered as tears streamed down her face.

For a moment, he only gave her a dismal, longing look. "Are you sure, Carny?"

She smiled through her tears. "Yeah, Brisco. Someday is now. It's a done deal."

He threw his arms around her then, burying his face against her neck, and held her so tight that he lifted her off the ground.

"I don't suppose you would marry me," he said as he set her down.

"Oh, I might be persuaded," she said through tears, "if you asked at the right time and place."

He set her down and touched her face. "And what would that time and place be?"

"Anytime, anyplace," she said.

Laughing, he kissed her as Jack barked up at them.

Logan used his persuasive talents to talk Hugh Berkstrom into throwing the wedding reception of the century on the back lawn of his estate, after they were pronounced man and wife at the Deep Waters Christian Church, where Logan had been baptized the week before.

Carny's parents wasted no time cornering Logan at the reception and trying to sell him on their own plan to set up a string of games at the back end of the park. "And if you'll listen to me, son," Dooley said, "I can give you a thousand ideas on how to turn a profit in other ways. We really need to talk."

Logan nodded toward Carny, who was dancing with Jason across the room. "You'll have to talk to my bride," he said. "The town just appointed her park commissioner. She's going to be in charge of keeping Hartland clean and legitimate. And she'll even have to clear the new hirees . . . you know, just to make sure that everything's kept aboveboard."

Lila's face fell. "She won't have time for that. Not with the airport expanding."

"Oh, Carny can handle a lot more than you think."

"But she don't trust anybody," her father said. "If you leave it up to her, the only people who get hired will be inexperienced townies who don't have a clue how to make a buck."

"We'll have some good, wholesome, decent people working in Hartland," Logan said. "There's nobody better qualified to do this job, or more passionate about doing it right. She's fair," he added with a chuckle. "Submit your proposals to her. She'll let you know."

Dooley and Lila were crestfallen as he walked away. He saw Ruth sitting in her golf cart, watching Carny and Jason dance, with a brilliant smile on her face. Strolling toward her, he followed her gaze. "She's really beautiful, isn't she, Ruth?"

"She's stunning," Ruth said. "You'd better be good to my baby, Logan."

"Don't worry, Ruth. I'll spend the rest of my life making her happy."

Ruth took his hand and patted it. "Somehow I think you will."

Jason left his mom to run off with Nathan. Cutting through the dancers, Logan took his wife in his arms. "Have time for a dance with your groom?" he asked.

"Of course." She laughed. "So what were my parents talking to you about?"

"Working for the park. I referred them to you."

"No wonder they looked so upset. They know they don't stand a chance with me."

Logan caught sight of Dooley across the lawn, animated as he talked to a group of guests who'd gathered around him. "Tell me something. Does your father make bets on card tricks?"

"Only if they're rigged."

"Well, he's liable to make a fortune at this

reception."

Carny looked over her shoulder and saw him engaging in the same tricks he'd used for years. "Oh, no. He never quits. We'd better break up the reception before he cleans everybody out."

They left for their honeymoon in Carny's truck — decorated with shaving cream, toilet paper, and tin cans — and headed for the airstrip, where earlier Logan had filled Carny's plane with white roses.

"Nassau, here we come!" Logan said, carrying her, wedding dress and all, to the plane. "Imagine Serenity raising the honeymoon money as our wedding gift. And I didn't con a single one of them."

"No, you didn't," she said, "Do you realize why they did it? They did it for you. With the pace you've been keeping, they were afraid you'd collapse before the park is finished."

"Oh, I have plenty of energy," he said. "And rest is the last thing I've planned for our honeymoon."

She laughed as he put her into her seat and dropped a handful of white rose petals into her lap. Breathing the aroma of the roses, she closed her eyes and smiled. Logan went down the pre-flight checklist, as she had taught him, then they took off into the sunny sky. "So what exactly *are* we going to do in Nassau?"

A wicked grin crept across his face. "Oh, I don't know. I hear there's a lot of money there, Carny. Montague always had this dream of hitting that place. And I had this great idea —"

"Don't even think about it."

Throwing back his head, he laughed. "Had you going for a minute, didn't I?"

She leaned closer to him and grinned up into his face. "I can see right through you, Logan Brisco. You know that, don't you?"

"And you married me anyway. Whoever said you can't con a con?"

A NOTE FROM THE AUTHOR

From 1983 to 1995, I wrote romance novels and women's fiction for publishers such as Harlequin, Silhouette, Dell, and Harper-Collins. As many of you know, I came under intense conviction at the end of that period, and decided to leave that career to write for the Christian market. I believed that God had given me a unique gift as a storyteller, and that I hadn't been using that gift as He intended. I started over with a Christian publisher, writing suspense instead of romance, and began using my real name — Terri Blackstock. I literally had to start over from scratch building my readership, but it was worth it to me so my readers wouldn't get confused about what I'd written when.

The last book I wrote for HarperCollins was the original version of this book, under a different name. Since my heart was already shifting toward Christian themes, I included those in that book, but some of them were edited out in an attempt to make it more "ecumenical." The original also contained some scenes that weren't completely appropriate for a Christian audience.

Despite my change of heart about what I was writing, this book has always had a special place in my heart. I was proud of this story and loved the characters as if they were my friends, and more than once I wished that my current readers could read and enjoy it.

When I was able to get the rights back, I had the opportunity to rewrite it. Technology had changed as much as my world view, so I did quite a bit of revising. When it came time to name it, my Facebook readers chose the title from several choices I gave them.

I really hope that you've been able to enjoy this story of redemption. Even as I rewrote it, I feared that some of my readers might feel that I was glorifying crime. I hope that's not the case. Instead, what I wanted to do was glorify Christ and his power to wipe the slate clean. The Bible tells us in Romans 5:8, "But God demonstrates His own love for us, in that while we were yet sinners, Christ died for us." His crucifixion paid the debt for our sins, and allowed us to start over new, as clean and pure as newborn babes. I hope you'll agree that

Logan Brisco's journey illustrates that.

Thanks for reading my books and passing them on to your friends. That's why my readership has grown since my first Christian novel came out in 1995. I value you more than you can ever know.

"For this reason I bow my knees to the Father of our Lord Jesus Christ, from whom every family in heaven and earth is named, that He would grant you, according to the riches of His glory, to be strengthened with might through His Spirit in the inner man, that Christ may dwell in your hearts through faith; that you, being rooted and grounded in love, may be able to comprehend with all the saints what *is* the width and length and depth and height — to know the love of Christ which passes knowledge; that you may be filled with all the fullness of God" (Ephesians 3:14 – 19 NKJV).

DISCUSSION QUESTIONS

1. If someone like Carny Sullivan or Logan Brisco came to your church, would you reject them or disciple them? Gossip about them or love them? What difference could your approach make in their lives?

2. If you sensed someone was conning people you loved, how would you react? What is that fine line between loving the lost and holding people accountable?

3. Have you ever known someone who you thought was unredeemable, then they were redeemed? Share that story.

4. Although you knew all along that Logan Brisco was a fraud, were there times when you were willing to forgive him and root for his relationship with Carny? Why or why not?

5. What does true change look like? Discuss the signs and evidence that someone has truly repented.

6. Should the town have forgiven Logan for

his past and continued with the plan to invest in the park?

7. What positive effect did Logan have on Jason? What impact did Jason have on Logan?

8. How does God use the "baggage" of our past for the purposes he has for us today?

9. Have you ever been to or lived in a town like Serenity, Texas? Do such communities exist? What makes them so attractive? Is there anything you can do to make your community more like Serenity?